John Bainbridge is the author of over thirty books, including novels, thrillers and historical fiction, as well as non-fiction and topographical books about Britain. He has also written widely for newspapers and magazines. John read literature and history at the University of East Anglia, specialising in the Victorian Underworld.

Fiction
The Shadow of William Quest
Deadly Quest
A Seaside Mourning
A Christmas Malice
Balmoral Kill
The Seafront Corpse
The Holly House Mystery
Loxley
Wolfshead
Villain

Non-Fiction
The Compleat Trespasser
Wayfarer's Dole
Footloose with George Borrow
Rambling – Some Thoughts on Country Walking
Footloose in Devon

Deadly Quest was first published in Great Britain in 2018 by Gaslight Crime.

Copyright © John Bainbridge 2018   Cover image © Shutterstock 2018

ISBN-13: 978-1722416898   ISBN-10:1722416890

DARK SHADOW

or The Vanishing of John Lardiner

John Bainbridge

Gaslight Crime

One

York 1854

Mr Lardiner is dead.

William Quest looked at the four words written boldly on the scrap of paper. It was dark in the room of the tavern. He reached out and turned up the gaslight. He wondered just who in hell Mr Lardiner was, and why it should matter so much that he'd shuffled off the mortal coil?

Why had his friends thought the death of a man he'd never heard of, so important that they'd summoned him all the way from London to York to find out?

And why had they insisted that he stay at this sprawling inn in Stonegate under his old name of William Marshall, ordering him not to try to make any contact with them until they sought him out?

Mr Lardiner is dead.

Now that he'd read the note several times, Quest found it hard to get those four words out of his head. He'd had a long and tiresome railway journey up to York, crammed into a compartment with several annoying travellers. He'd tried to sleep on the way but found it difficult.

In the longest period of rest, he'd had a nightmare that he was back on Jacob's Island, still killing the man who'd brought terror to the rookeries along the Thames. But some rational part of his mind knew that was a week ago and he was no longer in London.

As he woke, he reached out for Rosa. She wasn't there. He'd had to mutter an apology to a fat colporteur of religious literature who was staking a territorial claim to much of the seat. Quest realised, as he came back to consciousness, that he'd grabbed the man quite forcefully by the arm.

He'd reached inside his coat and brought out Isaac's letter, his eyes dancing across the words, the railway carriage shaking as it rumbled over a long set of points:

Will, urgently need your assistance if your business in London is completed. We are in York. A room at the ..... tavern in Stonegate has been taken for you in your old name, from Friday. Come alone. Do not seek us out. We will come to you. You are a commercial traveller working for the publishing establishment of Cazeley of Newgate Street. Carry some of their latest books with you. A further letter will be waiting and will be given to you by your host. Do not come unarmed. Send an unsigned note to the General Post Office in York addressed to me. If you can come by the above date, say simply that 'mother is better.' If you are delayed, and I pray that you are not, just say that 'mother is still unwell.' Isaac.

What in hell did it all mean and why couldn't Isaac Critzman be more specific? Quest was still asking himself that question when the locomotive let out a great belch of steam as it halted at the railway station.

Quest had walked up to the heart of the city, seeking out Stonegate. In all his many travels, he'd never been in York before. He'd had to ask the way several times before he found his lodgings. Even overcome by tiredness, he could admire the jumble of medieval streets leading up to the great towers of the Minster.

As he turned into the narrow street of Stonegate, the Minster's mighty bells chimed six, reminding him he'd been journeying for a number of hours. It could have been worse. At least there was a railway and he'd not had to make the journey by stage coach.

The tavern, where he was expected, dated back to at least medieval times. His host was a small man with a broad smile, used to welcoming the growing number of visitors seeking out the old city. He'd passed Quest a sealed letter, before showing him up to a tiny room which looked down on the street below.

'I'll be serving dinner in an hour, sir,' the landlord had said.

Quest had become aware that his host was staring at the terrible scars on his hand. He put it quickly behind his back. He noticed the embarrassment on the landlord's face.

'I apologise, sir, for staring at them old wounds. It's just that...'

The landlord held up his own right hand. The vivid white marks of old scars made four near parallel lines on its back. The original injuries must have been as deep as Quest's own. So deep, it was a wonder the man's hand could still function.

'Mine's a wound of battle, sir. I served with the East India Company and was captured by... well, 'twas a long time ago. I hope your wound doesn't trouble you, sir?'

'Not at all, really,' said Quest. 'Mine was caused by an... an accident in childhood, Mr...?'

'Cooper, sir. Nathaniel Cooper. You've me sympathy. I know how people notice these things. If I can be of service, please ask the maid to fetch me...'

He'd left and Quest had opened the sealed letter. As he unfolded it, a narrow slip of paper had fallen out. It had been crumpled at some time and bore those mysterious four words scrawled in an expansive hand...

Mr Lardiner is dead...

Quest studied the slip for some time before turning his attention to Isaac's accompanying note:

> *Will, I hope you had a satisfactory journey. Rest tonight, for tomorrow you must be busy. Do not attempt to seek us out. Be in Grape Lane as the Minster bells chime noon. You will be met by a clerical gentleman, who will approach you. Do not speak until he does. He will bring you to me. Take great notice of the street where you are met, for it is very relevant. I enclose a slip of paper which adds to the puzzle - which I shall explain to you. Be watchful, for there is great danger here. Isaac.*

What the devil could it all mean?

Until he'd received the original letter, Quest hadn't even known Isaac and his brother Josef were in York. Only that they were making a tour of the great cathedrals of England. A long-deserved period of rest from their usual occupation of running the secret society known to some as Monkshood. They had been absent from London throughout much of Quest's great battle against the murderous King of Jacob's Island. Jasper Feedle had sent them a written account, but there had been no response from the brothers.

Which in itself was strange...

The great clock of the Minster struck seven. Quest checked the time against his own hunter watch, put Isaac's letter and the slip of paper into his pocket, turned down the gaslight until it hardly glowed and went downstairs. He was usually careless about meals, but he hadn't eaten since leaving London and felt very hungry.

~

They stood at a point where an extremely narrow alley disgorged itself on to a stone-built bank of the Ouse. A dribble of water and raw sewage ran down a gutter in the middle of the cobbles, helping to turn the river an even murkier brown.

'He's come,' said the bluff man dressed in fustian and a cloth cap. His fingers tapped on the brick wall, oblivious to the fact that it was wet with running damp.

'Are you sure it's him?'

'He was followed from the railway station. He fits the description. And he's lodging where we expected him to lodge. There weren't many passengers on the train.'

'You know what you have to do, Faden?'

'Could be difficult. We can hardly get at him at the inn without being noticed. And tomorrow, he'll be with his friends. If we could deal with him openly, it'd help.'

'No!'

The man almost shouted, the word echoing up the ginnel. Faden tried to study his companion's face, but the tall hat was pulled down hard and there was a scarf across his mouth. In all their meetings, Faden had never got a glimpse of the face of the man who so often employed him.

The man was quieter when he spoke again.

'It has to be an accident, Faden. I'm not bothered about the two old men, but this new arrival's dangerous. He has a reputation. He could be a bother to me and my associates. Murdering him might be easy, but I don't want the detectives

8

of the city force prowling around. You never know what they might discover. I want him disposed of just as I said.'

'Very well,' said Faden, turning away.

He halted as a great weight pressed down on his shoulder. The leaden weight of his employer's life preserver. Faden had once been struck by the weapon. He was only too aware of its deadly capacity.

~

They sat by the fireside of a pleasant drawing room in a large house on the far side of the Minster. The two old men had begun a game of chess, but neither had made a move for a long time. Their minds were elsewhere.

'Do you think we've done the right thing, Isaac?' asked Josef Critzman, looking across at his brother. Despite so many years away from his birthplace, his Polish accent was still strong.

'Who else is there? If we are ever to solve the puzzle of John Lardiner? Will has the best chance, though I did welcome your alternative suggestion.'

'But you've read Jasper's account of the Jacob's Island business? Will has been through a terrible ordeal. And now Rosa has gone...'

Isaac smiled.

'Rosa will be back,' he said. 'She'll get bored with the stage, you'll see.'

'I'm not so sure. She and Will are both so strong-minded. They need peace and time together. And given the life Will leads, that's quite impossible. I sometimes wonder if it was fair of us to bring William Quest into Monkshood. Given the terrible events of his childhood.'

'He does it so well, Josef...'

Josef stared over his *pince-nez*.

'You are sometimes very callous, Isaac.'

The long-case clock in the hall struck eight, its chimes almost drowned out by the greater clangs of the Minster bell. The eight notes had barely finished before they heard the front door open and close. They could hear the mumblings of a conversation in the hall as a servant helped someone off with his coat.

'Our host is late,' said Isaac.

'His business at the Minster must have kept him longer than he anticipated. He may have some news for us.'

'Not the news he really wants, I fear,' said Isaac. 'Not the news that would mean Quest could go back to London. If the Reverend Clews had such a revelation, he wouldn't have waited to take off his coat.'

~

Quest walked up the narrow wooden staircase back to his room. The dinner had been good, but the three courses on an empty stomach, on top of a long journey, had made him very sleepy.

His room was at the end of a long corridor that ran the length of the inn. There were six doors before he reached his own.

The place was now full, according to Mr Cooper, who had talked to him before the dinner was served.

But Quest had been the first to leave the table, not feeling sociable enough to spend time with the other guests. No sounds came from any of the other rooms. Quest could hear the noises of the inhabitants from the dining room down below. They'd eaten well and were now quaffing Mr Cooper's best ale.

No lights came from under any of the six doors, only below the seventh, which was his own. A bright light too, though Quest had a clear memory of turning the gaslight down to just a glimmer.

He reached inside his pocket and took out the key, instinctively reaching back into an inner pocket and touching the stock of his little percussion pistol. Then he took his hand away.

Mustn't be so suspicious, he told himself. This wasn't a drinking den in St Giles rookery, but a respectable premise in York, much used by visitors to the city. There were a dozen reasons why the gaslight might have been turned higher. The maid might have come to turn up the bed or set the coals ablaze in the little fireplace.

He turned the key and opened the door. A glance showed the room was empty. But the coals in the fireplace were still unlit. The bed was still turned down and the curtains open. His bag lay on the chair where he'd put it and his walking cane was propped in the corner of the room.

But there was no denying the gaslight had been turned up. Not fully, not brightly, but a lot more than the glimmering state it had been in when he left for dinner.

Quest looked around the room and then examined his bag. Nothing seemed to have been touched.

Then he noticed the book he'd left on the table by the bed. A volume of *Lavengro* by Mr Borrow. He'd put it out in case he had trouble sleeping. But he remembered setting it with the spine facing the bed. Now it was the other way round. He thumbed through the book, but could see no evidence that it had been touched or looked through.

But his instinct told him it had.

Before dinner, he'd thought of concealing Isaac's slip of paper in the book, but he'd kept it folded instead, with the letter from Isaac, in his pocket book.

Perhaps just as well.

Quest turned the key in the door and lay down on the bed. Drowsiness was forcing him towards a deep sleep. But before sleep could take hold, he reached across to the chair where he'd slung his coat. He took out the pistol and put it within reach on the table.

Then he took out Isaac's letter and the slip of paper. He read the letter once again. Then studied the crumpled slip of paper, falling asleep with it still in his hand.

The four words danced into his dream.

Mr Lardiner is dead.

Two

Faden waited on the corner of the street, wondering about the character of the man he had to kill.

A dangerous man, he was told. Not a man to take risks with. Someone who'd killed men himself. An interesting challenge. Most of Faden's victims were harmless individuals. Just people who'd got in the way and needed to be disposed of.

Faden had murdered so many over the years and all for financial reward. Not once, in any of his slayings, had there been anything personal in it. He worked and slew only for hard money. Faden had begun his life as a rat-catcher. Now he disposed of men and women with exactly the same lack of passion and involvement.

He stood on the corner where Stonegate met St Helen's Square, the taverns of the narrow lane well within view. Faden had followed the man there from the railway station the day before.

Now it was all just a matter of waiting.

Faden had no plan of action. It was all right for his employer to tell him to make the death look accidental, but exactly how? Faden had puzzled on this for much of the night and not come to any conclusions.

He was more used to killing outright and making each slaughter look like a robbery undertaken by particularly vicious footpads. There was always a hue and cry, and the worthy citizens of York would shake their heads in despair and scream for more constables to be employed on patrol in the narrow streets.

Murders were bad business for the tavern-keepers and hoteliers who catered for the growing number of visitors coming to explore the medieval city. But there would be a long interval between killings and the place would revert to its quiet ways.

The dead were soon forgotten.

Faden watched as Stonegate became busier, with the shops and other trading places opening for business. Surely the taverns would have finished serving a breakfast by now. As the

Minster clock chimed nine, he began to consider that his victim might have left by some back entrance. This was, after all, a man who probably had considerable experience of evading pursuers...

But even as that doubt crept into his mind, the man appeared from the tavern nearest to the spot where he loitered. Faden waited as his victim walked up towards the Minster.

The man in the blue jacket was almost out of sight before he began to follow, weaving his way between the workers and the gawpers who now thronged Stonegate. He lost sight of his prey as the man turned left into Peter Gate.

Faden really hoped the man wouldn't spend an hour exploring the Minster. There would be no chance of attacking him in there, or in any part of these busy streets of York. He knew the man he was hunting had been brought to the city for a purpose, an employment, but he seemed very reluctant to get on with his work.

If the man had time on his hands, why didn't he go to one of the less salubrious parts of town? It might be too early for the brothels to open, but there were always desperate women offering knee-tremblers down in the Water Lanes by the river.

Somewhere down there would be ideal; the Water Lanes where poverty ruled and life was cheap. Where there were many dark corners in the even narrower streets. Abandoned places in every twist of a ginnel. Faden had killed there several times before.

It was one of the safest places in York to commit murder. If not there, then somewhere else on the banks of the river.

It would all depend on where the man decided to go.

~

Quest looked up the mighty towers of the Minster as the clock chimed the quarter.

He didn't quite have Josef's passion for the architecture of the great cathedrals, favouring the tiny churches of the countryside, but he had to admire the skills of the medieval

13

masons who'd constructed a building which inspired in him such a feeling of awe.

Quest was tempted to go in and look around, for he didn't have to meet the clerical gentleman in Grape Lane until the Minster clock struck noon. Nearly three hours was a long time to fill, but on consideration he thought it wiser to become better acquainted with the streets of the city.

This was not London; a place Quest knew probably better than anyone, from the growing respectable suburbs to the foulest rookery drinking dens down by the Thames.

York might be of slighter proportions, but Quest remembered how he'd needed to inquire from passers-by just how to find his accommodation on his walk up from the railway station.

It was important that he could at least find his way about. He might have to move suddenly and in the dark. Isaac had said there were dangers to be met. Having to stumble through strange streets was a risk too far...

Quest turned away from the Minster and walked swiftly back down Stonegate, towards what he perceived to be the heart of the city.

~

Faden smiled to himself as his victim took the streets that led down to the river. It had taken a while and the man had gawped at much of the city's architecture on the way there. But all good things come to an end. At least for this dangerous individual in the blue jacket.

Not that it was going to be easy. It was still the middle of the morning and there were a cursed number of people about. The river would be busy too, with labourers and boatmen working on the staithes. If only he could have waited until dark...

But the man had said that Faden's victim must be dead before noon. Just why Faden couldn't imagine? And his employer's insistence the death should look like an accident... how could that be achieved?

Faden had considered a host of possibilities from falling masonry to a runaway horse and carriage. But all improbable and not very practical. All beyond the bounds of possibility if they had to be done in a hurry.

The only sure way to murder someone was to get very close and wipe them from the face of the earth with a deadly weapon. If his employer didn't like it, well, to hell with him...

It was the only real option that was in Faden's mind. His usual tactic of making the killing look like a street robbery. Faden carried a lead-weighted life preserver. An easily concealed cosh that had killed so many before. One swing against the man's head from behind.

But where and when?

The man was admiring the church on the corner of Spurrier Gate. After several minutes his curiosity took him further along the street and then down a snicket, an alley of foul repute set between high walls leading to the river.

What a stupid thing to do, Faden considered. But then this man was a stranger to York and visitors liked to seek out the river. Liked to watch the labourers loading boats, seeing the colourful sails as they made passage down the Ouse. Perhaps the stranger was hoping to find a whore in the snicket's dark depths?

The man seemed unaware that Faden was dogging his footsteps. But then why should he be alarmed? Many folk walked the snickets of York at all hours. But for a man with such a reputation, not even to glance back?

He must be entranced by the old city. Many visitors were. People coming to York often imagined it was a less deadly place than London. Foolish of them. For its size, the old place was every bit as fatal.

The snicket dated back centuries, perhaps even to when the Norsemen needed to load their long ships as they went down the Ouse and back across the sea to the homelands of their ancestors. Its enclosing walls and its cobbled path and gutters had certainly been there since medieval days. To the times when the city was besieged in the great battles that Faden's grandfather had told him about. The days when soldiers manned the long city walls to keep out invading armies.

If the snicket could talk, Faden thought, it would chant a narrative of nightmares. Its cobbles would have run with blood on so many occasions. For this was a city that had seen more than its share of violence, both sanctioned and otherwise. Faden had murdered a man in this snicket, not a twelve-month before.

But that had been on a dark night.

And now it was broad daylight.

There was no longer a staith where the snicket met the river, just a steep paved bank and a drop of a yard into the swirling and murky water. And there the man stood, gazing at the old buildings on the far bank and then looking up to watch the people crossing the Ouse Bridge.

He seemed to be in a world of his own. Maybe he was tired after the previous day's journey, Faden thought. Or just so absolutely convinced there was no danger. Either way, he was being very stupid.

A thought crossed Faden's mind that the man might just be shamming his unawareness. That he knew perfectly well that he'd been stalked all the way across the city. A concerning thought crossed Faden's mind that *he* might be the man who didn't walk out of the snicket...

No point in thinking like that. If your rat-catching nerve has gone then find a new profession...

Faden swung the life preserver back across his shoulder in a great arc, then brought it crashing forward on to the side of the man's head, just below his right ear. The stranger flopped on to the cobbles like an item of washing fallen off a line. Lay there, his eyes fluttering and his arms twitching.

A handsome face, Faden considered, as he struck the man's head three times more, sending the stranger to oblivion. Not so dangerous an opponent as he'd been led to believe. The man had walked very easily to his own death.

Faden reached inside the man's blue jacket and discovered a little bag. He undid the lace and found inside a couple of sovereigns and a variety of smaller coins. He fastened it again and put it deep into the poacher's pocket of his own coat. Now it would look like a robbery.

Faden looked back up the snicket and found that it was still deserted. He risked a glance up to the bridge. It seemed quiet at the moment.

Now was the time to condemn the dead man to the cold mercies of the Ouse. Faden pushed his foot hard against the man's chest and sent him into the river. He slid into the brown water with scarcely a splash, floating out towards the current like some old sack thrown away by a careless labourer.

Faden walked swiftly back up the snicket.

The many church clocks all began to strike eleven.

~

Josef Critzman turned away from the window as the great bell of the Minster struck the hour. The massive building shadowed the room he was in. He'd been watching a workman on the roof, fearing a little for his safety. Josef had never liked heights.

His brother, Isaac, was playing chess with the Reverend Sebastian Clews on a little table in front of the fire. They were so engrossed in the game that they seemed oblivious to the time and the striking of the clock.

'Do you not think it is time to prepare?' Josef said.

Isaac looked up and then across at the clock.

'An hour yet, Josef. It'll take the good reverend here just minutes to stroll across to Grape Lane. I'm sure William's having a fine old time exploring the city.'

Unlike his brother, Isaac had completely lost his Polish accent. People, who didn't know him, thought of him as very much a bluff Englishman. Isaac was as fat as Josef was thin. It was many years since they'd fled their native country. Their experiences there had left Josef continually edgy. Isaac had used the years to learn how to relax.

'We have already lost John Lardiner,' said Josef. 'And I have a bad feeling.' He looked back through the window. 'York is a beautiful city, but there is a menace out there. We have seen its effects already. I am concerned about our friend William...'

'Will can look after himself,' said Isaac.

Josef said, 'William attracts danger. Trouble comes to him like a moth to a flame. I have a bad feeling about this enterprise.'

The Reverend Clews smiled at Isaac and stood.

'Our game can wait, Isaac,' he said. 'Best to get matters under way. I'll take a slow stroll across to the lane. I'll enjoy the fresh air. There's no harm in being early. I'm looking forward to meeting your friend Mr Quest.'

Isaac walked with Clews into the hall and helped him on with his long black frock coat, passing him his dark plush hat. The reverend picked up a silver-topped walking cane. Isaac notice the anxious look on the clergyman's face.

'You know what to do?' Isaac asked.

'I do... but...'

'But?'

Clews said, 'I'm concerned that I've brought you all into this situation. The mystery of John Lardiner should have remained my problem. What if Josef is right?'

'Quest lives for danger...'

'Yes, in London, perhaps. But not here.'

'But he's here now...'

Clews sighed.

'And I'll go and meet him, Isaac, but it's with a heavy heart.'

He let himself out through the front door.

Josef remained at the window, watching him walk slowly along College Street and turn into Minster Yard. He seemed lost in thought as Isaac came back into the drawing room.

'Josef...'

'Brother?'

'Quest won't be happy you've involved Decker in this business. You know they've never got on. Quest doesn't like private detectives. Especially men who've worked at Scotland Yard.'

Josef held out his hands in a gesture of despair.

'I wrote to Decker a week ago and invited him to investigate the problem. And only because I thought Will was still busy in London. We are old men, Isaac. We cannot be active in these matters.'

'Then you should have turned Decker back, when you knew Quest could come. Life will be uncomfortable with Quest and Decker tripping over each other.'

'Decker is efficient, Isaac. And despite his background in the police, he is sympathetic to us.'

'But he's not a member of Monkshood. We can only trust him so far. I mean, has he even been in touch yet?'

'I told him to wait for our instructions. I have sent a note round to his lodgings. He will call on us this evening. William need not know he is in York. Not yet.'

Isaac threw up his hands.

'This isn't London, Josef. York's a very small city. How long do you think it will be before they meet?'

~

The body had been in the water for just nine minutes when it was spotted by a pedestrian on the Ouse Bridge. A nervous lady from Harrogate who pointed and screamed, attracting the attention of a constable who was walking down from Micklegate.

The constable whirled his wooden rattle for assistance even as he ran, convinced there must be a street robbery in progress. But by the time he reached the bridge, the pavement was thronged with gawping bystanders, all looking down as the body turned again and again in the fierce current.

The constable ran down to the farther side of the bridge, where two men were clambering into a rowing boat. He jumped aboard and ordered them to retrieve the floating corpse.

Within twenty minutes of being in the water, Faden's victim was brought ashore. The constable looked down at the battered head and then up at two other constables who'd arrived at the scene.

'He didn't get that by tumbling in't river,' he said, indicating the wound on the side of the head. 'We'd best get a detective. 'Let's find out who he is...'

He reached inside the dead man's jacket. There was nothing there. The constable shook his head as he regarded his fellows.

'Street robbery gone wrong,' he said. 'He's a gentleman, that's clear enough. But not a penny on him, nor owt to say who he is.'

The constable plunged a hand deeper into the jacket pocket, his hand coming into contact with a scrap of paper.

'Except this...' he said.

'What is it, Bert?' asked one of the others.

'Letter. And the ink's not quite run.'

He scanned it quickly.

'Well, a bit of a letter,' he added. 'But there's an address on it. And a sender's name.'

'Anyone we know?'

'Funny looking name. Foreign. Critz... The ink's blotted there. Critzman. Josef Critzman.' He held the letter up. 'Look where he's staying.'

'Easy to find then' said the other. 'Best get this one down to the dead room. There's nowt doin' in leaving the poor beggar here.'

~

They were late coming. The clocks were all striking one and Josef Critzman hadn't left the window for much of the previous hour.

'Something has gone wrong,' he said to his brother.

'Nonsense! Will's just doing a thorough job of looking at the scene. You know what he's like? If something was wrong, the reverend would have come back here to tell us.'

He joined his brother at the window.

'It's the middle of the day, Josef. The city's thronging with people. What could possibly go wrong?'

Josef looked up at the towers of the Minster and then back at the street.

'That,' he said, pointing along the cobbles.

A tall man was walking hurriedly in the direction of the house, accompanied by a police constable.

Isaac was not known to panic, but he felt his stomach turn over at the determined look on the faces of the approaching visitors. There was a sharp rap on the door and they heard the Reverend Clews' servant admit them.

Isaac and Josef went out into the hall. The tall man and the constable regarded them curiously, not speaking for a long moment.

'I'm looking for a Mr Critzman,' the tall man said at last. 'I'm Sergeant Starkey of the detective office. City police.'

'I'm Isaac Critzman. This is my brother Josef.'

The detective looked them up and down. A good detective, Isaac thought. He could see the man's eyes noting every detail of Josef and himself.

'I regret to say a body's been found in the river, sir. Someone I feel who might be known to you. A gent in his thirties with dark hair.'

Josef sank down on one of the matching chairs set on either side of the door.

'Why do you believe he's known to me?' asked Isaac.

'He had a letter bearing the name and this address.'

'May I see it?'

'I don't have it with me,' said Starkey. 'It was wet from its time in the river. It's being dried out to preserve its contents. Do you have any idea who the dead man might be?'

'He had no papers on him... apart from this letter?'

'We believe the dead man was the victim of a robbery. His pockets were emptied before his corpse was tipped into the Ouse.'

'Where's the body now?'

'In our dead room,' said Starkey. 'I'd be grateful if you would come with me now and identify the...'

Isaac nodded.

'I'll come at once.' He turned to Josef. 'Brother, you'd better stay here and wait for...'

'No!' Josef thundered, getting to his feet. 'I will not wait here. I cannot just sit and wait for you to bring me the news. I want to see him...'

It was like the board room of any great business enterprise; oak-panelled walls and a long and heavy table placed on a sumptuous carpet, surrounded by chairs.

The three windows offered a splendid view of York Castle and the great earth mound topped by Clifford's Tower. A pigeon perched on the ledge outside for a moment, before flying off to seek sanctuary on the old city walls.

In each corner of the room was a leather armchair, the kind where men of business might relax when the discussions of the board were done. Each chair had as an accompaniment a little table, bearing sheets of paper and pen and ink, so that thoughts might be instantly noted down.

A pale-faced man, dressed all in black, sat on the one nearest the windows, though facing the room rather than looking at the view. Despite the earliness of the hour he sipped a glass of sherry, studying the manuscript on his lap.

There was a gentle tap on the door.

'What is it?' he called out.

A small man with huge eyes entered and walked the length of the room.

'Well?'

The little man gave a curt bow and a beaming smile.

'I've had word just now, sir,' he said. 'The threat has been dealt with.'

'Did Faden tell you that himself?'

'He did.'

'You've paid him?'

'I have, Mr Carver.'

The seated man sipped more sherry.

'Good,' he said. 'Thank you, Relkin. Have we heard from our other associate?'

Relkin frowned.

'I'm afraid not,' he said. 'He may have found it difficult to get away. These are busy times for him. No doubt he will report before evening.'

The seated man made a temple of his fingers and used them as a rest for his chin.

'I hope so, Relkin. Our enterprise works and survives on our efficiency. Security is all. Please be so good as to tell our associate that. When he deigns to appear.'

'Very good, sir.'

'And Relkin...'

'Sir?'

'The decanter is empty. Bring in some more sherry. It really does help me to think. I must leave in a moment. I've that other urgent business to see to. Despite everything, I really must be there. It would be dangerous not to at least put in an appearance.'

He waited until Relkin had gone before drinking what was left in the glass. It really was exceptionally good.

Then he looked down once more at the sheet of paper. He took a deep breath and rested the list on the little occasional table nearby. He took up a pen and dipped it in the inkwell, drawing a black line through some of the writing.

One more name eliminated.

He got to his feet and left the building, walking rapidly across the town. He hadn't expected to get such good news so soon.

~

It was not just the cold which made Josef Critzman shiver as he and his brother entered the dead room. It was a feeling that a whole chapter of his life might be coming to an end.

He had been the first to recognise the unusual talents of William Quest, when Will was just a boy called Billy Marshall. Josef had suggested to the members of Monkshood that here was a talent that should be nurtured, for the greater good of mankind.

The idea had been taken up very enthusiastically by his brother Isaac, then by so many others in a deadly and secret society fighting against the rich and the corrupt.

But then he, Josef, so enthusiastic at the beginning, had been the first to have doubts.

The first to recognise that William Quest was not just a hardened young street criminal working out of Seven Dials.

The boy had proved to be a damaged individual, cursed with an horrific childhood.

Someone who'd endured a terrible ordeal, darkening his very soul.

But by that time it was too late.

Once Quest had been brought into a world of vengeance and dark shadow, it had proved impossible to let him return to a peaceful life.

And here was the consequence of what Josef now regarded as an act of corruption. A corpse lying on a table in a police dead room. Whether his slaying was deliberate, or an act of casual violence by some street thief, was irrelevant. A dead man was a dead man. Whatever the reason.

William Quest had run out of good fortune.

Josef felt the dead room spin about him as Sergeant Starkey pulled back the sheet to reveal the face of the corpse. He glanced down for a moment at the dead man's head with the wound below the right ear.

Vicious and killing blows.

Then the sight and the stench of the room overcame Josef. He leant against the table, struggling to breathe. Then he slid to the floor.

Three

They walked back across the city. Isaac thought that his brother badly needed fresh air. At last they came to the green space by the Minster and sat down on a low wall.

'You are feeling better, Josef?' Isaac asked.

'No, brother. I am relieved that the dead man is not Will, but I have known Mr Decker for many years. I cannot believe that I brought him here to die.'

'We all live with death.'

'But he came to help us, brother! He didn't have to come all this way. I shall never forgive myself!'

'It was Decker's profession,' said Isaac.

'In the name of God, Isaac! The man had a wife! He had children!'

'Then we must at least catch his killer.'

'The police believe it to have been a robbery.'

Isaac shook his head.

'Well, I don't,' he said. 'We were warned not to investigate the puzzle of John Lardiner. We were told what would happen if we did. It seems that Lardiner's dead. Then we bring Decker here. He's hardly been here a day and they drag his corpse out of the river. This was no street robbery. There's some sinister purpose behind what's going on here.'

Josef looked up at the towers of the Minster.

'It is as though someone knows every move we make, Isaac. But what of William? He seems to have vanished off the face of the earth.'

'Brother! Will is a trifle late. He'll probably be there waiting for us when we get back.'

'I hope so,' he said, standing. 'Let us be on our way. I shall not rest easy in my mind until we are all together.'

They walked swiftly around the far side of the Minster and soon reached the house. Isaac jangled the bell and the door was opened for them by Clews' man Jessop.

'Has the reverend returned?' asked Josef.

'He has not, sir. But the archbishop's here and waiting for you. I told him where you'd gone, sir. He's very concerned...'

He was standing by the fireplace as they entered the room, a tall man in his sixties with a thin long face and nose. He held up his palms in a gesture of despair. Thomas Musgrave, Archbishop of York, looked old and tired.

The brothers had met him on their first day in York as they explored the Minster, taking an interest in the tomb of a pre-Reformation Cardinal. He'd admired their project of visiting the great cathedrals and abbeys of England, suggesting that they might be better accommodated with the Reverend Clews than in the modest tavern where they'd spent the previous night.

He'd visited to play chess on several occasions and guided them to the giddy heights of the Minster towers, comforting Josef in the more exposed places. They had been in this very room with him when the mystery of Mr John Lardiner had occurred.

Over their games, they had had long discussions about religious differences and the state of society. They had found Archbishop Musgrave liberal on social matters, deeply concerned about the plight of the poor.

'Jessop has told me the news,' said the Archbishop. 'Terrible news...'

'The dead man was Albert Decker, the detective we sent for from London,' said Isaac. 'Murdered, without a doubt. The police believe it to be a street robbery.'

'Do you believe that?' asked the Archbishop.

'It'd be a mighty coincidence,' said Isaac. 'Given what's happened in the past couple of weeks. No, I think this death is connected with what happened to Mr Lardiner.'

'What of your other friend, Mr Quest?'

Isaac shrugged, 'Not here either, though I don't yet fear the worst. The reverend was to meet William in Grape Lane at noon and then bring him back here. There's been no word and they are now late.'

Archbishop Musgrave sat down in the huge armchair by the fire.

'Grape Lane is safer these days than it once was,' he said, 'and its odious reputation consigned to history. It takes but a few minutes to walk from one end to the other. What could possibly go amiss?'

The Archbishop gave a sudden look of horror.

'For a moment I forgot,' he said, slapping his palm against his forehead. 'In all of this chaos and mystery, I forgot what happened to Lardiner.'

'Grape Lane,' said Josef. 'The same street. The same time of day. The same...'

Isaac picked up a chess piece from the set on the game table.

'We don't yet know anything has gone wrong, and...'

They heard the door to the street open and Clews give his familiar shout for Jessop. A moment later Clews ushered William Quest into the room.

Josef leapt to his feet and took Quest's arm.

'Thank God, my boy! It is so good to see you.'

Quest smiled at his two old friends and then noticed the old man in clerical dress who had stood up to be introduced. He had seen him once before in London, during a debate in the House of Lords, where the Archbishop had made a fine speech on the miseries of the poor.

'You are Mr Quest?'

'Your Grace...'

'I'm so pleased you've agreed to help us solve the mystery of Mr Lardiner,' said Archbishop Musgrave. 'But I hope we are not putting your life in peril. There have been too many deaths. Too many puzzles...'

'I have to confess I know very little about Mr Lardiner,' said Quest. 'I've been shown a street and the Reverend Clews here asked me to walk up and down it several times. I've seen a slip of paper propounding the idea that this Mr Lardiner is dead. But that's all I know.'

'Then I believe we should tell you our story from the beginning,' said the Archbishop. 'It's quite a tale and I feel we would all be better seated.'

Josef wrapped his hands tightly around Quest's arm.

'We went to the police dead room not an hour ago to identify your body, Will,' he said.

'*What?*'

'Mistaken identity,' said Isaac. 'A man murdered and something to do with this mystery. The corpse was Albert Decker.'

'Decker was here?'

'We brought him up to undertake a parallel investigation to your own. It was a mistake. He paid a terrible price. I've to write a letter yet to his wife. A sorry task and one I'm not looking forward to,' said Isaac. 'The police in London will inform her officially. But we have a responsibility...'

Josef looked up at Quest.

'Why did it take you so long to get here, Will?' he asked.

'It's not London, Josef. I walked too far and then had difficulty finding my way back. I was late for my appointment with the Reverend Clews. And there seemed to be some disturbance on the bridge over the river. Great crowds had gathered. It took me a while to push my way through.'

'That's when they found poor Decker's body,' said Isaac. 'But at least it wasn't yours. Tell us your impressions of Grape Lane, Will?'

~

Quest had pushed through a jumble of people to try and make sure he wasn't late for his appointment with the clerical gentleman. But the bells of the many churches were tolling noon, even as he struggled through the crowds gathered around the Ouse Bridge.

He walked uphill for a way, but could see no signs of the Minster. As the clocks rang out the first quarter, he found himself hard by the castle and realised, from the map he had studied in *The New Guide For Strangers and Residents in The City of York*, in the tavern the previous night, that he must have come the wrong way, for the Minster was surely on the other side of the city and Grape Lane not so far away.

He turned and walked back for a while into a jumble of streets that could have changed little since the Middle Ages. The churches rang out the second quarter as he found himself in Coney Street, a wider thoroughfare of shops and people dressed fashionably.

Not knowing where he was going was a novel experience for Quest. He knew every inch of London, and other cities like Norwich, but this place seemed to be a mystery and frustration to his sense of direction.

It was not that York was even particularly big, but its old pattern of streets were a puzzlement to him. They seemed to have grown almost organically through the ages, lost in time and history.

Quest would not have been surprised to see some ancient king and his army bursting the crowds apart as it marched over the cobbles. Nathaniel Cooper, his host at the tavern, had remarked that York was full of ghosts. Quest had smiled indulgently, but now, well, if it wasn't haunted, it ought to be. The long dead would have felt very at home in these unchanged streets.

As with most Englishmen, Quest thought it an anathema to actually ask the way, but he was weakening in his resolve. After all, only the day before, he'd inquired for his destination in Stonegate as he walked up from the railway station.

He reached the end of the street as the clocks were sending out an accusing third quarter.

He wondered vaguely what Rosa was doing in London at that moment. He wished Albert Sticks and Jasper Feedle were with him. They might have more easily been able to find their way around the place.

Jasper would know as little about York as he did himself, but Sticks knew the city well. He'd fought a prize-fighting bout out at the Knavesmire and lodged in York, while the promoters spent several weeks dodging the interfering magistrates who wanted to block the proceedings.

Knavesmire – an appropriate place for members of Monkshood. Surely where the highwayman Turpin had been 'turned off' by the hangman's noose? The thought of a hanging rope brought a feeling of nausea to Quest and triggered unpleasant memories of his own past.

Then up a narrow street to the right, Quest caught a glimpse of the towers of the Minster. He explored further and found himself back in Stonegate, the narrow highway where he was lodging.

With a sigh of relief, he walked swiftly along its length back to Peter Gate, turning right to where he knew Grape Lane to be, well aware that the bells would soon be marking the hour. If there was a menace in the city of York, he would really have to do much better than this. He must put some time aside to grasp an understanding of this maze.

A clerical gentleman in a black frock coat and plush hat was pacing up and down at the corner of the street, swinging a silver-topped cane to and fro. Quest, judging by the bored look on the man's face, knew this was the churchman he was supposed to meet. He'd expected someone older, but the man was about his own age, with a swarthy look and very black eyebrows.

He walked up to him and gave a little bow.

'My name's Quest,' he said. 'I do apologise for the lateness of my arrival. I find your city rather confusing and I lost my way. I regret we've not been properly introduced...'

'I'm the Reverend Clews. I'm currently on attachment to the Archbishop of York while doing research into old documents relating to the Minster.'

'And how have you come to know my friends, the Critzman brothers?'

'They're currently lodging with me,' said Clews. 'Teaching me things I never knew about the game of chess.'

Quest smiled, 'Yes, I know their talent for that. I long gave up playing them. They've other talents too. I presume that's why I'm here at this...' he looked up at the sign on the corner of the building above him, 'Grape Lane. Something to do with wine, I suppose?'

Clews' dark looks reddened under the afternoon sun.

'Not quite,' he said. 'The word's become corrupted over the years, even as the street itself has acquired more of an innocence. Its name was originally Grope Lane. Well, Grope and something much worse than that. It was a place of... how may I put it? Assignation. Where unfortunate women plied their trade.'

'I see.'

Quest looked down what now seemed to be a quiet thoroughfare. A few pedestrians were walking its length and a man was brushing away horse dung from near the entrance of

30

what appeared to be a Methodist chapel. It seemed little different from many of the streets he'd walked down that morning.

'It seems to be quiet enough now,' he said. 'Is it any different at other times of the day? At night perhaps? Do unfortunate women still ply their trade here?'

'There have been occasions,' said Clews, 'but they're soon moved on by the constable. There are, sadly, other parts of our city where such dreadful transactions occur. But that's not relevant to the mystery in hand.'

'Which is?'

'Mr John Lardiner...' Clews began. He threw up a hand in despair. 'I shouldn't have said his name. Mr Isaac Critzman was most keen that you got the feel of this street unencumbered by any other thoughts.'

Quest smiled at the clergyman.

'I know perfectly well I've been brought to York to see to a matter relating to a Mr Lardiner. I understand that the gentleman is dead?'

'We don't know that,' said Clews. 'Not for sure. Nobody knows that. We've seen the slip of paper, which Mr Isaac Critzman sent to you. But that's all. As for Mr Lardiner's body...'

He gestured towards the lane.

'I think it best if we carry out Mr Isaac's instructions. He's keen that you hear a full account of what happened to Mr Lardiner later. My task now is not to give you any information or pre-conceived thoughts. Only to let you get a detailed impression of Grape Lane.'

~

'I'm not quite sure what you expect me to say,' said Quest as he sat down near the fire. 'Grape Lane seems to be no different to any other street in York, though perhaps the buildings aren't quite as fine as in some.'

Isaac smiled, 'It's not the architecture that's of interest, Will. We really wanted you to get to know the lane without any pre-conceived notions.'

Quest sighed.

'Well, I've seen it and there's nothing extraordinary about the place. Certainly nothing sinister, though I take it there must be or you wouldn't have wanted me to look. Has it something to do with this man Lardiner?'

He noticed the look of concern on the face of the Archbishop. The Reverend Clews shook his head and sipped his sherry. Isaac and Josef exchanged glances.

Quest waved a hand in a gesture of despair.

'Perhaps you should start your tale at the beginning,' he said. 'I can't read minds, gentlemen. I've seen Grape Lane. Walked up and down it several times. It tells me nothing. It might be better to relate the story of this Mr John Lardiner.'

Josef turned to the Archbishop.

'Perhaps, Your Grace, you would care to relate the significance of Mr Lardiner. We can then tell William what happened when John Lardiner came to York. Then maybe he will grasp the importance of Grape Lane.'

Four

'Then I shall begin,' said the Archbishop, 'for Mr John Lardiner came to York at my bidding.' He looked at Quest. 'The name means nothing to you?'

'Until I arrived in York, I'd never heard of anyone called Lardiner,' said Quest.

He reached inside his coat and brought out the slip of paper. 'But this scribbled note suggests that Mr Lardiner is dead.'

'Well, that we don't know,' said Isaac. 'Nobody's seen Lardiner's body.'

'Only poor Decker's,' muttered Josef.

'Then I must tell you more than I anticipated,' said the Archbishop. 'John Lardiner began his life as a Fellow of King's College in Cambridge. As a Fellow he was obliged to take Holy Orders in the Church of England. He was a quite brilliant man of letters, an expert theologian, and would have gained great honours as a churchman. But he had a restless urge. Not for him the role of preacher in a parish. He'd a yearning to see the world, so sought employment by the Bible Society to distribute the testament in Russia.'

He saw the look on Quest's face and smiled.

'Fear not, Mr Quest. This isn't some long drawn out biblical tale. I can cut a corner here and say that Lardiner gained a great reputation in St Petersburg. Unlike many of his kind, he made friends in high places. He was not unfamiliar with the court of Tsar Nicholas, who became something of an associate. Lardiner was respected in many ways. He was allowed to travel all over Russia, met dignitaries and peasants alike. They stopped thinking of him as an Englishman at all. He was John Lardiner, a man beyond petty territorial boundaries.'

Quest sat back on the window seat.

'And now we are at war with Russia in the Crimea?' he said.

'We are indeed. A sad and unnecessary war. Two great Christian countries at each other's throats. It can only lead to the downfall of civilisation if it goes on,' Clews interrupted. 'I beg your pardon, Your Grace...'

'No. No. You need not apologise, Clews,' said the Archbishop. 'I'm sure that Mr Quest is well aware of just how opinions in our country are divided on this dreadful conflict.'

'I take it that with the outbreak of the war, Mr Lardiner was obliged to leave Russia?' said Quest.

'Not at first,' said the Archbishop. 'For you see, Lardiner was treated as more a citizen of the world than an Englishman. He remained friends with the Tsar and much of the Russian court. Pressure to leave Russia came not from the Russians, but from our own Prime Minister and Foreign Secretary. They sent a note to Lardiner, suggesting he might be considered a traitor unless he left Russia.'

'He obeyed them?' asked Quest.

'What choice did he have?' said Clews. 'These politicians of ours think of nothing but their own glory. Had John Lardiner remained in St Petersburg, he would have been a force for good and helped bring this mistaken struggle to a speedy end.'

'He had that much influence?'

'Who knows? But Lardiner would have been much more useful to those who prize peace, than he ever would as a vicar in an English parish,' said the Archbishop. 'Which is what he became some time ago. A small village in Wiltshire. His uncle – a feeble sot - owns the living and happens to be a friend of Lord Palmerston. Palmerston was particularly keen to have Lardiner away from Russia. Lardiner's uncle got a knighthood out of his cooperation.'

'Dreadful mongoose!' said Isaac. 'Palmerston's a pest!'

The Archbishop laughed.

'I've had my conflicts with him,' he said. 'But to continue: time went on, with Lardiner marooned amidst the downs of Wiltshire. And now we see our soldiers active in the Crimea and the war getting bloodier day by day.'

'And public opinion changes with it,' said Clews. 'No country wishes to lose face, but as the death toll mounts, any rational Englishman would seek to bring an end to this madness.'

'Exactly so,' said the Archbishop. 'And some of us, not just in the church but in wider political life, have come to the conclusion that overtures must be made to the Tsar to bring the war to an end. I have friends in Sweden willing to host a mission of peace between Britain and Russia. Our poor countries are crying out for such a move.'

Quest said, 'And you thought that John Lardiner would be the only man the Russians might trust to lead such a mission?'

'That was our hope,' said the Archbishop. 'So I invited Lardiner to York for a secret meeting. Few knew that he was coming. Some of those who did didn't know why, though it might have been easy to surmise.'

'And Lardiner never got to York?' suggested Quest.

The Archbishop grimaced.

'He got to York all right,' he said. 'But that's where this mystery begins. Lardiner arrived in York and then vanished off the face of the earth.'

'How so?'

'Perhaps you'd narrate the incident, Clews...' said the Archbishop. 'It was agreed that Clews and my clerk, Joshua Marples, should meet Lardiner at the railway station. They went down in my brougham to fetch him to me.'

'A two seater brougham?' asked Quest.

'Indeed.'

'How would there have been room for three?'

'Well, as it happens, my brougham has two folding seats at the front, but they weren't needed because Clews here took the place of my coachman. He's something of a specialist with horses, eh, Clews?'

'My father was a keen hunter on his little estate in Derbyshire,' said Clews. 'I like to think I've an affinity with the brute creation. I've had the privilege of driving several of His Grace's carriages.'

'So you met Lardiner at the railway station?'

'We did, Mr Quest, and we made our way back through the streets to the Minster.'

'What sort of mood was Lardiner in?' asked Quest. 'Did he seem worried or nervous?'

'Not in the least,' said Clews. 'He seemed overjoyed to see something of York, as we made our way through the streets. I was driving the brougham so I couldn't hear much of the conversation he was having with Joshua. They both sat within. But Lardiner seemed happy enough. At least at the beginning of our journey.'

'His mood changed?'

'We crossed the Ouse Bridge. There was a great deal of traffic and I was obliged to drive slowly. I took the brougham up through Colliergate and then into Peter Gate. It was there that Lardiner began acting strangely.'

'In what way?'

Clews sat back in his chair.

'We came to the junction with Grape Lane,' he said. 'I'd no intention of halting there, but Peter Gate was blocked by a drayman unloading casks. Then the door of the brougham suddenly flew open and Lardiner stepped out. He seemed to wave an arm to someone down Grape Lane and suddenly ran off down its length. He was shouting something, but I couldn't make out the words.'

'Did Joshua Marples hear what he shouted?'

Clews looked down at the carpet for a long moment.

'Ah well, poor old Joshua ran after him. As best as he could for a man of his age. I pulled the brougham over to a wider stretch of Peter Gate and took off after the pair of them.'

Quest noticed that all the occupants of the room were exchanging solemn glances.

The Archbishop broke the silence.

'Grape Lane, as you have seen, Mr Quest, is not a very long street, though it does curve round to the left into Swinegate. It was there that our mystery deepens.'

Quest noted that Clews seemed particularly agitated.

'I'd overtaken Joshua as I ran along the street,' he said. 'The poor devil was leaning against a wall, quite out of breath. He was, after all, over sixty. I came to the bend in the lane almost in Lardiner's footsteps...'

'And?'

'There wasn't a trace of Lardiner. He was nowhere in sight.'

'He could have gone into one of the houses...' Quest suggested.

'He could have,' Clews agreed. 'But I saw no doors open. Grape Lane was particularly quiet, given that it was the middle of the day. And why should he? Lardiner had never been to York before. He knew nobody in the place. I never saw who he waved to or heard what he shouted. It was pure circumstance that we halted by Grape Lane at all.'

'Did anyone else see this incident?' asked Quest.

'The drayman was interviewed by Sergeant Starkey of the detective force,' said Isaac Critzman. 'But he had his back turned at the crucial moment. He turned to see Reverend Clews chasing down Grape Lane.'

'There's been no sighting of Lardiner since?'

The Archbishop shook his head.

'Not a trace.'

Quest held out the familiar slip of paper.

'And this missive?'

'My servant found it on the carpet under my letterbox the next morning,' said Clews.

'Your clerk, Marples? What did he say about the incident?' asked Quest.

'I turned back along Grape Lane, thinking to get the brougham and drive around to the other end of Swinegate,' said Clews. 'I helped Joshua back to Peter Gate. He'd a weak heart and was overcome by his exertions. But he insisted on walking back to the Minster to report the incident to His Grace, so that I might take off after Lardiner. I scoured the streets for a good hour but there was no sign of him.'

Quest stood up from the window seat and looked out at the great towers of the Minster. He pictured in his mind his recent exploration of Grape Lane.

Turning to face the others, he said, 'It would be helpful to me if I might talk to Joshua Marples.'

The Archbishop sank forward in his chair.

'I wish it were possible...' he said.

'Joshua Marples is no more, Mr Quest,' said Clews. 'He died within an hour of the events I've just described.'

'He succumbed to his weak heart?' asked Quest.

'No!' there was anger in the Archbishop's voice. 'He did not succumb to his poor old heart. Weak though it was. He was murdered, Mr Quest. Found dead in the Choir of the Minster, with a portion of bell rope round his throat.'

Five

Quest walked back to the tavern in Stonegate, taking in Grape Lane once again on the way. The Reverend Clews had offered him a room in his house, but Quest thought it more useful to remain in the heart of the city.

For if the mystery of John Lardiner was to be solved, then he had the feeling the solution lay here in this muddle of medieval streets.

'Ah, Mr Marshall,' his host Nathaniel Cooper, greeted him, 'a pity you weren't here an hour ago. Someone came to the tavern to inquire after you.'

For a moment Quest's head reeled. He'd just left the only people he knew in York. And who would be inquiring after him using his original name?

'After me?'

'Yes, Mr Marshall. You've famous friends, it seems. Your visitor was Reuben Dudgeon. *The* Reuben Dudgeon. A chap I hold in great esteem.'

'I've never heard of Reuben Dudgeon,' said Quest.

Cooper looked at him in amazement.

'You've not been a follower of the fancy then? You look the sort of chap what might be.' He waved an arm around the taproom, 'We've had 'em all here over the years. Spring, Jem Cribb, Shelton, Sticks...'

'Sticks...'

Cooper nodded vigorously.

'Most of 'em stayed in these very walls,' he said. 'Some of the greatest prize-fighters in the history of England. Waiting on the magistrates to go away, so we could arrange a bout.' He looked sad. 'All gone now, for I fear the great days of the fancy are over. The only man of 'em left in York is Reuben Dudgeon, the black fighter.'

'Black?'

'A slave he was as a boy, taken from a Yankee ship by our own navy. Set free in Bristol. Oh, a rare gent is old Reuben. Works down on King's Staith and lives nearby. His fighting days are done, though I'd not risk crossing him.'

'He asked for me?'

'He certainly did, and waited for a while quaffing my ale, which I gives him for free, on account of his presence in my rooms bein' good for trade.'

'Did he say what he wanted with me?'

'That he didn't, Mr Marshall. But it'd be a honour for any visitor to York to shake his hand. You might seek him out tomorrow down on the staith. I said as how I'd ask you to go along there. The lass'll be putting up dinner in an hour, if you're craving food.'

Quest nodded and went up to his room. Now here was a fresh mystery. What business did a prize-fighter have with him? And could it be relevant to the disappearance of John Lardiner? Quest's brain seemed be buzzing with thoughts and he couldn't see any immediate way of resolving the conundrum which had brought him to this old place.

He threw himself back on the bed, thinking to sleep for a while before dinner, but thoughts of Grape Lane and the incident which occurred there kept flooding his mind.

He reached out and picked up the volume of *Lavengro* by his bedside. It opened at random to a chapter which ended with the words: *There are few positions, however difficult, from which dogged resolution and perseverance may not liberate you.*

It was one of Quest's favourite quotations, one he referred to often. He hoped that, on this occasion, Mr George Borrow's philosophy was to be proved right.

~

'Two of them, Relkin...'

Mr Carver looked out through the window as the late evening gawpers stared up at the walls of the castle. A light shower of rain had swept over York and the cobbles were glistening.

'I'm aware of that, sir,' said Relkin. 'But we weren't to know that the Critzman brothers had sent for this other man, as well as Decker. Why would they bother? Decker, I can understand. He was in the detective office at Scotland Yard. Then worked as a private inquirer. A valuable asset for this interference. But this other man?'

'His name is William Quest,' said Mr Carver. 'I've begun an investigation into his background. These Critzman brothers seem to prize him greatly. He could be a menace to us.'

Relkin's huge eyes seemed to grow even broader.

'William Quest? That's not the name he's using at the tavern. He calls himself Marshall there. Purports to be a commercial traveller in books.'

Mr Carver swung round.

'Well, he's certainly not that,' he barked.

'You want Faden to deal with him?'

Mr Carver considered for a moment.

'Yes,' he said at last, 'but not directly. No more bodies in the Ouse. No more robberies gone wrong. Better that he be destroyed in some street brawl. Get Faden to arrange it, Relkin. No later than tomorrow. I'm uneasy at the thought of this Quest being in York.'

'But the police will realise there's a connection,' said Relkin. 'Two men, presumably known to each other and killed within days of their arrival. How could there not be?'

Mr Carver sat down in his armchair.

'Who is dealing with this first killing?'

'Sergeant Starkey,' said Relkin, 'for his inspector's still recovering from the wounds our footpads inflicted on him last month.'

Mr Carver gave Relkin a grim smile.

'We made a mistake there, Relkin. Starkey is much cleverer than I imagined. His inspector was a dunderhead by comparison. We should have left well alone.'

'Starkey's run off his feet, sir. With the murder in the Minster and now Decker. And street crime has increased a great deal in recent weeks, thanks to Faden. A good idea of yours. Starkey's clever, I admit, but he can't be everywhere.'

'If Starkey annoys us too much, well, he'll have to be dealt with, as well. But I want this man Quest dead. By tomorrow night, Relkin.'

~

There was a thick fog over London that morning, as Inspector Anders negotiated his way through the crowds to Scotland Yard.

He'd had a tiresome week since the events on Jacob's Island. Police Commissioner Sir Richard Mayne had been incandescent with rage when he'd heard of the death of yet another man at the hands of William Quest, reluctant to accept the idea that it was self-defence.

It had taken Anders three whole days to talk the Commissioner out of pursuing an indictment for murder against Quest. Only the fact that Anders would have had to be a material witness for the defence had prevented any further action.

Then there'd been a suspicious death in The Regent's Park, which took up a further two days, before it was judged to be a suicide. The fog had set in during the night and made all journeyings difficult across the city, hampering many of Anders' minor investigations.

And to top it all, Sergeant Berry, the man Anders relied on among everyone else, had been struck down by the measles the day before.

As Anders entered the portals of the Yard, he was stopped by Constable Soames, a new recruit to the detective force.

'The Old Man wants to see you, Inspector. Says it's most urgent. He's in a foul temper. Something's upset him.'

'Something usually has,' Anders muttered to himself as he walked through the door and took the staircase up to the Commissioner's office.

Sir Richard Mayne looked wearier than ever and was certainly not in the best of tempers. Anders sighed with equal weariness, dreading any resurrected discussion on the activities of William Quest. There was no end to the Commissioner's obsession with that renegade.

'Sir?'

Mayne glanced up.

'Ah, Anders. I want you to go to York. At once.'

'York?'

Mayne passed a slip of paper across his desk.

'I've received this communication from the detective office in York. Bad news indeed, Anders. Please read it.'

Anders perused the message, which had clearly been transcribed from the electric telegraph.

'Poor Decker,' he said at last.

'Poor Decker, indeed,' Mayne echoed. 'Foully done to death and cast into the river.' He looked up at the inspector. 'He was one of ours, Anders. One of ours.'

'He did leave the Yard a good year ago, sir. He'd been having considerable success as a private inquirer, by all accounts. I'm not sure this tragedy is a matter which should concern us. It's well within the remit of the police in York.'

Mayne waved a second communication sheet.

'I've had this from York. The detective office in that city is completely overstretched. Two inspectors off with illness and a sergeant run off his feet. They've requested our co-operation in this matter.'

'But why me, Sir Richard? You know how much work we have here? And with Sergeant Berry unwell...'

'You trained Decker, Anders. You worked with him. Like I say, he was one of ours.'

'How long am I to remain in York?'

'For as long as it takes.'

Anders read the communication again.

'It suggests that Decker was the victim of a street robbery,' he said. 'It might be next to impossible to trace the culprit.'

Mayne rubbed his chin.

'I've visited Decker's wife... widow. She's distraught, Anders, as you might expect. I got very little sense out of her, except that Decker had been summoned to York to investigate some mystery there. And within a day of his arrival he's dead. His removal from the world could be to someone's advantage.'

'Do we know any more about this mystery?'

Mayne shook his head and produced a notebook.

'This is all we have,' he said. 'Decker was wont to keep a work journal in this book. Mrs Decker gave it to me. You may take it with you and study it. There might be a clue there as to his work in York. And Anders?'

'Sir?'

'Don't come back until you've nailed the bastard who put Albert Decker in the ground...'

~

Quest took a wrong turning on his way down to King's Staith and found himself out on the Ouse Bridge.

It was a fine morning and the crowds were about, mostly men and women on their way to work and strollers enjoying the splendours of the city. He halted on the bridge and looked down at the river. He could see the staith below him and the men unloading a few boats drawn up against its wooden piles.

The staith was one of the oldest loading places in York, though Nathaniel Cooper had remarked that its day was done and that most of the boats navigating into the city now tied up at the other staithes on the Ouse and the narrower Foss river. It was a very familiar scenario to Quest. How London had sprawled along the Thames since he'd first found out its secret places as a child pickpocket. It seemed that York was very much the same.

He made his way down on to the staith and watched the men at work for a while. None of them fitted the description of a black prize-fighter called Reuben Dudgeon, so when one of the labourers paused for breath he asked.

'Reuben?' The labourer looked Quest up and down and gave him a gap-toothed smile. 'Reuben's been and gone. He only works here in the early mornings.'

The clocks were just striking nine.

'Early?' Quest smiled.

'Reuben started at three,' said the man. 'Can be very busy at that time. All depends on how tide is to Naburn. Says what we do and when. You know old Reuben?'

'Never met him, though I feel I have. He's quite the man of fame where I'm lodging,' said Quest, naming the tavern.

'Ah, you're the gent staying with Nat Cooper? Reuben says as how you might be along, if your name's Marshall that is. And if it be that you are, I'm to tell you the way to Reuben's diggings. He's got a room not far from here.'

The labourer pointed up an alley leading back to Castle Gate. 'Go up there and take a turning to the right. I was to give you this.'

He passed Quest a scrap of paper with an address on it.

'Reuben's got fine diggings,' he said, 'for all that he mostly gets a view of the gaol through the winder...'

It was a long climbing alley with steps, the kind where whores linger in the dark hours and throats might be cut. But Quest wandered through it without harm.

He knew the gaol was next to the castle and walked on in that direction. But then he found himself hard by a prison wall. He followed this round and came to a river. It couldn't be the Ouse, so it must be the smaller River Foss. There were some cottages by its banks, but none of them looked back to the gaol. Quest turned and found a path that seemed to lead between the gaol's outer wall and the river.

A man sat on a stone by the bank looking in Quest's direction.

'Lost are yer, sir?' he asked. 'Cos no one's s'posed to be this near the gaol wall. Could get yer into a deal of trouble. Might already have done.'

There was the sound of a footstep behind him.

Quest turned his head.

There were five of them, six with the man who was no longer sitting on the stone. Toughs of the town, Quest thought. Labourers when they could get work, men who'd risk breaking the law when they couldn't. Even just outside the walls of a gaol which they must know intimately.

'I've no money with me,' said Quest to the man in front.

The tough gave a big grin.

'Yer must have summat,' he said. 'And we'll have a frisk. But that ain't really what this is all about.'

'Oh?'

Quest became aware that the men to his rear were stepping closer. He risked a quick glance. They seemed to have no weapons, just fists honed to hardness in a hundred fights and a carelessness about the battering they might get in return.

A succession of images rushed through Quest's mind. A long and violent gallery of the similar fights he'd been in. The times in London when he'd been surrounded, outnumbered by similar gangs of roughs.

And I'm still here, he told himself.

Sometimes by luck, but mostly by the ways he'd learnt to fight over the long and unpleasant days of his youth.

There were no secrets to survival, beyond being far more aggressive than your opponents. The man who wasn't prepared to really hand out hurt lost the battle. Fighting was always unpleasant. Because each fight was different and might be the one where your luck ran out.

But street roughs tended to fight in much the same way. And, once you knew what that was, you had a terrific advantage.

These roughs were predictable and, unless they struck lucky, that might well be their downfall.

Two of them were coming in at the obligatory distance apart to grasp his arms from the back. Their task to hold him steady while the others piled in with punches and kicks.

Almost by instinct, Quest timed the moment the two villains would reach out for his arms. He dropped his walking stick and prepared.

Then he gave a sudden twist sideways, bringing his right elbow crashing into one man's eyes and nose. Simultaneously, he kicked out backwards, grinding the heel of his left boot into the other rough's shin. Quest turned rapidly again, bringing the side of a hand hard against each man's throat in turn, sending them sprawling.

Even as they hit the ground, two of the other roughs came nearer, shouting obscenities. But Quest noticed that they seemed reluctant to close, keeping a good arm's length away from a victim they'd imagined would be an easy conquest. As Quest faced them he sensed the approach from behind of the man who'd done all the talking.

Time to increase their feeling of peril, he told himself.

He arced downwards and picked the walking stick up from the cobbles, pressing the little button in the handle as he came back upright. The two roughs must have sensed danger for they'd slowed.

But instinct told Quest that the first man was closer.

He yanked the handle of the stick, bringing out a concealed, thin but deadly blade.

Quest heard one of the men gasp, but he wasn't sure which one. He only noticed that the attacking pair had taken a step backwards.

As he turned, he saw that the lone attacker was very close. He pushed out the blade with the suddenness of a viper striking, sending the tiny point into the flesh of the man's forearm, withdrawing it as soon as he saw it had penetrated all the way. His stricken victim gave out a cry, a mixture of agony and disbelief, as he tumbled to his knees.

The three remaining roughs were hovering like damsel flies on the banks of the river, stepping forwards and backwards as though unsure just what to do.

'Finish him, you stupid bastards!'

The first rough, clutching his bloody arm, looked up at Quest.

'You're dead, you scum!' he muttered.

'A long way from dead, by the look of it.'

Another man had joined the party, a black man with grey-grizzled hair and a voice like velvet.

'You keep out of this, Dudgeon,' the stricken man cried out.

'I don't think so, Moth,' said the newcomer. 'I've warned you before about coming so near to the street where I live. Get back to the dung-pit where you sleep.'

'None of your concern, Dudgeon,' shouted Moth.

'Well, I'm making it my concern,' said Dudgeon, stepping towards the three men on the bank. 'Six against one don't seem to be exactly a fair fight.'

He waved a hand at Quest.

'You'll forgive me from interfering, my friend,' he said. 'I can see you're quite capable of dealing with these rats from the river, but I've an old quarrel with them that goes on the lists before yours.'

Dudgeon stepped down to the three men clustered on the river bank. They seemed unsure what to do, Quest thought. They had the swirling waters of the Foss at their backs and couldn't flee. All they could do was come forward and attack Dudgeon, unwilling as they seemed to engage him. If they'd been reluctant to seek battle before, they now seemed dead scared.

Quest watched as the three men went in together, fists swirling. Vicious no doubt. Brave in its way, and intimidating to any victim not used to brawling. But unscientific in any school of the fighting game.

Dudgeon brought matters to a close in the time it took Quest to draw in a breath. His first punch driving through the face of the man on the right with all the force of a railway engine on a speed run.

But, even as Dudgeon's right fist delivered and was hauled back, his left broke the jaw of the rough in the middle. Then the fighter's right seemed to come back from nowhere, crushing the nose and lips of the remaining rough, sending him with a splash into the filthy waters of the Foss.

Then the fighter turned his attention to the man on the ground.

'I'll spare you the river, Moth. But take this as my absolute warning. You stay out of this place, though I suppose I'll have to put up with your stench the next time they throw you in the gaol. Now go, before I change my mind...'

They watched as Moth slunk away, the pair that Quest had downed scuttling after him. Two of Dudgeon's victims lay unconscious on the cobbles. There was no sign of the footpad who'd ended up in the river.

Quest wiped his blade on a outcrop of yellowing grass and hid it away in his walking stick.

'York's a fascinating city, but I never recommend its visitors seek out such places as this,' said Dudgeon. 'You handled yourself with some skill, my friend. But best to avoid dark alleys and lonely places in the future.'

'If I did that I'd never find you, Mr Dudgeon. Mr Reuben Dudgeon I presume?'

The fighter smiled.

'You've the advantage of me, though as you know my first name I can only presume you're the visitor I expected. You were so late I came looking for you. Mr... Marshall, I take it?'

Quest gave a bow.

'The same,' he said. 'Though...'

'You live up to your reputation, I'll say that, Mr William Quest. Now, my room is but five minutes away. I don't know about you, but I'm in need of some tea. A man of my age shouldn't be indulging in street brawls. They give me the devil of a thirst!'

~

'I'm fascinated that you should take such an interest, Mr Dudgeon,' said Quest, sipping tea from a dainty china cup. 'I wasn't aware anyone in York knew of me.'

They were sitting in Dudgeon's tiny room at the top of a tall house, its solitary window overlooking the walls of the gaol. It was simply furnished with a bed, table, washstand and a chest topped with a long line of books. Interesting reading, Quest thought. Shakespeare, Bunyan, Dickens, Walter Scott, Pierce Egan, Daniel Defoe and George Borrow. Books that looked as though they were read very often.

Dudgeon glanced in the same direction.

'My little library,' he said. 'I've been recently corresponding with an old friend of mine who's also enamoured of books. He wrote me that you were in this town. Said you might appreciate a helping hand.'

'Your friend being?'

'Why, Albert Sticks, friend and ancient opponent. Though I know as how he hates the Albert. He told me he works alongside you, knowing me to be... sympathetic to your point of view on the ills of society. Said he wanted to be here to keep an eye on you, but had to mind some shop selling walking canes.' Dudgeon chuckled. 'I never pictured old Sticks as a shopkeeper...'

'You were a prize-fighter and so was Sticks,' said Quest. 'I take it you met in the course of that profession?'

'I beat old Sticks on his visit here. Out at Knavesmire. It went to forty rounds. He was very silly as he'd fought a bout not long before and not recovered. A month later we had another turn at each other near Alresford. On an old battlefield, which seemed appropriate. Spent the morning dodging the magistrates and the afternoon punching through thirty two rounds. He laid me out for the rest of the day.'

'Honours even, then?'

'Well, we had one more go at it in a big field near Redditch, where they make the needles. Fifty-two rounds... and we would have gone on all night had not the justices come and forced us into a draw. So we shook hands and bowed to each other and got very drunk.'

'A while ago then, for Sticks no longer drinks...'

'He told me that! And it took some believing. Not that I wreck myself these days. Just a slow tankard of ale. This old body ain't what it was.'

'Your fists served you well out there by the river.'

'Oh, water rats are easy pickings,' said Dudgeon. 'Though I'm kind of interested as to how you got on the wrong side of Moth?'

'Who is he?'

'He lives down in the Water Lanes. A small time villain who should have been transported or topped when he was very young. He's been lagged often enough, but not for much, you know. But he really should have got the hempen knot round his throat on various occasions.'

'A street footpad then?'

'And other things,' said Dudgeon. 'He does dirty work for men who don't want to get their own hands filthy. Moth has a cousin in the same line of work. A rascal called Faden. Now, it might be that Moth just wanted to get his grubby fingers on your sovereigns, or it could be that there's something a tad more menacing behind that little scene out there...'

'Tell me about this Faden?' asked Quest.

'Ah, Faden... now there's a character you don't want to meet on a dark night. He lives down on the Lanes too, not so far from his cousin. Faden worked as a rat-catcher in this place for years. Until someone pointed out to him that killing folk was a tad more profitable. Now he's a man who puts himself out for lease to any gent wanting to dispose of an enemy, or just someone who's become an inconvenience.'

Quest began to think of events since he'd arrived in York.

'There was a killing yesterday.'

Dudgeon nodded.

'Yes, the man who ended up in the Ouse with a blow to the head. It's the chatter of the town,' he said. 'Rumour has it that he was an inquiry agent here on a mission.'

'His name was Decker, a detective in a private capacity, though he used to work at Scotland Yard. Decker and I came to York to solve the same mystery. The disappearance of a man called John Lardiner. Decker died yesterday. I was meant to perish today. Moth indicated that his ambush of me was personal. Strange if there's no connection.'

Dudgeon rubbed a hand across his chin.

'Mr John Lardiner...'

'You know of him?' asked Quest.

'Only by reputation,' said Dudgeon. 'A good man by all accounts. But perhaps a dangerous man to the wrong people. I think, Mr Quest, you should tell me all you know? Then we might try to find out just how friend Faden's come to be involved in these matters.'

Six

Mrs Booth had lived in the house in Tanner Row for three weeks, though few of the neighbours had anything to do with her.

They saw her sitting in her window from time to time, watching the passengers who emerged from the nearby railway station. She seemed to take a great interest in new arrivals in York, but the neighbours put that down to the loneliness of the newly-bereaved.

She might wish them 'good day' if she met them in the street, but she would never linger to engage them in further conversation. And that was understandable. She was, after all, recently widowed and obviously still consumed by grief.

Rumour had it that her marriage had been a long and happy one and, with the passing of her husband, she could no longer bear her old home in Ripon. So she had come to York to make a new start. She was a woman at least in her sixties, her grey hair could be seen under the black veil she always wore in public and she walked with a stick, bent forwards, along the pavement.

Tanner Row was not exactly a fashionable location for a widow woman, though it was respectable enough – a thoroughfare of private houses and business premises for artisan workfolk. The railway station kept the street busy at certain times of the day, as busy as it had been two thousand years before when the Roman legions had more or less followed its course.

She kept one maid, a slatternly looking girl called Dolly, who came out of the house very infrequently, and never talked or gossiped with the other servants who helped in the better houses of Tanner Row. Neither Dolly or her mistress frequented the local shops, but deliveries were noted from time to time, from the better establishments of the city of York.

Mrs Booth came out of her property infrequently. Mostly in the early morning or late evenings. It had been noticed that she would take long perambulations into the heart of the town, always at a slow pace and with her ornamental walking stick tapping the stones of the pavement as she went.

But this morning the church bells were only tolling eleven when she made a unexpected appearance on the front steps of her house. The neighbours twitched their curtains as they noticed her pausing to look all round, before setting out towards North Street and the Ouse Bridge. Children playing in Tanner Row walked hurriedly out of her way, for the young of the district feared widows in black, associating the sense of recent death and its accompanying dark dress with the old tales of witches and the ghosts who populated York in the shadowy hours.

At the junction of North Street, where the pavement narrowed, Mrs Booth found a youth with a barrow of vegetables blocking her path. The veiled head looked in his direction and the walking cane tapped impatiently against the kerb. Mrs Booth emitted a sharp 'tut-tutting' sound and the lad pushed his barrow properly out on to the road.

Mrs Booth raised her shoulders and head a trifle and walked on.

~

'So where can I find this Faden?' Quest asked.

Dudgeon gave him a broad smile.

'Looks to me, he's already tried to find you,' he said. 'Rest assured, if Moth's taking an interest, then friend Faden knows all about it. And the chances are if John Lardiner has come into the clutches of either of them, he's already dead.'

Quest reached into his pocket and brought out the scrap of paper.

'Which is what this says,' he said, passing it over.

Dudgeon studied it for a long while.

'Where did this come from?' he asked.

'It was put through the door of the Reverend Clews' house near the Minster. His servant was the first to spot it lying on the mat. It was first thing in the morning, so it was probably delivered in the middle of the night.'

'A scrawl,' Reuben said at last. 'Written in a hurry, I'd say. But I ask you this, William – I might call you William? If Lardiner's dead, then where's the corpse? As you've seen with your detective friend, neither Moth or Faden ever go to much trouble to conceal their handiwork. If they wanted to get rid of John Lardiner, why not make it look like just another street robbery?'

'Well, of course, we only have this bit of paper to suggest he is dead. All we know is he went missing in Grape Lane.'

'There's nothing sinister in what happened in Grape Lane, William. There are a great many doors he could have gone into or even down a snicket. What's sinister is that if he did, why didn't he come out again? You've walked Grape Lane?'

Quest nodded.

'Well, the fact that John Lardiner didn't re-appear is our mystery,' said Dudgeon. 'The Reverend Clews said Lardiner waved to someone, gave a shout and rushed down there. It's next to impossible to discover what that was all about. So we need to tackle this conundrum from the other end.'

'The other end?'

'In the rats' nest that Moth and Faden call home. Down in the Water Lanes. We need to find out just how those two creatures came to be involved. Rest assured, someone's employing them to do this. Find that out and we might get close to discovering what happened to John Lardiner.'

'This place where they live... it's some kind of rookery?' asked Quest.

Reuben Dudgeon was silent for a while.

'It's a place where the poor live, William,' he said at last. 'Good, decent folk driven to misery by poverty. I'm not saying the wealthy folk of York don't do their best for them. Those Quakers are kindly people and very charitable. But it's too big a problem for just a few. And there's more than one individual in this fine city who likes to have the poor penned in quarters some distance from their own grand homes.'

'But villains like Moth and Faden hide there too?'

'The poor hate their likes as much as the rest of us, but what can they do? Just cross to the other side and keep silent. That's the safest way. They all know how vicious Moth and Faden can be. And the law gives them no protection. So, like I say, cross to the other side and keep silent. Their own lives depend on doing just that.'

The church clocks began to strike noon.

'Let's go then,' said Quest.

Reuben Dudgeon smiled and shook his head.

'Ah, not just yet, my friend,' he said. 'These rats are best cornered in the darkness. Go to the Lanes now and all you'll find are gents gone a-slumming. Artists painting a vivid scene. In the lonely corners there might be a dip or two lurking, or a girl selling herself for a penny. But that's just daily life. We need to go rat-catching after dark, when Moth and Faden think they're safe and that no one will pester them. And we'd better go with a change of clothes. We look a bit too respectable to be haunting the Lanes in our current rig. Better that this is a midnight expedition.'

~

Mrs Booth had wandered up into the heart of the city, crossing the Ouse Bridge, then along Spurrier Gate and into Coney Street.

A poor widow woman out for her constitutional, thought Constable Barratt of the detective force, who happened to pass her as she came off the bridge. He'd seen her a couple of times in the past week, as they both roamed the streets of York.

He would never have particularly noticed her – there were a great many widows in York – but for her very fine walking cane. A lovely malacca with a golden eagle-head handle.

Charles Barratt was something of a connoisseur where walking sticks were concerned. In his boyhood, in the countryside near Helmsley, he'd spent much of his time cutting rough sticks, which his father made into canes of considerable variety and quality.

This old lady's metal top cane was a beauty, made by a real craftsman, someone at least as good as Charles Barratt's father. He'd like to have asked her where she got it, but felt that a policeman asking such a question might cause offence. He'd learned from bitter experience that the widow women of York were best left alone. They cherished any opportunity to unload their grief.

Barratt watched her walk on and then resumed his own journey, down to the staithes around the Ouse Bridge. A waste of a day, Barratt thought. If anyone had seen anything of the demise of this London man, Decker, then surely they would have come forward by now? But Sergeant Starkey had insisted he give it a go before the inspector arrived from Scotland Yard.

Inspector Abraham Anders.

Even Barratt had heard of the reputation of this Inspector Anders. The detective's cases often earned paragraphs in the pages of the Leeds *Intelligencer*, which was required reading in the detective office; not least because it gave fair coverage to their own triumphs against vice and crime.

Inspector Anders was a detective of some influence, perhaps, and Barratt – unlike Sergeant Starkey – was a young man of ambition who quite favoured the prospect of relocating himself to Scotland Yard. As he looked down at the murky and ponging waters of the Ouse, Barratt considered how he might make himself useful to this *doyen* of London detectives...

He shuddered at the stench from the river, wondering how the workers on the staith could bear to be so close to it all day. Perhaps they became immune to the smell? They were a rough bunch. They might even enjoy it. But as a country lad, Barratt found it obnoxious, especially on those breezy days when the foul odours of the Ouse and Foss swept up into the muddled streets of the town.

He was altogether glad he hadn't been one of those constables who'd had to dip hands into the Ouse's grimy waters to retrieve the corpse of the unfortunate Decker.

Barratt crossed the bridge and descended to the Queen's Staith. But even as he approached the first group of labourers, he became aware of a distraction from the river. A long rowing boat was coming up from the confluence with the Foss. A man in its bow was waving furiously in his direction.

Then he heard the man shouting his name. As the boat drew nearer, Barratt recognised him. The old man was called Skeever, a former catcher of eels who now found a greater profit by transporting tourists on the river, though how any of them could put up with the stink baffled Barratt.

'Pleased to sithee, Constable,' said Skeever, as the boat came alongside the staith. 'Found this 'un floating where t'Foss comes in.'

He pointed down into the boat. A man lay on some old sacks, his nose broken and his face crushed.

It took Barratt a few moments to recognise him. Davy, that was his name, one of the low-lifes who made a living dipping into pockets and rolling gullible gents, lured into dark snickets by the more despicable whores. One of Moth's cronies and the two rarely far apart.

'He's been given a reet goin' over,' said Skeever. 'Somehow he clung to a bit of timber on't way down. Otherwise he'd a bin drownded.'

Skeever and his two oarsmen lifted the stricken man out of the boat and lay him down on the cold stones of the staith.

'Has he said anything?' Barratt asked.

'Nowt,' said Skeever. 'Dead t'world, gaspin' up blood, but nought else but moans.'

'You'd better get him up to the workhouse doctor, Skeever. Tell him I'll send a constable down. Tell him that should he recover, he's not to be allowed to leave.'

'He'll not be goin' nowhere in hurry,' said Skeever.

Barratt watched as they constructed a makeshift stretcher and carried the man away, drips of river water turned scarlet with blood, leaving a trail on the ground.

Yet another man in the rivers of York.

Sergeant Starkey would be even more alarmed.

~

Quest walked up from Dudgeon's lodgings, determined to have a quiet afternoon before his expedition to the Water Lanes but, as the servant, Jessop admitted him to Clews' house, he heard a great deal of talk coming from the morning room. An unfamiliar voice. The reverend must have a visitor.

Quest cursed inwardly. He'd wanted to report confidentially to the Critzman brothers, before heading back to the tavern for a refreshing sleep. It would be difficult in front of a stranger.

'My dear Quest,' said Clews, as he was announced. 'This is opportune. I'd like you to meet my step-brother, Gaius. Mr William Quest – Mr Gaius Pritchard.'

Quest could see a likeness between the two half-brothers, though Gaius Pritchard was stouter, shorter and several years older.

Quest gave a low bow.

'Pleased to make your acquaintance, sir... or is it reverend?'

Gaius Pritchard laughed.

'No, I've nothing to do with the church, Mr Quest,' he said. 'I'm a lawyer by profession, though no longer in practice. I am, as they say, of independent means. But I do my best to support my step-brother in his good works. When time allows, I give my assistance to his searches amongst the old manuscripts of the Minster library. We catalogue much, but discover few new revelations.'

'That is the curse of the cataloguer,' smiled Clews.

'However, I'm aware of the reason you're in York,' said Gaius Pritchard. 'Poor Joshua Marples was an old friend of mine. His terrible death in the Minster quite shook me up. I also had the privilege of being a close acquaintance of John Lardiner. It was partly on my suggestion that he was summoned to York. So you see, Mr Quest, I feel a double responsibility for these terrible events.'

'Mr John Lardiner knew no one else in York?' Quest asked.

'Not a soul,' said Gaius Pritchard. 'I confess to being completely baffled by his disappearance. So out of character for John to run off like that. I do wonder if he had some kind of confusion of the mind. He'd spent so many years living a hazardous life and was always kept so busy in his labours. There's no doubt he found it hard adapting to life as a priest in an English country parish.'

'In Wiltshire I believe?' said Quest.

'That's correct,' said Pritchard. 'A little place a dozen miles from Swindon. I had correspondence suggesting he found his modest duties irksome. Which is understandable, given the life he'd led before. He felt that society was punishing him for his beliefs, by forcing him to exist in such a place. He very much wanted to return to Russia.'

'There's no evidence that's what he's done?'

'None whatever,' said Clews. 'It would have been difficult for him to slip out of the country in any regular way. Lord Palmerston thought John Lardiner a potential danger. An eye was being kept on him.'

'How?'

'John believed he was being watched,' said Gaius Pritchard. 'He wrote to me that there were several strangers in his village and in the nearby town. He thought he was being followed, even on his parochial expeditions.'

'Palmerston has a most impressive collection of spies at his disposal,' said Isaac Critzman. 'Some friends of ours have fallen foul of them in the past.'

Gaius Pritchard sat back on the window seat.

'Could I ask if you've made any progress, Mr Quest?'

Quest looked round the room.

'Nothing about Mr Lardiner,' he said. 'But I may have discovered some knowledge about the man who murdered Decker. Whether there's a connection between the two, I can't say.'

'You know who killed Decker, Will?' asked Josef Critzman.

'Not for sure, though a name's been suggested to me. A villain called Faden.'

'I know of him,' said Clews. 'He's been up before the magistrates several times, but never got much more than a rap on the knuckles. A dangerous character. Difficult to get anyone to testify against him. He's detested and feared in the poorer parts of this town.'

'Could this man Faden have murdered Joshua Marples?' asked Isaac.

'In the Minster? Certainly not,' said Pritchard. 'The Lord's House might be open to all, but Faden would certainly be noticed if he pushed through its doors. The better folk of York would protest if a man like Faden was allowed unsupervised access. There'd certainly be no opportunity for him to be alone long enough to take the life of dear Joshua.'

'But someone did,' said Clews, 'and Faden has a reputation for brutality, even if he's never been arraigned on a capital charge.'

Isaac looked up at Quest.

'Do you intend to seek out this Faden?' he asked.

'It would seem a good way to begin,' said Quest.

~

Mrs Booth glanced up at the great towers of the Minster before making a slow progress back through the city to Tanner Row.

A flock of pigeons gathered at her feet as she turned into North Street. She waved her stick to send them flying away. The dusk threw the street into shadow and the widow glanced around, as though fearful of who might be lurking in the darkness.

A late train had arrived at the station and a long line of passengers swept against her as they marched in the opposite direction.

It was the longest walk she'd done since arriving in York. Her neighbours in Tanner Row commented on the lateness of the hour as they observed her climbing the four steps of her house, rap on the door with her stick, and be admitted by that ugly girl who worked as her maid.

A young boy called Marcus, who sometimes earned a penny carrying luggage for passengers, watched her from the entrance to the railway station.

Widows in black always made him shudder with fear. The cholera had taken away his own parents, and Marcus hated any association with death. But he did wonder whether the old lady might like some errands run. She was comfortable and grieving. She might have a generous nature to go with a deep purse. Fearful and dressed in black as she might be.

Seven

'I'm glad to have you here, Inspector,' said Sergeant Starkey. 'I trust your journey from London wasn't too arduous?'

Anders smiled.

'Well, as I get older, I rather dislike the boredom of long journeys, whatever the transport,' he said. 'I can't get used to the railway, though, fast as it is. Mind, I used to hate the stage coaches. Now I rather yearn for them.'

'I've seldom been out of Yorkshire,' said Starkey, 'and only used the railways locally. Then only on police business. I couldn't afford the fares to travel on my own account.'

Anders had rather taken to the young policeman on their journey up from the railway station. A fresh-faced lad with fair hair that seemed uncontrollable. Every few minutes Starkey would brush a stray lock away from his eyes. There was something about Starkey that reminded Anders of his own early police days in Wiltshire.

There was something else Anders had noticed. Here was a policeman who was no plodder, but a man who thought through his cases.

Starkey had given him an account of the death of Decker. Then shrewdly pointed out there might be a connection with the disappearance of a Mr John Lardiner and the murder of a certain Joshua Marples, clerk to the archbishop, in the Choir of the Minster.

'Coincidence?' Anders had thrown out the word as an invitation for the young policeman to speculate.

'Hardly, sir. Decker was invited here to investigate the disappearance of Lardiner. Joshua Marples was a witness to his vanishing. I believe that'd be too much of a coincidence.'

Anders smiled.

'Too much of a coincidence,' he agreed. 'Now, who are these individuals who invited Mr John Lardiner to York?'

'Well, it was done with the blessing of Archbishop Musgrave. The suggestion was apparently made by Mr Gaius Pritchard, a man well-known about this town. He was once a lawyer of some repute, but he no longer practises. His half-brother, the Reverend Clews, is an aide to the archbishop.'

'Why was Lardiner invited to York?'

Starkey shrugged, 'The gentlemen seemed reluctant to tell me the purpose of his visit. There's some great secret there...'

'Then we must find out what this great secret is, Sergeant. You didn't force the question?'

'A sergeant of police has very little authority in this place, Inspector. The detective force of York is a relatively new institution. Some of the gents of the town think we are intrusive by our very nature. Policemen are not considered much above domestic servants. When we go calling we're often sent round to the back of their houses – to the tradesmen's entrances.'

Anders frowned. He'd faced the same difficulty during his own career in the police. He was getting more than a little tired of the scenario.

'Well, we may have to see about that,' he said. 'What I want to know is who brought Decker up here? Decker was well-known in London. I worked alongside him myself at Scotland Yard. But I wouldn't have thought that anyone in York would have heard of him.'

Starkey produced a little pocket notebook and sought out the relevant page.

'It seems Decker was invited here at the suggestion of two gents who're staying as guests of Reverend Clews. Two brothers from London. Isaac and Josef Critzman.'

Anders jumped from his chair.

'The Critzman brothers? What the hell are they doing here?'

'You know them, Inspector? Are they criminals? They seemed respectable enough when I took them to view Decker's body.'

'They're respectable enough in their way,' said Anders, sitting down again. 'Tell me, are they alone in York?'

'Alone?'

'Is there anyone else from London staying with them?'

'Not that I'm aware of,' said Starkey. 'As I understand it, the Critzman brothers are making a tour of old church buildings. They were befriended by the archbishop and Reverend Clews. They just seemed to be here when Mr Lardiner disappeared. But I do know they invited Decker.'

'Mmm.'

'Do you wish to interview them?'

Anders thought for a moment before replying.

'Perhaps tomorrow,' he said at last. 'I understand there's been a spate of street robberies in York? Men attacked and some ending up in the river?'

Starkey brushed the hair out of his eyes.

'Over the past few weeks there's been an increase in such felonies,' he said. 'A matter of great concern in our detective office. Attacks on men, of a particularly vicious nature. Pedestrians murdered as they walk the streets of the town. They all seem to have been robbed. Few have survived and those that have remember nothing of their ordeal.'

'Unusual for York?'

Starkey spent a moment gathering his thoughts.

'Like any town, there's crime,' he said. 'The people who run *this* town like to press the idea that York's a lawful place. But there's a dark side too. Rookeries where crime breeds. Villains outside the law who the well-to-do don't seem to want pursued too hard.'

'Why would that be?'

'My personal view is that some of the rogues are handy for the more ambitious men of business in York. They can't settle old scores themselves, so they employ the dregs of the gutter.'

'Are these matters investigated?'

'Only so far,' said Starkey. 'We investigate every attack and slaying, but, as there are few clues, we aren't encouraged to devote much time to each crime. A while ago my superior, Inspector Appleton, was beaten near to death by footpads in the Water Lanes. He may never make a complete recovery. I doubt he'll ever resume his duties.'

'Policemen do risk such assaults,' said Anders.

'Inspector Appleton was investigating possible ties between the rascals of the streets and the men of business in this town. Only on the day of the attack he told me he was getting close to solving what he called "the great conundrum". Now he lies abed with his mind gone. He remembers nothing.'

Anders leaned forward.

'Do you believe that Decker fell afoul of these same folk?'

'It's a possibility,' said Starkey. 'There were certainly similarities in the method of attack. Inspector Appleton had been dragged down to the river's edge, but not thrown in. I believe his attackers were disturbed by honest staith workers who were returning home from a nearby tavern.'

'Have you voiced your suspicions to your superiors?'

Starkey gave a grim smile.

'I rather fear that if I did that, Inspector, I might be put back into uniform and sent out into the countryside to pursue poachers.'

'I see. Do you have any suspicion as to who might be behind these attacks?'

Starkey nodded, 'I've a name or two in mind.'

'Then perhaps you and I should seek these gentry out. Without telling your superiors.'

The sergeant gave Anders a broad smile.

'It's what I've been trying to do, ever since Inspector Appleton was attacked. It's become my own personal quest, Mr Anders.'

Anders rocked back in the hard wooden chair.

'Quest,' he said. 'Now there's a word.'

~

Marcus, the station boy, took a deep breath and walked across the street to the home of Mrs Booth, climbed the four steps and tapped gently with his fist. There was a door knocker in the shape of a fox's head, but he hadn't the courage to use it.

Nobody answered the door.

He looked all around. The last train had come into the station a while ago and the street was deserted. Darkness had fallen and only the gaslights and the illumination from the railway station lit Tanner Row.

Marcus took another deep breath and rapped slightly harder on the door.

At first, he thought he would be ignored again, but then he heard someone approaching across the bare boards of the hall. Someone with heavy steps, muttering aloud.

The door opened a fraction and a hideous face glared out at him, a visage as round as a pumpkin with straggly brown hair. Marcus recognised the slattern as Dolly, Mrs Booth's maid. Not that anyone knew her very well in Tanner Row. Dolly, like her mistress, kept herself to herself and ignored all greetings from neighbouring residents.

'Wotcher want?'

'I was...' Marcus began.

'Wot?'

'I wondered... er, if Mrs Booth wants any errands runnin',' he said. 'Or odd jobs doin'. I work for pennies, when I'm not wanted at the station to carry luggage. I'm Marcus Braithwaite.'

The maid opened the door wide and looked Marcus up and down, her lips clamped tight together in contempt.

'No she don't!' she said. 'And if she did, I'd be doing it for her. Now clear out lest I thwack you one!'

'Dolly, who is it?'

It was a quiet voice from the darkness of the hall.

'Just this ragamuffin lookin' for errands, ma'am.'

'So I understand,' said Mrs Booth, coming into the light from the Row. 'But leaving the boy on the street is no way to repay a kind offer, Dolly. Bring him into the hall...'

Mrs Booth gestured with her hand and Marcus was inside the house almost without realising he'd walked forward.

It was a narrow hall, with a flight of stairs at the far end and four doors, all firmly closed. There was a long table with two burning candles and a solitary chair along one wall.

Marcus heard the maid shut the door. He looked up at Mrs Booth, who stood before him, her left hand clutching a walking cane decorated with the head of an eagle. Even in the bad light Marcus noticed the silver band bearing some odd inscription.

'What is your name, boy?'

The old lady spoke gently in a refined way. Not from Yorkshire, Marcus thought, for all that she'd dwelt in Ripon. If she was, she'd been better brought up than some. He could see a narrow, pinched face behind the widow's veil.

'Marcus, ma'am,' he replied. 'Marcus Braithwaite. I carry parcels and luggage from the railway station.'

Mrs Booth gave a brisk nod.

'Yes, I've seen you about,' she said. 'Where do you live, Marcus?'

'I've a bed in a lodging house, up by th'House of Correction. Well, I have when I've enough pennies to pay keeper. On bad days it's streets for me. There's a gap under city walls that does well, for all it might be freezin'.'

The old lady gave another slight nod.

'These are hard times for the poor,' she said. 'Have you no parents, Marcus?'

The boy shook his head.

'Nay, cholera took 'em, back end afore last. I was lucky to be spared, for it carried off both me brothers and me three sisters and all. But it ne'er touched me.'

'Fortunate indeed,' said Mrs Booth.

She looked at him for a long while, before speaking again.

'I'm a widow, Marcus,' she said at last. 'People take advantage of widows, so I have to be sure I may trust anyone I employ. You understand that?'

Marcus nodded.

'I'm straight enough, ma'am. Mr Jenkins at the station'll vouch for me. I work hard, ma'am. I can fetch and carry and run with messages. Owt really...'

'But are you discreet, Marcus?'

'Dis... Sorry ma'am?'

'Can you keep secrets, Marcus? You see, people around here are always prying into my business. I value my privacy, boy.'

'They'd hear nowt from me,' Marcus protested, turning red.

Mrs Booth gave a little laugh.

'No, I can see they wouldn't,' she said, looking across at the maid. 'I think we may trust this boy, Dolly. It will save you having to leave the house so much. I think, Marcus, you might be of great use to me.'

She reached out and took the boy's hand and shook it very gently. Marcus noted that her gloves were made of fine silk. Even in the poor light he detected a smile behind the veil.

'Come back tomorrow after the morning train,' she said. 'I'll have a message for you to be taken into the city. We'll look upon it as a trial for us both, Marcus. We'll look upon it as a trial...'

~

'You don't have a change of clothes?'

Reuben Dudgeon looked Quest up and down and shook his head.

'I came to York at very short notice,' said Quest. 'In London I've plenty of disguises. I wasn't anticipating having to raid a rookery when I got the invitation.'

Reuben let out a deep breath.

'In daylight you might get away with wandering into the Water Lanes dressed like a toff,' he said. 'Men go there to paint the scene in water

65

colours and oils. They're indulged by the residents. But at night, no one risks their neck by parading its alleys looking like that! Even toffs seeking a whore only journey to the fringes.'

'Is there a slop shop still open?'

Reuben laughed, 'I think I can do better than a slop shop.'

He walked over to a dark corner of his room and dragged a great chest towards the lamplight. He threw back the lid and reached in with his battered hands.

'You're not built hardy enough to fit any of these exactly, not having been a prize-fighter, but I've an old outfit of fustian that might just do. A trifle big, but it's all I have. Clothes that don't fit are a hallmark for the poorer people of this place. You'll look no different, my friend.'

Quest changed into the moth-eaten set of clothes and dirtied his face with soot from the tiny fire hearth.

'I can see you're an old master at this game,' said Reuben. 'We'll need to go armed, of course. Do you have anything?'

'Always this,' said Quest, holding up the walking cane with its concealed blade.

'Might do in the rookeries of London, but not down there. The kind of folk who haunt the Water Lanes don't usually carry walking sticks. Best you leave it here.'

'Then there's this,' said Quest, reaching into the hidden interior pocket of his own coat and producing the little percussion-cap pistol.

Reuben smiled, 'That's better, though wise not to use it unless your life's in danger. If you shoot a man, even down by the river, they'll stretch your neck in York Prison.'

He knelt down and fumbled under the bed, looking and rejecting several hidden items in turn. At last, he produced a lead-weighted life preserver, perhaps a foot in length.

'Try this old neddy,' he said. 'It's broken a score of heads since I've had it and never let me down. Easy to hide and effective in its powers of destruction.'

Quest took it from him and waved it through the air.

'Just right,' he said, 'and beautifully made.'

'A gift from my old adversary and friend, Mr Albert Sticks,' said Reuben. 'An old Gypsy created it and offered it as a prize in a little bout Sticks and I had together. Sticks won the bout, but made me a gift of the cosh. I've appreciated his kind gesture many times since.'

'Perfect,' said Quest, hiding the weapon in the fustian jacket.

Reuben walked to the window and looked out at the black night.

'No moon and no stars,' he said. 'Just a church clock striking midnight. Time we were away, William. Let slip the dogs of war, huh?'

Quest laughed.

'You're a very dangerous man to know, Reuben.'

'Why, that's just what Sticks said about you.'

~

At the top of the house in Tanner Row, Mrs Booth put the candle closer to a mirror set on the little table underneath the window and lifted up the veil. There were fresh signs of age in the face, though more powder would attend to that. Always more powder until that face became positively white.

A sickening sight without the veil.

Across the road, the lights were being put out at the railway station. There would be no more trains until the morning. Mrs Booth wondered just who might come to the city and pose a danger? As if there were not enough perils on the streets of York, as it was.

Mrs Booth considered the boy Marcus. He could be of use, because he was not as noticeable as the maid Dolly. But what to tell him? A good story would have to be considered. Something a boy might understand, though it would have to be a long way from the truth.

Was there danger in trusting the boy?

Mrs Booth had rather taken to the urchin, but there was undoubted intelligence in his brown eyes. That could be good if he proved as useful as desired, but a risk if it put questions into his mind.

He had no family, but what of his friends? He'd mentioned nobody but a Mr Jenkins at the railway station. There might be a menace there. Railway employees could be both inquisitive and garrulous. Both habits produced danger and questions. The boy would need to be examined further before he was given any task of importance.

Mrs Booth pictured again the eager look on the boy's face as he stood in the hall. He might be ideal for the purpose.

And, if not – would anyone really miss a street boy who carried luggage?

Mrs Booth took a damp cloth from a little red bowl and began to clean off the face powder for the night.

Eight

'Once we leave Castle Gate our adventure begins,' said Reuben, pushing up his coat collar and pulling a canvas cap further down on to his head, 'and the danger too.'

He and Quest walked slowly away from the walls of the gaol, into the heart of the city. The street was poorly lit and they attracted little attention as they pushed their way through crowds of men and women who seemed mostly drunk.

'Not a vast place to search?' said Quest.

'Not vast, but full of people, good and bad,' said Reuben. 'Like one of those tiny rookery acres in London. Small but filled with danger. The one blessing is that people come and go in the Water Lanes and poor strangers are not unknown. Moth has a room just up from the staith. Faden tends to move around.'

'We have no plan,' said Quest.

Reuben chuckled, 'How could we have? We don't even know if they're there. They might be elsewhere in York on their own foul mission. Who's to say? But we got to start somewhere.'

They were walking along Castle Gate, and were outside a church when Reuben nodded towards a vile looking alley on the far side of the street.

'That's the first of the Water Lanes,' he said. 'Our friend Moth's likely to be in a room at the top of a slum in the next lane along.'

'And Faden?'

'Ah, he's a more difficult fish to catch. As I said he moves around. Never spending more than a few days in one place. The street gossips do say he can find shelter with some of the people who employ him – the kind of creatures who live in the smarter parts of town.'

Quest considered. 'You think Faden's the more dangerous of the two?'

Reuben shrugged.

'Certainly the more cunning, that's why he's lived so long. Moth's just the worst kind of footpad. A vicious streak, but not much brain. Faden's a nastier and cleverer proposition. To get Faden we really need to persuade Moth to talk.'

'You think he'd blow on his own cousin?'

Reuben gave Quest a humourless smile.

'It all depends on just how persuasive we can be,' he said.

They walked on a few yards until they were nearly opposite the second lane. Castle Gate was busier here as late workers returned from long hours of labour on the staithes. Inebriated men and women staggered away from the low taverns and drinking dens.

Reuben was about to cross the street when Quest took his arm and led him back against a shadowy wall on their own side of the road. In the far-flung light from a gas lamp, he saw the questioning look on the old prize-fighter's face.

'Over there,' Quest whispered, pointing to where a lamp shone brightly at the entrance to the second Water Lane. The crowds parted for a moment and Reuben could see a well-dressed man talking to a scruffy youth.

'Some gent out slumming, that's all,' Reuben said.

The pair seemed to be having an animated conversation, the youth waving his arms and the man nodding his head. Quest and Dudgeon could hear, but not make out the loud words echoing across the street.

At last, the youth seemed to calm down. The toff reached inside his long coat and produced something which he gave to the boy. The boy nodded and knuckled his forehead before sidling away down the alley.

'Do you know those two?' asked Quest, as the man walked smartly away down Castle Gate.

'Seen the boy about,' said Reuben. 'Country lad, not been in York very long. Don't know more than that. I know the gent better, though I've not seen him frequenting this place before.'

'You know who he is?'

'Not by name.'

'I met him earlier today,' Quest said. 'In more salubrious surroundings. He's a lawyer called Gaius Pritchard. He was mostly responsible for John Lardiner coming to York.'

'Now that is interesting.'

Quest watched as Gaius Pritchard turned right into Coppergate.

'I'd give a lot to know why a respectable lawyer like Pritchard is having a meeting with someone in this neck of the woods?'

'Nothing we can do about it tonight, William. Best get on with the task in hand. Let's get this done...'

They crossed the street to the spot where Pritchard and the youth had been standing. The glare of the gaslight made the dark alley beyond seem even blacker. As they walked down its long slope, it took Quest a few moments for his eyes to adjust to the dimmer light, though the stench of the alley, and the Ouse which ran along its foot, was overwhelming.

A shrivelled young girl with a hungry look on her face, launched herself off the step of the first building, exposing naked breasts and reaching out a hand.

But something about the two men, probably their determined pace, persuaded her to withdraw just as swiftly. She might have been twelve years old, Quest thought. Dudgeon had said the whores came cheap and desperate in the Water Lanes. She might do better with a wharfinger returning home with shillings in his pocket.

Two drunken men lay on the ground, with their backs to one of the houses. They were both snoring loudly, their clothes disarrayed as though some wilier inhabitant of the Lanes had fingered through their pockets in search of a penny.

It was all familiar to Quest. Poverty and injustice created these places, but they were all much the same. He'd spent his own youth scrabbling for pennies in just such a rookery, though a larger sprawl of slums, in the supposed greatest city of the Empire.

They were nearly at the river before Reuben held out an arm in front of him, pointing to an open doorway. Quest turned and looked inside. A narrow and broken staircase led upwards. There seemed to be no rooms at ground level, perhaps because the inhabitants were wary of a river which so often flooded.

'Moth has the room at the top,' Reuben whispered, taking out a life preserver. 'Better prepare for trouble as we climb the stairs, though in truth, friend Moth's usually drunk by this hour.'

Quest took out the cudgel that Reuben had lent him, a lead-weighted life preserver covered in hard leather, marked and scratched from previous violent encounters. It had a good feel to it, Quest thought. Nicely balanced and not too heavy to limit speed in use.

They climbed the stairs as quietly as possible, not easy given the noise the wooden treads made as they put any weight upon them. There was no light in the stairwell and the darkness was overwhelming, but Reuben seemed to have no difficulty in seeing his way.

The two men reached a landing with a flimsy door leading off it. A woman was on the other side, singing a bawdy song. A baby was crying in harmony with the words.

'Not at the top yet,' whispered Reuben. 'This is Molly, Moth's neighbour. There's a rumour he spawned the child. But then there are a hundred other possible paternities. Molly's a lady who's free with her favours.'

Quest's eyes were getting used to the dimness. He could make out a much longer flight of stairs, narrow now, almost a ladder, leading way up into the dark. The steep ascent led to a door, which seemed to be partly open.

'Given his reputation, would Moth really leave his door ajar?' asked Quest. 'I'd hate to think he's expecting us?'

He could see the concern on Reuben's face.

'Can't see why he would be,' he said. 'Well, only one way to find out. Pity these stairs are quite so noisy. Better rush them and go in low.'

Before Quest could reply, Reuben was dashing up the staircase, two and three steps at a time. When they reached the doorway, Reuben fell to the ground and tumbled like a ball into the room, regaining his feet with remarkable speed.

Reuben just stood there, the arm carrying the life preserver falling to his side. There was something wrong, Quest could see that. Something in the room that Reuben hadn't expected to see. There was certainly nothing to show he was preparing to fight.

Reuben waved the life preserver at the far side of the room as Quest came through the doorway, waving his other hand through the gloom.

'Not what I anticipated,' Reuben said. 'Not what I anticipated at all.'

The room was bare, except for a table, a chair and a grubby bed. A blanket that covered the lone window had been pulled down, one corner of the grey wool clutched in Moth's hand.

Moth lay partly on the low bed, but with one leg on the floor. His head lay half hanging over the foot of the bed, eyes bulging and tongue protruding from between his remaining teeth. The footpad's free hand clutched his throat as though trying to unravel the tight piece of rope which had choked the life from him.

'I really think it would be better if we were not here,' said Reuben.

~

Gaius Pritchard sat in the study of his house in Goodram Gate, a modest property wedged between two grander establishments. It was well past midnight and he reached out towards the fire to take away the chill of the night. He'd come in from his journey across the city, cold to the bone. So cold, he hadn't yet removed his coat. Pritchard had turned up the gaslight to take away the shadows that seemed to creep out from the corners of the room.

Shame.

He said the word out loud, trying not to let his eyes rest on the pair of pictures on either side of the window. They were small portraits, rather well done, people often commented, of his mother and father. Stern looking individuals who often seemed to look down and judge him in his weaker moments.

Shame.

Gaius Pritchard spat the word across the room. Every time he participated, he felt like this, wondering whether it was all worth the bother.

There was a battered flint upon his work table, deep black with white striations. He'd found it near an ancient barrow on the Wiltshire Downs. Some man in antediluvian times had worked it to a sharp edge, probably to scrape out the bloodier parts of an animal skin. It had not lost its sharpness in all those thousands of years. Even the flatter surfaces were rough and brutal.

Shame.

He said the word even louder.

Then he smashed the palm of his hand down on to the flint's hardness. Smashed it down again and again, until the agony swept through his body and the skin was broken and blooded.

At last he desisted, took out a handkerchief and wrapped it around his palm. He was breathing heavily, but felt that he had assuaged his guilt. The flint was marred red with his blood. He'd need to wash it, lest the maid be alarmed by the sight when she came to make up the morning fire.

Gaius Pritchard considered: What was shame after all?

Shame.

Just a word...

A word of others. Not mine.

~

The screaming of the trull had brought a crowd to the doorway in the Water Lane, her cries still breaking the silence of the alley, as Anders and Starkey walked down from Coppergate. Her words between the screams were hardly understandable, though Anders – from long experience – knew that murder must have come to haunt the slum dwelling.

'Molly!'

Starkey grasped the woman by the shoulders and forced her to look up at him.

'What is it, Molly?'

Her eyes widened and her head twisted towards the doorway.

'Mo... Moth...' she gasped out the words.

Starkey ran up the stairs, the inspector following behind at a gentler pace. Anders envied the police sergeant his youth and stamina. He'd been like that once. A very long time ago. Besides, it wasn't always a good idea to run upstairs in a rookery. You didn't know what might be waiting for you.

As he reached the landing, Anders heard the sound of a police rattle somewhere below in the alley. The local beat constable, no doubt disturbed by the screams of the bereaved woman. Funny how a woman could keen so dramatically for even the vilest of humans.

'This was Moth,' said Starkey, as Anders walked through the doorway.

Anders glanced at the body.

'Well, there's a tongue that'll never wag again,' he said drily. 'Almost as though someone knew we were coming for him.'

'There might be no connection,' said Starkey. 'Moth had a lot of enemies. His death might have nothing to do with the killing of Decker or anything else.'

Anders shook his head.

'I'll put money on it that it does,' he said. 'Call it detective's intuition, if you like. And...'

He was interrupted as a police constable burst into the room. The young man halted at the sight of Starkey and gave a perfunctory salute. Charles Barratt looked with interest at Abraham Anders. So this was the famous Scotland Yard detective. He'd caught a fleeting glimpse of the celebrity earlier in the day at the police station, but there hadn't been time to note much about the man.

'This is Constable Barratt,' said Starkey. 'He knows a lot about this part of York. And a fair bit about our victim as well.'

Barratt looked down at Moth.

'What do you think, Constable?' asked Anders.

He always respected the gained local knowledge of the man on the beat.

Barratt walked nearer to the corpse, having a good look around the room on the way. He examined the tight piece of rope around Moth's throat. He remained silent, as though considering several possibilities.

Better than some, Anders thought. Many a constable would leap in straight away with his thoughts, trying to impress. Barratt was a thinker. And thinkers made good detectives.

'Not unexpected, sir,' said Barratt. 'Violent men usually meet violent ends. Moth had a lot of foes in this part of town...'

Anders detected a question in the way the words were put.

'But?'

'Something wrong with it, sir,' Barratt went on. 'Not unusual for *women* to be strangled in the Lanes, though mostly it's done with the bare hands of their husbands or ponces. But when men get killed, they're mostly stabbed or bludgeoned to death. They're certainly not strangled. Not least with a piece of cord like that.'

'Smart thinking, Constable,' Anders said. 'Down here by the river you'd expect to see a length of tarred rope. Or the kind that's tied around the goods on a wharf. But that... that piece of cord's quite singular. I don't know what it is, but I suspect it had its origins a long way from here.'

'Garrotting with a rope's unusual,' Starkey concurred. 'And it's the second strangulation in the past few weeks.'

'Ah, the clerk Marples in the Minster?' said Anders.

'Just so, sir,' said Starkey, 'though that wasn't a cord like this. I saw the body. Marples was slain with much thicker rope. Bell rope, in fact. Just as you might expect to find in a house of God.'

'You might, but surely only strung beneath a bell?' said Anders.

'The ringers had been replacing a bell rope the day before. There were a few lengths of the old one lying around, waiting to be taken away.'

'That's interesting,' said Anders.

'Sir?'

'Well think about it, Sergeant. It suggests that Marples was murdered on the spur of the moment. His killer didn't go prepared to murder him. With a piece of cord like that, for instance. He grabbed what was nearest to hand. Had it not been the bell rope, he'd have had to find something else. Or use his bare hands. But a garrotte's quicker and gives less chance for the victim to make a noise. Once the doctor's seen this body and it's taken to your dead room, I'd like to have that cord, Sergeant. Its origins might be the solution to this mystery.'

'We should talk to Davy, sir,' said Barratt.

'Who's Davy?' asked Anders.

'A fellow villain of this man Moth. We hauled him out of the river earlier,' said Barratt. 'He'd been badly beaten and half-drowned. He was still unconscious when they took him to the workhouse infirmary. If he lives, he might peach – for a consideration.'

'Do you know who attacked him?'

'No, sir. Only that it was a very bad beating. Davy was lucky to live.' Barratt waved a hand towards the corpse. 'There might be a connection with this slaying, I suspect. Davy usually preyed on passers-by with a few other miscreants. Might be worth hunting them all down.'

'We'll go and see this Davy in the morning. And if you can feel the collars of any of his associates, it might be helpful, Constable,' said Anders. He turned to Starkey. 'I'd like to see the spot in the Minster where Marples was murdered.'

Starkey nodded, 'I agree with you, Inspector. Moth dead and possibly linked to the murder of Mr Decker. And Mr Decker brought here to investigate the disappearance of John Lardiner. Marples – one of the last men to see Lardiner alive - slain within the hour in the Minster. It all adds up to something very unpleasant.'

~

Back at Reuben's lodgings, William Quest was voicing the same conclusion to the prize-fighter.

'Take your point, William,' said Reuben. 'What we need to find out is who killed Moth? Moth was the weakest link in the chain. A vicious creation, but well-known to talk too much in his cups. And the way he was killed? Hardly the technique of a Water Lane villain.'

'Perhaps he was topped by his cousin?' suggested Quest.

'Well, I wouldn't say friend Faden was strong on family feeling, but I'm not sure he'd go that far. And he's a bludgeoner by reputation. Killing with a length of cord's hardly his method.'

'If we can hunt him down we can find out,' said Quest.

'What about this man Gaius Pritchard? You think he's involved in all this in some way?'

Quest sat back in the chair.

'Let me just say, I find it interesting that the man who brought John Lardiner to York was a few yards away from where Moth was murdered. And there at the time of his death.'

'You think he killed Moth?'

'There's a probability. Can you think of another reason why a respectable gentleman about town should be down by the Water Lanes late at night?'

'So do we tail this man Pritchard or confront him?'

'I'd like a watch set on him,' said Quest. 'And we need to find the youth Pritchard was talking to. He might have played a part in Moth's death.'

He thought for a moment.

'But we need to go canny, Reuben. Gaius Pritchard's well connected and if we scare him off, we might find out nothing. He knew Lardiner, knew Decker was in York, and was well aware I'd been summoned here as well. He certainly knew I was coming to the Water Lanes tonight in search of Faden.'

'Then he could be a most dangerous man.'

Nine

'Relkin!'

Mr Carver stood looking through the window. The servant noticed that his hand was shaking, which it sometimes did when his employer was particularly agitated. The street outside was busy and noisy with the morning's activity.

'Sir?'

'Where is Faden?'

'Don't know, sir. I left the usual messages. He hasn't been in touch. But there's a hue and cry about the killing of Moth.'

'Is there?'

Mr Carver gave Relkin a thin-lipped smile.

'Moth was clumsy. Not clever enough to be in my employ. He failed in his attack on this William Quest. Worse than that, Davy is in the workhouse infirmary under police guard. Now what am I to do about that?'

Relkin had known his master long enough to recognise that the question was rhetorical.

'Davy may talk,' suggested Relkin. 'He's a blabbermouth at the best of times. Even more if they pour gin down his throat. A liability, sir.'

'Indeed he is. He needs to go the same way as Moth. But that won't be easy to achieve. As I understand it, Davy is not actually under arrest?'

'No, sir, but that makes little difference. There's a constable been posted by his bedside, though Davy's not conscious yet.'

'Better that he never is... conscious.'

Relkin shook his head.

'Normally, we'd employ Faden to undertake his removal. But the disposal of Moth must have frightened him. And they were related.'

'It couldn't be helped, Relkin. If Moth hadn't been killed, he'd be Quest's prisoner by now. He might have hinted where I may be found. Just as Faden may do.'

'Then surely Faden should go. Once he's discovered.'

'And who's to do the deed?' Carver almost shouted. 'Moth was easy. Battered and drunk when he was turned off. Not difficult at all. But Faden's a difficult proposition. He'll not let himself be caught as easily.' He looked through the window. 'He's out there now, slinking in the snickets or the back lanes of some rookery. Not knowing whether he may trust me anymore.'

'With respect, sir, it was a mistake to ever trust Faden. An error to accommodate him in this very house when he had to lie low. He might not know your name or position, but he could certainly point the finger.'

'He's never seen my face, Relkin. There is that. I've never met him here. Only encountered him in dark ginnels with my features covered, to give him his instructions.'

Relkin looked up at his employer, nervous of saying the words. He gulped and wet his lips with his tongue. Then, at last...

'He could be at the detective office right now, sir. Turning Queen's Evidence.'

With a roar, Mr Carver grabbed Relkin by the collar and shook the little man, squeezing tighter and tighter on to the fleshy skin of his throat.

'Imbecile! Do you think I don't know that?'

He let him go as Relkin's eyes turned upwards. The little man fell backwards on to a chair, clasping his neck and struggling to breathe. When he'd recovered, he looked again at his master.

'I ... never mean to offend...' he began.

Mr Carver held up the palm of his hand.

'No... no. I shouldn't have done that, Relkin. This is not your fault. But you must understand, I act only as the agent of others. If I fail, well, the price I'd have to pay is very high.'

'We have a dilemma though, sir. Faden was the bludger we employed to undertake these unpleasant physical tasks. Moth was easy to deal with because he was alone and inebriated. But attending to Davy, under police guard? Removing Faden himself?... how might it be achieved?'

Mr Carver say down on the window seat.

'I don't know Relkin. I really don't know.'

'Sir?'

'Relkin?'

The little man stood and came closer.

'Given the circumstances, sir... the difficulties we face...' he waved a hand in the direction of the heart of the city. 'Do you not think that *he*... after all, protecting *him* is what this is all about... Do you not think that *he* might share some of the risks and be prepared to remove Davy and Faden. He's gone that far with Moth?'

Relkin saw the look of fear on the man's face.

'You think I dare ask, Relkin? You don't know what he's like. Everyone knows his reputation, but they've never seen that side of him. Well, I have. He's not pleasant, Relkin. Not pleasant at all. If he thought that Faden and Davy had become nuisances, well... he might come to believe the same about you and I. Better to leave York and fade into obscurity than risk that.'

'Then what can we do?'

'Only one way out,' said Mr Carver. 'We'll have to approach him about the matter, though God knows what mood he'll be in. And we still need William Quest dead. He's possibly the greatest menace of all.'

~

'Then we cannot trust anyone, Will?' said Josef Critzman.

Quest and the two Critzman brothers were walking on the green by the Minster, in the long shadows of the great building. It was a beautiful, warm morning and early visitors to the city had begun to promenade in anticipation of the first religious service of the day.

'Well, certainly not Gaius Pritchard, until we're sure what he was doing down by the Water Lanes at such a strange hour. But we must tread warily. If Pritchard knows we're suspicious of him, he might go to ground and not go anywhere near those strange haunts.'

'It'll be hard to suddenly clam up,' said Isaac. 'He was instrumental in bringing John Lardiner to York. He knows we're looking for him. To tell Gaius Pritchard little will put him on his guard.'

They sat down on a low wall.

'Then we must keep him interested,' said Quest. 'We'll learn nothing if we frighten him into abandoning his own course of action. There's something here we're missing. I wish I knew what it is?'

'Let's recap then,' said Isaac. 'The one man who might be able to broker a deal bringing an end to the war in the Crimea is invited to York, mostly at Pritchard's initiation. Lardiner vanishes in mysterious circumstances before he can do anything at all. One of the witnesses to his disappearance is murdered. So is Decker, who was brought here to investigate this puzzle. And so nearly were you, Will.'

'Exactly so,' said Quest, 'so we need to ask ourselves who profits by removing Lardiner from the scene. And is Lardiner vanished or is he dead, as the scrawl on the slip of paper suggests?'

'We know that his disappearance was out of character,' said Josef.

Quest shook his head.

'With respect, old friend, we know nothing of the kind,' he said. 'Lardiner has a certain reputation. We know a lot about this moral figurehead, but very little about the breathing man. Most men live several lives. We know only of Lardiner's religious piety and his skill as some kind of diplomat. But what we don't know is what Lardiner, the private man is like.'

'Ah, you think he had a darker side?' said Isaac.

'Don't we all?' asked Quest.

'But he had never been to York before,' said Josef. 'Who was he waving at and why should he flee down this Grape Lane? It makes no sense...'

'No, it doesn't,' said Quest.

They got up and strolled towards the great doorway of the Minster.

'There are many people who'd like the war brought to an end,' said Isaac, at last. 'It's ruining all the countries involved.'

'And they would be the last people to seek the removal of John Lardiner,' said Josef. 'The one man who might fulfil their ambitions. Surely the danger to Mr Lardiner comes from men who might wish to prolong the conflict?'

'Those are my thoughts,' said Quest. 'If Lardiner's disappearance has anything to do with the war, then those are the folk we should be looking at. If Lardiner vanished because of some other matter, then we might search for a solution for ever.'

'So what do we do now?' asked Isaac.

'Find Faden,' said Quest. 'He's a paid murderer, like the late and unlamented Moth. If we get our hands on Faden I'm sure we can prevail upon him to talk. Reuben Dudgeon and I'll begin that task. In the meantime I want Gaius Pritchard tailed. I want to know more about his interest in the Water Lanes.'

'Could be difficult,' said Isaac. 'We're hardly awash with individuals adept at following men around in a place like this. Leave it with me, I'll see what I can do. What now?'

They were at the foot of the steps leading up to the Minster.

'I suppose we might as well see the place where Joshua Marples was murdered,' said Quest. 'Then I'll go and seek out Reuben. It looks as though the pair of us have a busy time ahead.'

But as they neared the wooden door, they were stopped in their tracks.

Three other men emerged from the darkness, one a police constable in uniform. The tallest of the men stopped dead and clutched at the stonework of the arch, shaking his head in a mixture of disbelief and annoyance. He gathered himself and banged his walking cane hard on the ground.

'Quest!'

'Inspector Anders... what the devil are you doing here?'

For a moment, Quest had a flash of memory of the last time he'd seen the policeman, only just over a week before and near to the tattered bridge at Jacob's Island. It seemed as if his destiny was to be forever entangled with this ageing detective.

~

Faden crouched down in a corner of the ginnel, his breath coming deep and hard.

Someone was about and after him, that was for sure. He was lucky to be alive. He hadn't been back to his own room all night, having spent the previous evening with a cheap whore. He'd learned of Moth's death only from the hue and cry on the streets.

It was only a matter of time before Moth was topped, of course. His cousin had lacked Faden's cleverness and instinct for survival. And he'd drunk too much, leaving himself insensible during the dark hours.

Only a matter of time.

Had he been stabbed or bludgeoned, Faden wouldn't have thought twice about his end. But a cord round the throat? No, that wasn't the way of the Water Lanes at all...

Faden knew, to the cold heart of his bones, that time was running out. Those who employed him had run out of patience. The killing of Decker hadn't been enough to satisfy them. The failure to slaughter this man Quest, and the fact that the garrulous Davy was now more or less in custody, had exposed the weakness of Faden and his band. Faden knew that he knew too much.

The next piece of cord might well be around his own throat.

What could be done? Faden knew nowhere as well as York. Even escaping from the city would be a struggle and would expose him to danger.

He thought vaguely about seeking out and murdering the man who employed him, but he would scarce know where to start. He might, he considered, turn Queen's Evidence. They might spare him the noose if he sent the foul men who ran all the crime and corruption in York to the gallows...

But would they?

Faden knew that he had few provable crimes against his name, but the suspicions would be there. The very people he might have to deal with could well be connected with the sinister individual who'd retained his services in the past.

Besides, Davy had been under police guard for hours now. To save his miserable neck, he might already have fingered everyone in the gang.

Being blown upon had always been Faden's greatest fear.

He pushed hard back against the dripping wall, wishing that the bricks might swallow him. There was someone entering the ginnel, coming up from the direction of Fossgate. He reached inside his coat and felt the comforting weight of his lead-weighted cudgel. One swing could take out a man's brains. He had his dagger with him as well, with its blade so broad and heavy.

Let them come.

Let them all come.

But no, that was the courage of last night's ale talking. Better to slip away and not let them know where he was. He could easily deal with one, but say there were more? Perhaps he was already sealed up in this ginnel like a rat in a trap?

The intruder was nearer now, his feet padding softly down the steps halfway up the alley. It sounded like a solitary man, but could anyone be sure?

Something had to be done.

The footsteps were too close.

He would see Faden at any moment.

There the intruder, or rather the outline of the man in the narrow darkness between the two high walls. Better to be sure, Faden thought. Better to kill than be butchered yourself. He reached inside his coat and brought out the cudgel, that stout weapon that had brought so many breathing men to their ends.

Faden stepped out suddenly, aware of a face looking up at him. He raised the cudgel and brought it smashing into the side of the man's head.

He heard the bones and teeth splinter, as it caught his victim in front of his ear. There was no cry, not even a whimper, as the man hit the ground. Faden brought the cudgel down three more times until the head was just a bloody mass, hardly distinguishable from the foul brown mud lying on the cobbles.

Faden's breath was coming in sharp and painful gasps. He looked at the cudgel, which was stained with very little blood but spattered with the disgusting remnants of the man's brain. This faithful old weapon had had its day. He could hardly carry it through the streets of York, and he felt a reluctance to put it back in the deep pocket of his coat. The cudgel clattered to the ground.

Faden rested a hand against the dank wall as he gathered his breath and listened. The ginnel was quiet enough. Perhaps the man had been alone.

He had to go, to leave, to get well away from this ginnel and the corpse at his feet. Whatever the risk of there being anyone else waiting in ambush. To stay here was to die. He reached back in his coat and wrapped his fingers around the handle of the dagger, its weight and heavy blade a comfort to him.

Having killed, Faden felt bolder.

Let them come.

'Let them all come. Let them come now. I'll slash out their guts!'

He turned and loped away in the direction of the Foss River.

~

Mr Carver hadn't realised that anyone had come into the room. He'd been sitting quietly in one of the corner chairs, reading a letter from his contact in London.

Then he'd looked up.

The sight of the unexpected visitor quite startled him.

'You're taking quite a risk coming here in the middle of the day,' Mr Carver said. 'I thought we'd agreed just to send messages, particularly with this man Quest and a London detective in York?'

His visitor leaned against the great table.

'It seems to me that too many risks are being taken,' he said. 'We play for great stakes. You are becoming quite a liability.'

'I am?' said Mr Carver.

'Yes, you are,' said his visitor. 'Faden a fugitive and likely to be taken soon. Bungled attempts to see off this William Quest. Deaths that should have seemed to be accidents, but which scream murder. This is a small city, my old friend, and you are increasing the risk of putting a rope round both our throats.'

'You've a nerve to throw accusations at me,' Carver protested. 'Who put the cord around Moth's neck?'

'Somebody had to account for Moth,' said the visitor. 'He should never have been given your trust. Faden was an unwise move. You should have handled these slayings yourself. Like I've had to do.'

Mr Carver jumped to his feet.

'You know who I am?' he blustered. 'As you say, this is a small place. I'm well known here... unlike you. I'm having to live a double life and there's great danger in it for me. I come here every day with only Relkin to keep intruders away. It wasn't such a good idea to base ourselves in York. We should have undertook this mission in a place where nobody knew us.'

His visitor gave him a grim smile.

'You see the lengths I've had to go to?' he said. 'And all for your convenience. We must conclude this business soon or we could well lose our heads. Bring this to a conclusion, my friend, so I may leave York. I've had to kill twice. And account for Mr John Lardiner.' He gave a humourless laugh. 'Time to see you getting your hands dirty.'

Mr Carver sank back into the chair.

'Our paymasters are keen that we end matters soon,' he waved towards the table. 'You see that book?'

It was a black covered volume, narrow like a ledger. His visitor reached out and turned over the pages.

'Is this for me?' he asked.

'In that book I've written appraisals of all those who employ us. Very damaging some of the details. But the knowledge therein might be used by us if we should be forced to leave England with speedy expedition.'

His visitor thumbed the pages for a while, before turning back with a smile.

'At least that is satisfactory. I think I shall take it with me. I'm not convinced that this is a safe place for it to be kept.'

'I'd rather you didn't,' said Mr Carver.

'I insist. One other matter...'

'What is it?'

'I want Faden dead. Before he falls into the wrong hands.'

'But there's nobody who...'

'Then see to it yourself. And you will communicate with our paymasters. Tell them we want to end this affair within the week. And I want to know that our agreed reward is deposited. Tell them that I won't conclude matters until it's confirmed.'

The visitor picked up the book and swiftly left the room.

~

They had walked back into the Minster, Quest and Anders together.

Starkey and Barratt had returned to the detective office, and Isaac and Josef Critzman were undertaking a mission in the city - Isaac had remarked that he needed to send an urgent message by way of the electric telegraph.

Before they departed, they had given Anders and Starkey a full account of what was known about the disappearance of Mr John Lardiner.

'Sergeant Starkey tells me that this is where they found the body of Joshua Marples,' said Anders, indicating the long seat in the Minster Choir. 'A quiet enough place when not in use or when there are no visitors about.'

'So anyone could have slipped in here and strangled him,' said Quest. 'Someone skilled in the use of the garrotte could turn a man off in seconds at a peaceful time of the day.'

'They could,' Anders agreed. 'But why?'

'Well, this was no random slaying. No casual murderer would risk his neck to come in here for such a purpose. Joshua Marples' death must be connected to what happened in the previous hour - with Lardiner's disappearance.'

Anders sat down on the end of the seat.

'Can I ask you something, Quest?'

'Of course.'

'Do you know more about this matter than I've just been told?'

'You've been told all I know about the vanishing of John Lardiner.'

'That may be so,' said Anders, 'but what about these other matters that have occurred in York? The killing of this man Moth, for instance? Was that down to you?'

Quest sat down.

'You're a Scotland Yard detective,' he said. 'If I'd topped Moth, I'd scarcely confess and put my head in a noose.'

Anders smiled, 'I don't seriously imagine you killed Moth. A cord around the throat's hardly one of your methods. But I do sense that you know more about it than you're telling. As long as you're not involved in the man's death, I'll use my discretion about any other matters you confide to me.'

Quest looked up into the farthest reaches of the Minster's roof, considering what might be for the best.

'There is more,' he said at last, 'though I'll deny all of this conversation if it's used against my associates or myself. I trust you, Bram, because I know you trust me.'

Anders had been completely unaware that Quest even knew his first name was Abraham. He felt curiously moved, particularly by the contraction, which only his real friends ever used.

'I trust you about as far as I could throw you, Quest,' he said. 'But I don't believe you killed Moth.'

'No, I didn't, though I did have an altercation with him earlier.'

Quest related how Moth and his gang had waylaid him down by the gaol. He admitted that he'd been responsible for Davy going into the filthy waters of the Foss, but made no mention of the fact that it was Reuben who'd struck the man and sent him tumbling into the river.

'The law does allow self-defence,' said Anders. 'It seems you were considerably outnumbered. I doubt that any charges could be laid against you and this man Dudgeon.'

'You say that this footpad Davy lives?'

'In the workhouse infirmary,' said Anders. 'He wasn't conscious last night, but may have come round by now. I intend to pay him a visit this morning. Perhaps you might care to accompany me? A sight of you might persuade him to peach.'

'How much does Sergeant Starkey need to know? It might hamper my own inquiries if he puts me in a cell until self-defence is established?'

'He won't, given the way I'll explain the circumstances,' said Anders. 'After all, this Davy might well be linked to the murder of Decker.' He gave Quest a stern look. 'But please bear in mind that you've no right to be involved in these matters at all. Criminals are investigated by the detective force, not by you. Step across the line and I *will* arrest you...'

'I'm not quite sure what the line is?'

'No, that's always been your trouble.'

He looked across at Quest.

'I know so much of what you've done in the past,' he said. 'I know the men you've killed. If I'd the proof, I could have had you swung a dozen times. Even though your victims deserved it. But while we're in York, I'd be grateful if you played by the rules. No killings, no violence, though I do give you the right to defend yourself. And Quest...'

'Inspector?'

'No secrets, Quest. I want to know everything. What you find out, who you see... everything. And you're not to undertake any of your usual felonious expeditions without consulting me first...'

'A beautiful alliance then?'

'I wouldn't go that far,' said Anders. 'You'll probably be the death of me, Quest. And one day I'll have you in Newgate. But in the meantime, let's get these matters resolved and get back to London.'

~

Mrs Booth was returning home from her journey into the heart of the city when she was accosted by the street urchins in North Street. Grubby, filthy children, the kind who went further than begging for scraps.

There were seven of them, their eyes gazing at her like vicious feral animals, their hands everywhere. Far more than beggars, undoubtedly dips. Clumsy pickpockets, but thieves none the less. The less cunning and skilful kind who'd get put away through their desperation and inefficiency.

Mrs Booth had noticed them first on the Ouse Bridge. Seen the ways their eyes took in her respectability and the slim package she had under one arm. She'd noticed them scampering along the street behind her, then crossing the road and dashing way in front. Now they had crossed back and were on the pavement, impeding her progress. Mrs

Booth became aware that there were others behind. She heard them mumbling, coughing and gasping.

There seemed to be nobody else in the street. She was alone with these ragamuffins and there was no way she could ease out of their path.

One of them, a girl, though the child's sex was hard to tell by the shreds she wore, stood directly in her path, hand outstretched.

'Penny?'

The child coughed out the word.

'I've nothing for you,' said Mrs Booth.

The girl's mouth stretched wide in a smile of discoloured broken teeth.

'Penny!'

More insistent now, almost a barked order. The child reached forward and her filthy hand grasped Mrs Booth's clothing. The waif's face looked up at her.

'Penny!'

Mrs Booth used her package to sweep the clutching hand away. The child gave her a venomous look and snarled out another word.

'Bitch!'

The child clutched Mrs Booth's outside jacket with both hands, tightly, pulling the old lady forwards. Mrs Booth brought down the heavy package on them with considerable force.

'Take... your... filthy... hands... off... me!' she said.

Mrs Booth became aware that a boy had edged to her side, a hand reaching out towards her left arm, the grimy fingers playing with the brown paper wrapped around her package. The girl moved forwards and seized her clothing once more, a harder grasp now as though as though she was trying to pull the old lady down to the ground. More fingers rubbed lightly across her back.

The girl was staring her right in the eye, her face turned up just inches from Mrs Booth's own.

'Want it all...' the girl sent out the words in one fetid breath. 'Want all you got...'

There was a long moment of silence.

'Want it all,' the girl said again.

Mrs Booth gazed down through her veil.

'You shall have it...' she said quietly.

The girl gave her a look of wonder and triumph, her mouth open.

'Here...' said Mrs Booth.

In one swift movement, her walking cane with the eagle's head came forwards, the sharp beak of the ornamental bird raking down the side of the child's cheek, opening the skin very deeply and forming a thin line of blood on the grimed face.

Mrs Booth saw the brat's expression change from wonder to terror. The girl's hands wandered up to where she could feel the cold river of scarlet. Her eyes widened even more as the pain struck and she realised she'd been maimed.

The other dips had stepped back at the sight of gore on the face of their ringleader. They were used to harsh blows, and scarcely got through a week without cuts and bruises. But no lady had ever fought back in this way.

Mrs Booth turned, her back to the wall as she faced them all. She tapped the walking cane against the bricks and a short and slim blade came from its end. Mrs Booth waved the stick around in a great horizontal arc, forcing her attackers back even further. But there was no longer any threat.

The bleeding girl was staggering away along the street, hands clutching her torn face, her mouth uttering a scream that drowned all the other noises of the city. The other pickpockets followed her, walking backwards, seemingly frightened of turning their backs on the old lady.

Mrs Booth watched them until they were out of sight, before turning to continue her walk to her home in Tanner Row. She twisted the eagle's head on her walking cane and the blade in the ferrule and the razor edge on the beak of the bird disappeared. But she halted almost as soon as she'd moved.

A boy was running along the pavement towards her. She hesitated about re-arming the stick.

It was Marcus Braithwaite.

'I saw...' he gasped. 'I were coming to help and...'

He looked admiringly at the walking cane.

'A gift from my late husband,' Mrs Booth said. 'It was his desire that I should be able to protect myself, Marcus. Though I confess the need had never arisen until today.'

'I would have helped,' he insisted. 'Had I been closer.'

89

But she could see the fear on his face.

'I know, Marcus. I know. Please will you carry my package for me? We'll go to my home and I'll get Dolly to find you something to eat. This has been a most distressing day!'

Ten

Davy was propped up in one of a long line of beds in the workhouse infirmary. He'd been conscious for a good hour and wished he had the strength to walk away.

A constable was sitting in a chair at the bedside. Davy contemplated asking him to fetch some water, in the hope that he might be able to sneak off, but the footpad felt that his legs didn't belong to him and feared he wouldn't get very far.

The traps were on to him, that was a sure thing, but how much did they know? Had the man they'd attacked involved the police? If he had, then the gaol beckoned... or perhaps the constable was only there because he imagined Davy the victim of an assault?

As he gathered his wits, Davy doubted that possibility. He was known to every policeman in York. He'd done his time, both in the House of Correction and the city prison. Nobody would ever believe he was an innocent victim.

'Got summat to say, Davy?' asked the constable.

'Nowt for you!' he replied.

'What about talking to us, then?'

Davy jumped with fright. He hadn't noticed the three men standing near the head of the bed on the other side. He knew two of the men, Sergeant Starkey of the city police and, worst of all, the man he'd tried to bludgeon on the banks of the Foss. The supposed victim who'd known how to fight back, alongside that bastard Reuben Dudgeon. The third man standing there was older, with almost white hair and long grey whiskers.

'So what about talking to us, Davy?' Sergeant Starkey persisted. 'Lest this gent lays an information against you. And not just assault, Davy. More like attempted murder, and that makes it serious. They probably wouldn't stretch your neck, but they haven't quite done with transportation. Or hard labour in some place fouler than York Gaol.'

'I've nowt to say!'

He tried to look away, but the grim expression on the oldest man's face dragged his eyes back.

Anders leaned across the bed, his mouth close to Davy's ear.

'Hard labour, even transportation... that's not the worst though, is it, Davy? A man was murdered in York the other day. The name of

Decker. Mean anything to you? Well, I'll tell you something about Mr Decker. He used to be in the detective office at Scotland Yard. Had a lot of friends, Davy. And now he's topped.'

'Nowt to do with me!'

He tried to turn away, but Anders grabbed the side of his head and forced him to look up.

'My name's Anders, Davy. I'm from Scotland Yard. I've sent many a bludger to the gallows. You could be next. You don't have to have topped Decker yourself. Understand that. You can be swung just for knowing and not telling.'

'I don't...'

'Oh, think warily before you speak, Davy. Don't be stupid. Moth knew who killed Decker, even if *he* didn't murder him. And shall I tell you something, Davy? Moth was murdered last night. Throttled. No doubt to keep him quiet.'

Davy's stomach heaved.

He wanted to vomit.

Wanted to soil himself.

But there was something about the look on this old man's face that banished all such thoughts.

Davy had once watched a man charm a snake, keeping his face near to the creature's tongue and fangs. All the snake's aggressiveness had vanished in the fakir's gaze. Now he felt the same. There was no world except the few inches between this man's eyes and his own.

'Faden's gone, Davy,' Anders went on. 'Run away in fear? Perhaps. But more likely dead. Slain by whoever topped Moth. And whoever that is, Davy... well, by now he'll know you're in here. And we can't leave this constable to guard you for ever. If we let you leave, how long d'you think you'll last?'

Davy tried to speak. It was as though his lips, his mouth, didn't belong to him.

Anders nodded.

'You wouldn't last the hour, Davy. You're not in a good condition to put up much of a fight. And I'd have it spread round the rookeries of York just when you were being thrown out of this place.'

'What...'

'What are you to do? Oh, well, I can make that easy for you, Davy. There's such a thing as turning Queen's Evidence. Telling all you know...'

'Peachin'...'

'Well, some call it that...'

'I'd be safer in gaol,' Davy muttered. 'If they...'

'You wouldn't be safer in gaol,' said Anders. 'Think about it. Moth dead. Probably Faden too. And it's so easy to turn off a prisoner in gaol. So many in there willing to knot a bit of rag across your throat, or cut you with a chiv. Just so they might be nicely rewarded when they get out. There's nowhere safe for you, Davy. Not unless I help you. And I will, Davy. I promise you that.'

'But if they're blown upon...'

'Oh, don't fear them, Davy. Fear me...'

Davy sank back against the hard pillow. There was no strength in his body and he knew that even if he could get out of the infirmary, he wouldn't travel far.

'What am I to do?' he cried out.

'If you'll tell all, I can get you away from York, Davy,' said Anders. 'Far away. Anywhere in England. Somewhere they'll never find you. Come on, man! What's there to think about? They'll get you in gaol or out there on the streets.'

'How do I know I can trust you?'

'Can you trust the men who murdered Moth?'

Davy looked up. Someone in parson's clothes was standing at the foot of the bed. Davy had a feeling the preacher had come to read him the last rites.

'The inspector's a good man,' said the Reverend Clews. 'You may trust him, Davy. You've my word that I'll oversee your treatment by the police. I'm a man of the cloth.'

'I need time,' said Davy.

'I can give you an hour,' said Anders, 'and the constable will stay with you for that period. You'll not be left unattended. But think hard, man! Step out of this place and you're at the mercy of whoever killed Moth.'

Davy coughed and spluttered.

'I need to throw up,' he said.

'Sir...'

They looked round to see Constable Barratt standing, hesitating, in the middle of the ward. Anders noticed that Davy turned his head away. This policeman walked pavements and ginnels that Davy was very familiar with. They must have known each other very well. Quite likely that Barratt had felt this thief's collar on more than one occasion.

'What is it, Barratt? I said we weren't to be disturbed...' said Starkey.

'Important, Sergeant,' Barratt persisted. 'Something all of these gents might care to hear.'

They got up and joined him.

'What the hell is it, Barratt?' asked Starkey. 'We're on the verge of getting that villain to peach.'

Barratt lowered his voice.

'A man dead, Sergeant,' he said. 'In a ginnel near Fossgate. His head smashed in and a cudgel lying nearby. A very brutal murder. I've just come from there.'

Starkey asked the question that was on all their lips.

'Is it Faden?'

'It could be anybody by the state the face is in, but no, it's not Faden. A shorter man. By the papers he had on him, he was Mr Jardine, the spectacle maker who had premises in Church Street. Done to death in the most brutal way.'

'Was he robbed?' asked Anders.

'No, Mr Anders sir. He had his purse in his pocket, with sovereigns in it. He wasn't slain for his money. Something more. The cudgel was lying nearby. Very like a weapon I took from Faden and which he must have taken back, when I couldn't get a conviction against him.'

'Very like Faden's cudgel or exactly it?'

'I'd swear it was the same cudgel, Inspector.'

'Is the victim still in the ginnel?' asked Starkey.

'Yes sir. The police doctor's there now and constables posted at each end of the place. I knew you'd want to see the scene, Sergeant.'

'Let's get over there,' said Anders. 'And I'd like you to send for every constable you can spare. If it's Faden, he's probably not far away. This is a small city. I doubt he'll go far in daylight.'

'What about Davy?' asked Quest.

'He's got the constable with him,' said Starkey. 'And it'll give him more time to consider his position. If Faden's in that part of the city, I want him brought to heel.'

~

Faden leaned against the wall of the disused warehouse down by the Foss River, one of those old places abandoned as trade moved down to the newer staithes on the Ouse.

There was some talk of developing the building as a charity home for lowly but honest labourers. For the time being, its great gate rattled in the breeze and the dusty windows gazed across the filthy waters of the Foss like the pointless eyes of dead men.

Every vagabond who wanted to evade the poor house sought shelter there on cold nights. It wasn't a safe place to lurk, but Faden had worked there in a brief but honest period when he was young. He knew a secret or two about the old building.

But you never knew who might be scouring the old staith? Faden regretted casting away his cudgel. He still had his blade and that was his one comfort, but he yearned for the heavy feel of that old club.

He paused by the gate and listened. Vagrants were often drunk and noisy and you could usually tell if the warehouse was occupied. There was no sound. Nothing. It might be possible to seek out the secret hiding place he had in mind, without disturbance.

Faden crossed the warehouse cobbles and climbed the rickety steps leading to the three upper storeys. The place stank of vomit and human soil. He heard the rats scuttle away as he ascended.

From a window at the very top, he looked out across the city. There were the sounds of men not far away. He could see builders renovating a warehouse higher up the river. Far enough away to make no difference. He thought he could hear the crackling of police constables' warning rattles, but he couldn't be sure.

At the back of the building there was a narrow slot, which had once held a glass window that had opened. He put his head and shoulders through and looked around. A tall building at the back hid him from view, the gap between the two structures being a blind alley. Faden reached out with a hand and found the protruding brick he remembered from so long ago.

He sat on the ledge of the window and reached for it with his foot, pulling himself round and then heaving upwards. There was a small enclosure just above, where the walls supporting the roof came together. A niche just a few yards across, with very low walls on three sides, open on the fourth, and covered by the edge of the roof.

It was a place where Faden had often hidden when he was an apprentice boy, from a warehouse master who'd enjoyed giving him a good leathering with his stick. An employer who was the very devil when he was in his drink, but kindly and jovial when sober.

A place to be safe until he could get away from York.

Faden reached inside his jacket and brought out a crust of bread. It wouldn't last long and there was little chance of finding any more food. He felt an overwhelming desire to kill the man who'd employed him so often. Faden had no doubt that this creature must be responsible for the death of Moth.

He also had no doubt that the bastard was trying to wipe out the men he'd used for his slaughters.

Faden knew he must be at the top of the list.

~

'You may as well move the body,' said Anders, looking down at the battered corpse of Mr Jardine, spectacle maker. 'It's a ghastly business, gentlemen, but there's nothing more we can do here. Best to put out a hue and cry across the county for Faden. It might help to bring him to heel.'

'And Davy?' asked Starkey.

'Let's get back and attend to him. Are you coming, Quest?'

Quest glanced up and down the alley.

'If Faden murdered this man, we can assume it was a spur of the moment killing,' he said. 'Perhaps done in panic. You tell me that Faden's well known in York? Then he can't travel far without being seen..'

'Your point?' asked Anders.

'Well, unless Faden has someone to hide him, he'll have found some shelter for the day and will try and sneak away in the hours of darkness. I doubt he's far from here. If the sergeant keeps his constables posted all day, we can limit his movements. We must be back here at dusk to hunt Faden down.'

'With respect, Mr Quest, you're not an officer of the law,' said Starkey. 'My masters wouldn't tolerate the involvement of members of the public in this way. It would look as though the police couldn't cope.'

Anders looked at them both.

'I'd be inclined to agree with you, Sergeant,' he said. 'But Quest has unusual abilities and we'd be foolish not to make use of his talents. But with this proviso, Quest. You may seek out Faden, but you're not to lay a hand on him, is that understood? Well, not unless your life's in danger.'

'Very well,' said Quest.

'Oh, and Quest?'

'Mmm?'

'I've no objection to you carrying a stick or a life preserver, but nothing deadlier than that... understood? I want this Faden in one piece if it's at all possible.'

~

'I'm not bloody having it!'

Long Ted never noticed his little girl when he was drunk, but this week pennies had been hard to come by and he was both sober and angry.

Even he was revolted by the long cut down his daughter's cheek. The gash was raw and red with blood. The strike from Mrs Booth's cane had gone right into Madge's mouth in at least two places. Her mother had fainted at the sight of the injury and, coming round, had insisted that she be taken to the workhouse infirmary.

Long Ted, staith worker and occasional thief, had bashed on the great gate and had demanded the attentions of the matron and the master.

'She needs sewin' up,' he roared. 'Right now, lest she bleeds to death. Dreadful... my little girl can't walk the streets in safety. And I want the traps here. I want the old bitch what's done this taken in charge. D'ye hear me?'

'I've sent for the doctor,' the master said. 'He'll be here in minutes and'll stitch her up. But it's up to you to pursue her attacker. Nothing to do with the workhouse...'

'So that's how it is,' yelled Long Ted. 'Cos I said as how it was a lady what done this. You'd get the traps soon enough, if you thought I'd bashed her...'

Madge gave her father a sideways look. She was quite used to being bashed and bruised by her father when he was in his cups. Her chest and back were still black from the last beating.

'I can finger the old hag,' he shouted. 'Finger her, I tell ye. She lives in Tanner Row. Everyone knows of her. If she was one of us, she'd soon be in the gaol or even the mad house. I wants her taken up d'ye hear me? I wants money for the injury she's done my child.'

'As I've said, there's nothing we can...'

Long Ted grasped the workhouse master by the collar and lifted the little man from the floor. The matron backed away and screamed for assistance.

The constable, who'd been guarding Davy, had been escorting his prisoner to the disgusting piss-hole in the corner of the ward. The man said he needed to relieve himself.

Hearing the row from the entrance hall and fearing there might be an attempt to come in and seize Davy, he left his prisoner sitting on the wooden seat of the stone lavatory and rushed in the direction of the disturbance. As he went, he glanced back along the ward. It wasn't deserted. There was a workhouse helper in the distance and a woman visiting a patient not far away.

He knew Long Ted of old. Had collared him on more than one occasion for drunkenness and lewd behaviour in the streets. He knew his little girl too. Too much of a compliment to call her a dip. She emptied pockets with intimidation, rather than skill. One for the reformatory if he could ever catch her in the act.

But even Constable Parfitt was appalled at the sight of the child's face.

He made Long Ted release the master and asked what was up, provoking a long and blasphemous explanation.

'I've seen her about,' Parfitt said. 'The old woman from Tanner Row. But if you want to lay an information, you need to get yourself down to the police station. I'm about other duties here and can't be spared to deal with this.'

'Ah, but if it had been a nob, one of the Class who'd had their child maimed, you'd soon go a-running,' Long Ted protested. 'Always the same. The poor suffer and the well-off get away with murder.'

'I've told you what to do...'

Long Ted looked down at him.

'And I'm tellin' you. Now are you goin' to...'

'What the devil's going on here, Parfitt?'

The constable tuned to see Sergeant Starkey by the gate, Anders, Quest and Barratt at his side.

'I told you to stick by Davy,' said Starkey. 'What's going on?'

Parfitt explained.

'Well, that's none of your business, now get back to our man...'

'What about her?' Long Ted jabbed a grimy finger at his daughter. 'Or do I have to take my pals down to Tanner Row to deal with the old woman?'

Starkey faced up to him.

'You'll do no such bloody thing,' he said. 'Or I'll have you in the gaol so fast, your feet won't touch.' He turned to Constable Barratt. 'Constable, you go down to Tanner Row right away and find the lady. Get her side of this yarn.'

'Yes, Sergeant.'

As he turned to leave, Starkey grabbed him by the sleeve.

'Two sides to every story,' he whispered. 'If this old biddy's of the Quality, go easy. She might well be a victim in all this. I know all about that dreadful child.'

Barratt nodded understandingly and left.

Starkey turned back to Long Ted.

'Be warned,' he said to him. 'Nobody takes the law into their own hands in this place. Get your daughter stitched up and go home. I'll send a constable round later to get her account. But you stay well clear of Tanner Row and this old woman. I'm itching to put you away and you'll make it so easy for me by crossing the line.'

They walked back towards the infirmary ward, dodging workhouse inmates and casual visitors as they went

'Has Davy said anything?' Anders asked Parfitt.

'No Inspector, though he's wide awake. I left him in the, er...'

'You shouldn't have left him at all!' said Starkey.

'Safe enough, Sergeant,' Parfitt said. 'The ward's full and there was a workhouse attendant and a sick visitor close by. Davy can't escape without coming past us. I know him well enough.'

'But he's not in his bed is he?' Starkey said as they entered the ward.

'He'll still be in the piss-hole... er, privy, Sergeant.' said Parfitt. 'Over here...'

He pulled open the flimsy wooden door at the end of the ward.

Anders had already pictured what they'd find, long before Parfitt staggered backwards. His instinct for these matters was almost supernatural.

Davy lay across the wooden seat, one arm down the dark and stinking hole, staring at them in wide-eyed amazement. His purple tongue stuck far out between the blue lips. A neat piece of cord was cutting hard into the dead man's throat.

'Well, there's another tongue that won't wag,' said Anders.

Eleven

Barratt had almost given up on interviewing Mrs Booth, for nobody appeared to be at home when he first tapped the door. But as he was turning away, the old lady appeared, looking hot and flustered, her maid running behind, bearing a large package.

The old lady explained that she'd had urgent business in the town.

Now she sat in a dark corner of her sitting room, her head nodding as Constable Barratt gave an account of Long Ted's complaint.

She tapped her stick on the carpet with some impatience, as he came to the end of his account.

'But what was I supposed to do, Constable?' she asked. 'I was surrounded by these dreadful people and feared for my safety. They were most aggressive and I feared they might be carrying knives.'

'Then in that case, you had every right to defend yourself,' said Barratt. 'The question in law is the degree of force you used. There's no doubt the child was badly maimed.'

Mrs Booth leaned forward.

'Which I bitterly regret,' she said. 'I appreciate that poverty drives these people to crime, but I am an old lady. A defenceless widow.'

'The law might say... hardly defensive,' Barratt pointed at the walking cane.

Mrs Booth ran a gloved hand over the eagle-headed handle.

'My dear, late husband had it made for me,' she said. 'During the disturbances of the 'thirties. He wanted me to be able to protect myself. The sharpness of the beak and the blade at the end were his idea.'

'May I?' asked Barratt, reaching out a hand.

Mrs Booth hesitated for a moment, and then handed over the cane. Barratt studied the eagle-head and then the ferrule at the tip which concealed the short dagger.

'Most unusual,' he said. 'I've an interest, ma'am, for you see, my father made such canes and sticks as an amusement.'

'He must have been a very talented man...'

'Ah, he was... I must say, this eagle is unusual. Not like our native ones at all. Was it based on one that Mr Booth had actually seen?'

Mrs Booth shook her head.

'I really don't know, I've never thought about it. My late husband was a much-travelled man in the days before we were married. Tell me, Constable, it is against the law to carry such a cane in public?'

'Certainly not, though there would be limits to its offensive use.'

'Have I over-stepped the mark?'

Barratt considered.

'Probably not, ma'am, though I shall have to submit a report to my superiors. But it seems to me that it was purely a case of self-defence. I doubt any action will be taken.'

'And the girl's father? Am I in any danger from him?'

'He's been warned, ma'am. I doubt he'll bother you. But I should avoid the lonely places of the city for a while. Try and stay where there are other people.'

'I will, indeed.'

After the slatternly maid had shown him out, Barratt had a good stroll up and down Tanner Row, half-expecting Long Ted to be hiding nearby. But the street was busy only with passengers from the railway station. A great cloud of steam indicated the arrival of the midday train.

He walked down into North Street, which had a reputation for being a haunt of the loathsome girl, Madge and her gang of footpads, but there was no sign of any potential trouble there.

Mrs Booth was a game old girl, he thought to himself. He couldn't blame her for protecting herself, and would suggest to Starkey that no action be taken against her. Old ladies should have the right to walk the streets in peace and safety.

Barratt envied her that marvellous cane. He had a modest collection of gadget sticks himself and would dearly like to have possessed that one. Such a strange eagle too. Being a country boy, he knew a lot about birds. He really must thumb the pages of his *Compendium of World Birds* and look that one up.

~

'I've just heard the terrible news!'

Gaius Pritchard came along the corridor leading into the entrance hall of the workhouse. Anders, Quest and Starkey turned on hearing his voice. Anders thought that Pritchard seemed particularly flustered.

'Here, in the open ward of our infirmary... who would believe it?' Gaius Pritchard went on. 'I suppose it was his accomplice, Faden, though how he could have got past the officials is beyond me?'

'I didn't realise you had a connection with the workhouse?' said Quest.

'I'm a member of the Board,' said Pritchard. 'I advise the Guardians on matters legal. I keep an office here for that purpose. I was upstairs when I heard the commotion. And this gentleman is...?'

He was looking at Anders.

'This is Inspector Anders of Scotland Yard,' said Starkey.

'Oh yes, of course. I know something of your reputation, Inspector. It's a privilege to meet you. You come to our lovely city at such a distressing hour.'

'This is Mr Gaius Pritchard, Anders,' said Quest. 'I've told you of him.'

'Yes, of course. You're the Mr Pritchard who invited John Lardiner to York.'

'Indeed I am, though I wish now the thought had never crossed my mind. I've simply made a bad situation much worse. But about this dreadful killing? Am I to understand that nobody in the infirmary ward saw anything?'

'It appears not,' said Starkey. 'There's a blind spot by the doorway of the privy. Only someone walking in or out of the ward would have seen anyone enter. According to our constable, there were two people in the ward, apart from the patients. One was a workhouse attendant seeing to a dying man at the far end. He observed nothing. The other was a woman visiting her consumptive husband.'

'The Guardians will be most distressed,' said Pritchard. 'I must report to them at once, if you'll excuse me.'

He gave a bow and dashed away.

'There's little more we can do here,' said Starkey. 'We must prepare for a night's work hunting down Faden. I'll meet you gentleman later at the detective office. Say about eight. We'll leave from there.'

After he'd gone, Anders said to Quest: 'Perhaps you'll take a turn with me through the streets, Quest. I've been giving these matters a great deal of thought and I'd value your opinion.'

They strolled up towards the Minster.

'Tell me, what do you think is the most puzzling aspect of this whole business?' asked Anders.

'I suppose the vanishing of John Lardiner,' said Quest.

'I don't think so,' said Anders. 'To me there's a greater puzzle. A matter overshadowed by that particular mystery.'

'Which is?'

'I'm more interested in the murder of Joshua Marples in the sanctity of the Minster. That's the greater puzzle. It was clearly a calculated slaying, but we know that his killer didn't go prepared in his desire to commit murder, hence the use of the bell-rope. But it seems there was an urgency, a desperation, to have Joshua Marples dead. Why there and why then? His killer could have waited and murdered the man at any time or in any place. Why take the considerable risk of killing Marples in somewhere as public as the Minster?'

Quest considered.

'I see your point,' he said at last. 'By all accounts, Marples was an inoffensive man with no enemies. Yet someone needed to slay him at that precise moment. But why? To silence him?'

Anders gave him a grim smile.

'Precisely so,' he said. 'To silence him before he could relate something he'd seen regarding the disappearance of Lardiner. It's the only thing that makes sense. Why did he go to the Minster at all?'

'To report to the Archbishop.'

'Yes, but report what? He dashes after this Lardiner as the man runs down Grape Lane, but Lardiner evades him. Or so we believe. But did Marples see something? Something of such great importance that, despite his exhaustion and weak heart, he needed to tell the Archbishop straight away.'

'So he got as far as the Choir and was obliged to rest,' said Quest. 'We know from Clews that he was exhausted, even in Grape Lane. He was searching the Minster for the Archbishop when his ill-health overcame him. He sat down and...'

'An easy target for his killer,' said Anders. 'The Choir is a discreet place, not as open as much of the building. He did his killer a favour by resting there.'

'But what's the mystery of Grape Lane? What could he have seen that was of such importance?'

Anders shrugged.

'It cost poor Marples his life,' he said. 'Something vital, Quest. That old man paid a high price for that piece of knowledge.'

~

Mrs Booth looked up as Dolly the maid entered the sitting room.

'I asked not to be disturbed,' she said.

'It's that boy, wants to know if you've a job for him?'

'I don't think I have... no, wait, show him in.'

Dolly waved Marcus into the room. The boy stood on the carpet in front of the old lady, cap in hand.

'Ah, Marcus... you say you know all about that girl who attacked me?'

'Name's Madge, her father works down on't staith. Least Long Ted does when he's not drunk or in the Correction House. Bashed my head once!'

'You know where he lives?'

'He's got a room, down by the Bailey.'

Mrs Booth considered.

'Would you go there for me, Marcus?'

The boy shuffled on the carpet, giving her an apprehensive look.

'He don't like me much, ma'am. Might bash me again.'

'I don't think he will, Marcus,' said Mrs Booth. 'You see, I want you to take him some money.'

'Money, ma'am?'

'Two sovereigns, Marcus. Here, I'll put it in this...'

She reached into a drawer of the bureau near to the fireside and drew out a little leather pouch. She took two golden coins from a small pile on the table, put them in the pouch and pulled the drawstring tight.

'There... and I must write this Long Ted a note.'

'Pardon, ma'am, but I doubt he can read.'

'Then you must relay my message to him. You will tell him that this money is in compensation for the wound I inflicted on his daughter. Can you remember that, Marcus? You will add that I don't expect to hear from him again.'

The boy looked uneasy.

'What is it?' asked Mrs Booth.

'Don't think it's wise to pay him. Long Ted'll just keep coming back for more. The police'll do nowt anyway. They've had trouble enough with Long Ted.'

'Nevertheless, it's what I want you to do. Bring back his reply and there'll be a shilling in it for you.'

'I'll try and catch him down at the staith. He'll be less likely to belt me there, with other folk standing by.'

He glanced at her again and left the room.

Dolly saw him out and came back.

'You heard that?' asked Mrs Booth.

'What's to stop the brat taking off with your sovereigns?' said Dolly.

'Oh, I think he's trustworthy enough. It'll be a useful test. If he accomplishes this, I'll know I can trust him with more important matters.'

'You're taking a risk...'

Mrs Booth looked up at her.

'Our life is full of risks,' she said. 'Because of my condition, I'm limited in what I may do. There comes a time when you have to trust someone...'

~

There was somebody in his room. No doubt about it. Quest could see a shadow move across the light coming under the door. A floorboard inside gave a faint creak.

Perhaps the maid, though in Quest's experience, maids were usually noisy creatures as they went about their work. The maid in this tavern invariably left the door open as she tended the fire and made the bed. She also had a habit of singing to herself as she did her tasks.

Quest had returned to the inn for an hours sleep, before the night's expedition in search of Faden. He'd felt weary since coming to York. His struggles in London, against the King of Jacob's Island, had exhausted him beyond measure. Quest no longer had the energy he'd enjoyed as a younger man.

And he was missing Rosa...

Someone sat down in the chair in his room. He heard one of the legs scuff across the bare, wooden floorboards. Instinctively, he reached into the inner pocket of his coat, in search of his little percussion pistol. He realised, with some frustration, he'd left it in his room when he set out that morning.

Oh well, nothing for it but to go in...

It was probably a quite innocent visitor. Important not to react to every event of life as a drama.

Quest turned the door handle and walked in.

There was his pistol. Not hidden away as he'd left it, but being pointed in his direction. Aimed directly at his heart. Held by the man sitting in the chair by the window.

'Ah, Mr Quest,' said the intruder. 'You're here at last.'

~

Inspector Anders and Sergeant Starkey had walked down to a workshop along from the Manor Shore. It overlooked the filthy waters of the Ouse. Anders thought the river a good match for the Thames as a source of stenches, but he was too polite to mention it to his companion.

A sign above the gate of the long building said that it was the premises of Alvar Zinion, manufacturer of ropes and cords.

'What old Alvar doesn't know about rope isn't worth the knowledge,' said Starkey, as they strolled along the cobbles outside. 'He came over from Prussia forty years ago, during the wars against Napoleon. His ropes were much used on the warships of the day.'

'He must be old,' said Anders. 'Older than me,' he added with a chuckle.

'Alvar has three sons who run the business now, but he's always here taking an interest. Here's the man himself...'

A tall stringy man with a huge white beard and even longer hair came out of the workshop and nodded a greeting.

'Good to see you, Sergeant. A long time since you've paid me a visit. Not since that business with the theft of my old cart.'

'Alvar, this is Inspector Anders of Scotland Yard. He has a length of cord he wants you to look at, in relation to a case. We wondered whether it might be a product of your manufactory?'

Anders held out the cord used to strangle Davy in the workhouse. Alvar Zinion looked at it for a moment as Anders stretched it to its full length between his two hands. He reached down for his *pince-nez* spectacles, which hung on a ribbon to his jacket pocket, and perched them on his nose.

'Let me see, please,' he said, holding out a hand.

The old man sucked in a breath, as he looked at the cord with great deliberation. He made no comment for several minutes as he looked at it again and again, testing the fibre of the cord between two fingers. He sniffed at the cord and then held it up against the afternoon sun.

He passed it back to Anders, shaking his head.

'No, gentlemen, that cord was not made here nor anywhere else in York,' he said.

'You are sure?' asked Anders.

'Oh, quite sure,' said Mr Zinion. 'The methods of making rope and cord vary little, but rope-makers in most countries have differing styles. I can say, with some certainty, that this cord was not even manufactured in England.'

'Then where?' asked Starkey.

'It's of a type we see quite often in vessels coming up-river to York. Ships from the Baltic. But I say of a type, for this was never used on a ship. This is the kind of cord more used to secure lengths of timber. I almost made a fundamental error in thinking that it originated in one of the Scandinavian countries...'

'So it's not from the Baltic?' said Anders.

'Forgive me, it almost certainly is, but not from most of the countries which trade with York. This cord comes from the very head of the Baltic. Probably the shores of the Gulf of Finland. I might suggest that it was used to secure timber in the dark forests along the banks of the River Neva, for look there are traces of bark on the braiding. Russia perhaps, but that would be a surmise.'

'Russia...' said Anders.

'I've no doubt that this cord comes from the manufactory, no, that is too grand a word, the small rope-works of some very able Russian, either in Russia itself or possibly Finland.'

~

Quest waved in the direction of the pistol.

'I didn't leave it loaded,' he said. 'Unless you've taken the trouble?'

Nathaniel Cooper, landlord of the tavern, held the pistol in his own scarred right hand for a long moment, and then placed it on the table by the bed.

'I haven't,' he said. 'Pistols are dangerous weapons to leave lying around in my rooms, Mr Quest. Suppose my maid had stumbled upon it?'

'I did leave it well hidden,' said Quest.

Cooper smiled, 'You did indeed, but I knew you had one and thought it best to discover its whereabouts. You intrigue me, Mr Quest...'

'Marshall...' said Quest.

Cooper laughed, 'I don't think so, Mr Quest. It's a wise conspirator who knows his own name. You were Marshall once, but now you are Mr William Quest of London and Hope Down. You are in York to investigate the vanishing of a Mr John Lardiner. Who, I confess, I'd never heard of until an hour or two ago.'

Quest took off his coat and hung it on the hook on the door.

'Do you search all of your guest's rooms?' he asked as he turned to face the innkeeper.

'Only the ones I'm particularly warned about.'

'Not the first time you've examined my possessions. You came in here while I was dining, on my very first night. You left the gaslight turned up and placed my book there the wrong way round.'

Cooper drew in a breath. He picked up the copy of *Lavengro*.

'That was clumsy of me,' he said. 'You know I had the good fortune to meet its author, Mr George Borrow, once. At a prize fight. A giant of a man with white hair. I'm an admirer of his works, though he was in a grumpy mood that day.'

'You were privileged,' said Quest. 'I'd like to strike up an acquaintance with him myself.'

'A man handy with his fists. I wouldn't like to get into a brawl with him. They say he was instructed in the art by John Thurtell, the murderer of William Weare.'

'Thurtell got his neck stretched for that crime,' said Quest.

'I'm told you're fortunate not to have had the rope around yours?'

'Some people have said that.'

'Yet now I understand you're working with the detective force?'

'A means to an end,' said Quest. 'But you have the advantage, Mr Cooper. You know all about me. I'm intrigued to know why and how? I take it you're not my enemy, or you'd never have put the pistol down?'

Nathaniel Cooper sighed.

'Not your enemy,' he said. 'More a friend of a friend. I was requested to give you support in this dangerous quest.' He smiled at the word. 'Quest, a man who lives in danger, I'm told.'

'Who made this request?'

'An old friend of mine,' said Cooper. 'A prize-fighter of great renown. Someone who's enjoyed the hospitality of these four walls on more than one occasion. No less a bruiser than Albert Sticks.'

'I should have guessed,' said Quest. 'Particularly as you mentioned him on my arrival.'

'Sticks wrote to me even before you left London. Explained the circumstances. You confided in him where you were to stay in York. An admirable coincidence that it should have been here. Sticks said you might need an ally – in the absence of your usual comrades. I'm handy with my fists and a great many weapons, My years with the East India Company weren't wasted. So here I am.'

'But how do you know about John Lardiner? Sticks knew nothing about the reason for my visit?'

'I only learned the details some little while ago. From another old friend of both Sticks and myself...'

'Reuben Dudgeon!'

'Exactly so, Mr Quest. May I call you William? I think we can dispense with the formality of host and customer. My friends call me Nat.'

Quest sat down on the bed.

'Has Sticks written to all his old pals in York?' Quest grinned. 'May I ask why you didn't greet me in this way when I arrived?'

'Regrettable,' said Cooper. 'But there are devious individuals operating in the city. I had to make absolutely sure you really were William Quest. I've had spies foisted on me before. Sticks described to me your pistol. A splendid example, tested by the gun provers of Brummagem. He also mentioned this wonderful book.'

'What am I to say?'

'I'm not in the first flush of youth, William. But a trained man never forgets the fighting arts. You might appreciate someone to watch your back... when you set out tonight to hunt down that dangerous wretch Faden...'

'Seems as though it's all been arranged,' said Quest. 'How can I refuse?'

Cooper clapped his hands.

'A long time since I've had an adventure,' he said. 'We'll toast the enterprise with my best sherry and then you might relish a nap before we take to the streets.'

~

Faden watched as the dusk settled over the jumbled streets of the old city. It was going to be a dry evening. He fingered the hilt of the dagger in his inside pocket. A weapon he'd used to stab so many.

If anyone obstructed him tonight, they would surely die.

Twelve

'The constables are sure that Faden hasn't slipped the net,' said Starkey, as the hunters gathered at the city end of Fossgate. 'If our man's in this part of York, we'll have him.'

'It'll mean searching a lot of buildings, Sergeant,' said Constable Barratt. 'For all we know, he has allies who could help him keep his head down for weeks.'

Anders looked towards the river.

'It depends if he trusts his allies,' he said. 'Given what's happened, I suspect this Faden has become a liability. Instinct tells me he's lying low. Friendless and full of fear. He'll run and I suspect it'll be tonight.'

'I hope so,' said Starkey. 'We don't have the men for a house to house search. We can barely contain this small area. There's many a street and ginnel he can use to slip away.'

'What do you think, Quest?' asked Anders. 'You've evaded search parties in the past?'

Quest smiled.

'I'd have no difficulty on the streets of London. Here, well, I'm not so sure. It's a small place compared to the Metropolis. Faden's well known and probably has no access to disguises. There's miles of countryside beyond the city walls. He has to move at night or he'd be noticed. As long as he has no access to food or shelter, he'll go tonight.'

'He's hemmed in by the walls of the prison in one direction. Then there's the great curve of the river. I've men on the bridges and all the boats secured. Unless he takes to the water, he can't go that way.' Starkey looked at his watch. 'It's gone eight. My men will have started their sweep from the direction of the city. If our rat's here, we'll flush him out.'

Starkey looked uneasily in the direction of Quest, who stood by a wall with Reuben Dudgeon and Nathaniel Cooper at his side.

'I trust that none of you gents are carrying weapons?' he said.

'We've no pistols or blades,' Quest replied. 'You sanctioned the use of life preservers, Sergeant. We all have one of those.'

'For self-defence only, Quest,' said Anders. 'That was the agreement. I want this villain taken alive. I want him to talk. I want chapter and verse about the men who employ him.'

Quest gave a sidelong glance towards Cooper and Dudgeon.

~

Gaius Pritchard strode along Colliergate on the way to the Foss bridge, trying to keep up with the faster pace of his half-brother. Sebastian Clews had always been the athlete in the family, even when they were boys.

'You believe we'll be welcomed?' asked Pritchard, breathing heavily. 'The city police don't usually encourage the involvement of amateurs.'

'Quest and his friends are there,' said Clews. 'Sergeant Starkey can hardly object to our participation. If anything, we've the greater right to be in at the kill. If this man Faden's involved in any way with the disappearance of John Lardiner, then we've a responsibility to help bring him to heel.'

'I was just saying...'

'You are too cautious, Gaius.'

'Forgive me, I'm no man of action.'

Clews stopped and faced him.

'Perhaps you should go back, Gaius. What'll happen if we encounter this villain? Do you know how to use the cosh you carry, bub? You'll recall I used to box at school and when I was at Cambridge. But I remember the difficulty you had when young, when you were bully-ragged...'

'That was a while ago, Sebastian.'

'Even so.'

Gaius Pritchard looked up at the dark sky.

'I'd feel dishonoured not to be part of this night's adventure,' he said. 'Whatever the consequences.'

Clews sighed.

'So be it,' he said.

~

It was like the harsh sound of a horde of demented crickets, echoing along the darkened streets and narrow ginnels of the old city. The noise of the police rattle, turned by Constable Barratt, was taken up by the policemen forming a line parallel to the River Foss.

It was the signal to move in and take Faden.

Quest found himself breathing heavily. The sound of the rattles brought back a score of memories. The times when he'd been hunted by the police in a similar fashion.

113

He'd always managed to elude his pursuers, even with the mightier River Thames at his back. There were mysterious alleys. Holes that linked one house to another. Secret routes across rooftops. A myriad of escapes for a determined fugitive. Faden would know them all in this place, just as Quest knew them in London.

There were just two factors to take into account.

Was Faden even *in* the search area?

How *good* was Faden?

Quest looked at Anders' face. He knew that this very skilled policeman was making the same calculations. After a long moment, Anders caught Quest's eye and gave a brisk nod.

Man-hunting was never a pleasant activity.

~

Faden had climbed down from his rooftop lair, descended through the old workshop and crept out into the narrow street beyond. It seemed deserted, apart from one old drunkard sprawled across the cobbles. The street led to a ginnel which coiled around the gasworks, worked its way alongside the Foss and then journeyed towards Union Street and the river bridge leading towards Heworth.

Worth a try, though he feared the police would have sealed the crossing. If they had, there would be no alternative but to cross the city, relying on the sheer number of people to distract the hunt.

Faden felt the dagger again, concealed under his coat. If they were going to swing him, he'd make it well worth the rough feel of the rope on his throat.

He'd take as many of the bastards with him as he could.

~

Quest felt a surge of excitement run through his body as they turned out of Hungate into a particularly foul ginnel. A police rattle and the cries of policemen broke the silence of the night. Barratt, who'd got ahead of the main party, was calling out for assistance.

'Come on...' Starkey yelled.

They ran in the direction of the disturbance.

The shouts were louder now. More than one police rattle was being turned furiously. Quest could hear the note of triumph in some constable's voice.

114

As they turned a corner, Quest could see a great struggle in progress. Barratt and two other constables had seized some villain wearing a battered tall hat and a torn coat of fustian.

The man was trying to fight back, his fists flailing and his right leg kicking out at his captors. He was crying out indistinguishable words, which then ended in a great cry of anger and frustration.

The light of their bullseye lanterns reflected the silver gleam of a knife, fallen on to the cobbles. A ferocious looking weapon, Quest noted. Designed for no other purpose than stabbing.

At last, the captive was subdued, head bowed forward as he gasped for breath. Two of the constables had him by an arm each, which they'd twisted behind his back. Barratt had his forearm around the man's throat.

Starkey shone his lantern into the face of the prisoner.

He mumbled an obscenity.

'Sergeant?' said Anders.

'It's not Faden,' Starkey said, 'this one's called Adair. A footpad of the worst sort. Not the one we want...'

Quest had often heard his hunting neighbours at Hope Down moan that a stray fox had crossed the line of the animal they'd been pursuing, throwing the hounds off the scent. It seemed to particularly annoy them. Quest, who never participated in hunting, was always baffled by their passion and frustration.

Sergeant Starkey seemed similarly frustrated.

'You know Faden?' he almost spat the words at Adair.

'No,' the footpad replied.

'Yes, you bloody do, Adair. You've been on the rob with him in the past. Served time in the House of Correction alongside him. Lie to me and you'll rot in the gaol for years.'

'I know Faden,' said Adair.

'Have you seen him today.'

'Not for a week nor more...'

'You'd better not be lying to me, Adair.'

'I ain't.'

'Where would he be in this district? If he was hiding out?'

'Can't tell you that, Mr Starkey...'

The sergeant stepped nearer to the footpad.

'You'll tell me, Adair. Or it's the gaol for you. And my lads here might not be too gentle getting you there.'

One of the constables twisted Adair's arm a tad further up his back, making the footpad groan.

'All right, all right, but when you take him, don't let on I peached?'

'I won't,' said Starkey. 'Where?'

'Only one place he's like to hide,' said Adair. 'Old Cutler warehouse, down by t'Foss. He was apprenticed there and old man Cutler gave him many a beating. I suspicion Faden turned the old man off. Drownded him in the river.'

'Where is this place?' asked Anders.

'A few hundred yards from here,' Starkey said. 'It's derelict now. A good place to hide.'

He turned to Barratt.

'Move the men in towards the Cutler warehouse, Constable. Seal all the ground between there and the two bridges. Then take some men into the warehouse and tear it apart. If Faden's not there, he won't be far away.'

If he's there at all, thought Quest, as Barratt dashed off.

'What about this one?' Anders nodded at the prisoner.

'We've nothing to hold him on,' Starkey replied.

He turned to Adair.

'Get out of my sight,' he said. 'Into the city, back to the Lanes. I can't spare any men to take you in or I'd give you a long session at the detective office.'

They watched as the footpad loped away from them, along the dinge of the ginnel and up towards Hungate. Starkey bent down and picked up the fallen dagger.

~

Faden pulled himself into the corner of a building in Union Street. Not much of a place to hide, but there was at least some dark shadow. A solitary bell was tolling from St Cuthbert's church at his back. Its sound crashed through his brain.

The disgusting stench of the Foss river came up to him as it flowed below the Layerthorpe Bridge. Faden could remember when the old bridge spanned the river, with its postern gate. He'd picked the pocket of an aged gent hard by the gate. The first of many dips in his long years of crime.

But the gate and the old bridge were gone now and the new crossing offered no concealment either for a villain or the law.

At a first glance, Faden had thought the bridge unguarded. He'd started to walk towards it with his usual boldness. But then a constable appeared on the Heworth bank, flashing a bullseye. He was joined by two others and they stepped out on to the bridge.

One of them shouted something and two more police came from the direction of Jewbury and joined them. They stood, a human barricade, across Faden's end of the bridge.

He cursed at his decision to move so soon. He should have waited until the hue and cry died down, but the coldness of his rooftop perch and the need for food had proved too much. Faden never really believed that the city police force would make such an effort to take him by the heels.

He slunk backwards, keeping deep in the shadows of the wall, back past the church. He crossed Peasholme when he was out of sight of the constables, and headed into a ginnel that would take him back to Cutler's warehouse.

Better more days on the cold rooftop with hunger gnawing his belly, than the feel of the rope at his throat.

~

Adair had scarcely vanished into the darkness when two other men walked down the ginnel accompanied by a police constable. Anders held up his arms in a gesture of annoyance at the sight of the Reverend Clews and Gaius Pritchard.

'This is a manhunt, not a public spectacle,' he declared.

'My brother and I thought that...' Pritchard began.

Starkey stepped forward.

'We appreciate your offer of assistance, gentlemen,' he said. 'I know you've a vested interest in us collaring this villain, but these matters are best left to trained policemen.'

'But Mr Quest is here,' protested Pritchard.

'He may well be,' said Anders. 'But Quest has certain talents which make him invaluable in these circumstances.'

'And these gentlemen?' asked Clews, indicating Reuben Dudgeon and Nathaniel Cooper.

'Quest's assistants,' muttered Anders.

'But this is one man you're seeking,' said Pritchard. 'There are a number of us. Surely we are in no danger?'

'Faden's a killer,' said Starkey. 'Who's to know how a desperate fugitive might strike out?'

'If he's so threatening, then surely we are better remaining with your party, Sergeant, than retracing our steps through the darkened streets?'

'Inspector?' Starkey turned to Anders.

Anders grunted.

'Very well, but keep out of the way. Now let's close in on this Cutler's warehouse. Time this matter was resolved one way or another.'

~

Faden stopped dead as he reached the entrance to the Cutler warehouse. He'd closed the wooden gate when he'd left. Now it stood open. Voices came from the gloom of the building. Shouts as men searched its derelict levels. A half-turn of a police rattle.

The constables had stopped up his earth.

No shelter for him there.

Faden's face and back were wet with sweat. Its salty taste ran down from his eyes and on to his lips. Breaths came in tiny gasps. He took out the dagger from beneath his coat. His hand was shaking.

The sound of one police rattle was met by another, and all on the city side from where he was. There were shouts as one constable cried out to his companion. In the ginnel leading down to the narrow lane by the warehouse, there was the noise of several men talking.

Footsteps coming closer, echoing in the ginnel like the drumbeats of a hellish army.

He could hear the hiss of the water from the Foss river. No escape that way.

No more liberty.

No more freedom.

This was it then.

Faden hit his shaking hand against the dripping wall, as if the pain induced might give it extra strength and power. He looked down at the blade of the dagger as it caught the reflection of the gaslight.

His hand stopped its shuddering.

He was ready to kill.

They'd top him anyway.

Better to die with a reputation.

~

William Quest turned the corner. Out of the ginnel and into the lane. He was a yard ahead of the rest of the hunters. He could see the gate of the warehouse in the flickering light of the gas lamp, but didn't see the wanted man for a moment or two.

Faden had sunk himself hard against the filthy wall, as though he wanted to be part of it, his dark clothing rendering him almost invisible in the gloom. But then Starkey came out of the ginnel, his bullseye lantern sending out a beam towards the warehouse door.

Then Quest saw Faden. As clear as could be. Pinioned in the ray of light. For the rest of his days, Quest never forgot the desperate and haunting look on the face of the fugitive.

Or how quickly the expression changed from fear to fury.

'It's all up, Faden,' shouted Starkey. 'Put down that knife. Don't make it any worse for yourself.'

Police always said that, Quest thought.

Stupid...

If you're going to be topped anyway, how could it be any worse?

As the others turned the corner, Faden was fixed in the beams of several lanterns. His mouth wide open, his breathing echoing into the doorway of the warehouse.

'Go to hell, Sergeant!' Faden yelled.

'There's no way out, Faden,' said Starkey.

Faden looked along the line of men surrounding him, all of them with grim expressions on their faces. He glanced down at the dagger. It might be possible to slash one or two of them, but the end was inevitable.

Faden could feel the rope tightening across his throat.

In the dazzle of the lanterns, it took him a moment to notice the pistol clutched by Starkey. The detective had it pointing down at the ground.

Faden thought...

Better to die swiftly here than face the weeks rotting in the prison. Then the inevitable moment of being trundled out of the condemned cell, the hood placed on his head, the falling away as he plummeted through the drop, the hempen rope cutting into his throat.

One swift shot and...

'Listen, my friend...'

One of the men had stepped forward to the side of him.

'Listen, my friend,' said Gaius Pritchard, coming closer. 'There's no escape. Don't ruin any more lives...'

Faden looked the man up and down. Noted the life preserver clutched in one hand. Saw the expression on his face.

'Resist and the sergeant will shoot you down,' Pritchard went on, taking another step nearer. 'It's that or the gallows. Both are quick deaths really.'

The smug bastard was urging him to get shot dead!

Faden edged along the wall towards Pritchard. If he could get the man between the armed detective and himself, he could at least plunge his dagger through the heart of this fool.

Then he became aware of another man by Pritchard's shoulder. Noted the resemblance between the two. He'd seen them around the town together. In happier days when he'd been on the dip. Brothers, someone had remarked.

'Get back, Gaius,' Clews shouted. 'He'll not hesitate to slay you. He'll not show you mercy...'

Quest also took a step forward, his own cosh out and ready. Prepared to charge forward and grapple with Faden. But something made him pause. A look of astonishment on the villain's face.

Astonishment that turned to fury.

'You bastard!' Faden screamed.

He swung away from the wall and dashed forward, raising the dagger to strike a blow. Quest saw Gaius Pritchard raise his life preserver and, more by luck than skill, ward off the blade as he wielded it upwards.

Faden held on to the hilt of the weapon. With his other hand, he pushed Pritchard on the shoulder, trying to get him down on the ground. He pulled back the knife, preparing to make a vicious swipe. He was looking up and yelling something. Some word indistinguishable in the accompanying scream.

'Juuu...'

Quest was just a yard away when Starkey's pistol cracked. He smelt the powder. The flash of its discharge made him blink. The ball broke through the air within a foot of him. So close, he veered to one side as he dashed forward.

Quest saw a bright red hole open in the middle of Faden's forehead. Heard the dagger clatter to the ground. Faden's eyes turned upwards, white in the light of the lanterns. His arms flung out. His hands smashing backwards against the dripping walls of the warehouse.

Quest collided with Pritchard, having to hold out his own hands against the wall to halt his momentum.

When he looked again, Faden lay dead, caught in the gutter between the cobbles of the lane and the bricks of the warehouse wall.

His mouth still open from his last desperate cry.

Thirteen

William Quest slept, disturbed with bad dreams and waking memories. Not sure at any time whether he was conscious or not. Something was haunting him about the night's adventure, but he couldn't quite think what it was...

There was something about the encounter with Faden that bothered him. A matter that had sunk into his subconscious, even as he'd charged at the footpad.

That thought had been lost to his mind even as it occurred, only coming back as a nagging botheration as they all walked away from the warehouse.

They'd retired to Nathaniel Cooper's tavern, where their host had given them a generous feast and lots to drink. At last, in the early hours of the morning, Quest had gone to his room, asking not to be disturbed for several hours.

But even as he sprawled on the bed, he knew there was something he was trying to remember. Something from the death scene of Faden. But try as he would, he couldn't recapture the initial thought. As he drifted into sleep, he replayed the moments of Faden's death in his mind.

Something...

No, whatever it was, it evaded him.

Then there were the dreams, the nightmares. Faden in front of him dying again and again in different ways, yelling out so many single words that seemed meaningless.

He woke, or thought he woke for a moment, saw the dawn of a new day beyond the window. Heard the clatter of a cart on the cobbles of Stonegate. Just for a second... the lost thought was nearly there.

Faden charging at Gaius Pritchard...

Then Quest was in a deeper sleep.

The nightmares were not of York, but back in a Norfolk woodland. A scene from his own childhood. His father and brothers swinging in the wind, hanging from the branches of a tree...

Quest shot up from the bed, his eyes opened against the daylight streaming in through the window. The brightness snapped back the memory he was seeking, bringing the moments of Faden's death back into his conscious mind.

~

The boy Marcus was in the sitting room of Mrs Booth's house in Tanner Row, admiring the small picture on the wall above the fireplace. A strange-looking building, set against the backdrop of a wide square. A building the like of which he'd never seen. Not anywhere near York, that was certain sure.

The old lady was penning a letter on the writing slope set on the table. An urgent message that needed taking right across the town. So vital that the maid Dolly had come to fetch him from the railway station, demanding his immediate presence at the house across the way. As there was no train expected for two hours, Marcus hadn't hesitated in complying with the request.

Mrs Booth blotted and sealed the letter and turning her head, noticed him looking up at the picture.

'Yes, it is a strange looking place, isn't it Marcus?' the old lady said, as though she'd read his mind. 'Do you like the picture?'

'It's a fine picture, ma'am,' he said.

Mrs Booth waved a hand dismissively.

'I wish I could have painted it better,' she said. 'But it was a long time ago and I was in a rush.'

'You painted it, ma'am?'

The old lady sat back in the chair.

'Oh, I used to paint a great deal in my moments of leisure, Marcus. I wish I still had time.'

'It's very good, ma'am.'

'Oh, a trifle,' said Mrs Booth. 'A mere trifle...'

'Is it by your old home in Ripon?' he asked.

He could sense rather than see the smile under her widow's veil.

'No, Marcus. Not Ripon. Somewhere I lived a while ago. When I was younger. But no matter... Here is the letter. I'd be grateful if you would convey it straight away.' She pointed at the address she'd written on the outside. 'Here is the place to take it to... knock on the door and give it to the clerk. He's expecting it and will definitely be in. Wait there and he'll give you a reply, which you are to bring straight back to me.'

'Yes, ma'am.'

'Now, just before you go, Marcus, tell me what happened when you took my two sovereigns to Long Ted? He accepted the money?'

123

Marcus frowned.

'Clipped me ear, ma'am, for all he was workin' down on the staith in front of folk. Though t'others scolded him for it. He were drunk, ma'am. But he took your money and gave a nod when I told him what you said.'

'Do you think he will leave me alone, Marcus?'

The boy looked agitated.

'Dunno, ma'am. Probably while he drinks away your gold, but how long after that? I should keep your door bolted for a while, ma'am, and look through the winder afore you lets anyone in. No one knows which way that old... Long Ted'll jump.'

'I'll take your advice, Marcus,' she said, as she rang the little bell on the table for the maid to see him out. 'Here is something for your trouble.'

She pushed a coin across the table with her gloved hand.

~

Inspector Abraham Anders was taking a morning stroll around the city walls when he found Quest sitting on a stone, apparently lost in thought as he gazed across to the great heights of the Minster.

He halted for a moment, unsure whether to disturb him, taking a deep breath. These were such peculiar circumstances. Quest was a killer, a man outside the law, a rebel. By rights he should be shackling the darbies upon him. Dragging him into Newgate Gaol and watching the hangman put a noose around his neck.

Yet, here they were in this strange alliance. Hunting fugitives in the narrow alleys of York. Seeking out the mysterious fate of Mr John Lardiner.

But more than that. From the moment he'd first met Quest, Anders had liked the man. Anders had few friends beyond Sergeant Berry, whom he worked alongside for many hours at a time in London. His work at Scotland Yard ruled out much of a social life. He not only liked Quest, but had an empathy for his ambitions to right the wrongs of society.

That was a dangerous path to take – for Quest wanted to clear up those ills beyond the pale of the law. As a police detective, Anders couldn't tolerate such renegade behaviour.

Then Anders became aware of someone standing at his shoulder. He turned to see the broad and smiling face of Isaac Critzman. The newcomer nodded in Quest's direction.

'He'll sit like that for hours on end,' Isaac said. 'I've seen it so often. By the river in London. In the little churchyard at Hope Down. In many a wild and lonely place. Sometimes he's quiet as he wrestles with a problem. Like a dog with a bone, squeezing out the last drop of marrow. But more often he's lost in memories. And you know how painful some of Will's memories are?'

'Should we disturb him?' asked Anders.

'Probably not,' said Isaac. 'If it's a problem he's grappling with, then better to give him time to resolve it. If he's dwelling on a nightmare, then better that he has the peace to get it out of his system. Perhaps we should return along the walls and leave him alone.'

They were starting to turn when Quest called them back.

'A fine morning, gentlemen,' he said.

'You've recovered from the exertions of last night, Will?' asked Isaac.

'I had rather a troubled night of dreams,' said Quest. 'More than that... thoughts about the death of Faden.'

'This place is better off without him,' said Anders. 'I wouldn't let his passing be a bother to you.'

'The fact that Faden's gone from this world's no matter to me,' said Quest. 'More the consideration of how he behaved in the moments of his death.'

'How do you mean?'

Quest stretched out his arms in the warm sunlight and yawned.

'There was something I noticed in those final moments,' he said. 'It disturbed me at the time, but as he died so violently, it went out of my mind. I didn't think about it afterwards, until I lay abed. Then, when I tried to recapture those initial thoughts I couldn't retrieve them.'

'Sounds like trying to remember a dream,' suggested Anders.

'Exactly like that,' said Quest.

'And now it's come back to you?'

'It has indeed.'

'Are you going to tell us?' asked Isaac.

'May be nothing,' said Quest.

'It bothered you all night, though?' said Anders.

Quest smiled and nodded.

He was silent for a long moment and then he began.

'You'll recall when we had Faden pinned against the wall. Surrounded. Nowhere to flee. You saw his look as he faced us? Angry and frustrated. Defiant, and yet hopeless. You remember where we all stood?'

'We stood facing him,' said Anders. 'Sergeant Starkey, you and myself, with Barratt and the other constables. Your friends Dudgeon and Cooper to one side of him. Then further along the alley, and to his other side, Pritchard and Clews.'

'Surrounded, with no escape?'

'Exactly,' said Anders. 'Then he flew at Gaius Pritchard...'

'Why?' asked Quest.

'Why? What does it matter?' asked Anders. 'Faden was a desperate man with no future. He clearly wanted to take at least one of his pursuers with him.'

'But why Gaius Pritchard?'

'Who can say?' said Anders. 'In the circumstances, Faden was probably deranged. He could see that the men were clearly not policeman, but members of the public. He might have had one last thought of escape and thought that the easiest way to go...'

'Even though he knew Starkey had a pistol?'

'Men in such circumstances rarely act rationally.'

'But you'll recall, Anders, that Faden didn't charge until he heard Gaius Pritchard speak. Seemed to me that he recognised his voice. That's why he swung in Pritchard's direction.'

'But so what? Pritchard's a man about town. Faden may have encountered him before.'

'You recall what Faden called out?' said Quest.

'He yelled an insult at us,' said Anders.

'The word he used was bastard,' said Quest.

'So?'

'Faden is facing capture,' said Quest. 'Surrounded by us all. Reasonable that he calls us bastards. But bastard? The singular? And looking right at Gaius Pritchard as he said it? It was no insult aimed at all of us, Anders. That word bastard was aimed squarely at Gaius Pritchard.'

126

'I don't see the relevance,' said Anders. 'Frankly, I can't remember exactly what he said. Are you suggesting that Faden had some personal grudge against Pritchard?'

'He attacked him...'

'He did. But he might have picked any one of us at random.'

Quest considered.

'I might not give Faden's choice of victim much importance,' he said at last. 'Except for another incident involving Mr Gaius Pritchard.'

'You mean the incident at the Water Lanes?' said Isaac.

'What incident?' asked Anders.

'The night Moth was murdered, Reuben Dudgeon and I happened to be in Coppergate. Down by the Water Lanes. At the top of the very alley where Moth lived,' said Quest.

'Why?' asked Anders, suspiciously.

'We'd gone hunting,' said Quest. 'Hunting for Faden really, though Moth was our first target.'

'So, I'll ask you again, Quest. Did you kill Moth?' said Anders.

'No. He was dead when we got there.'

'Then you were in his room? It would have been helpful if you'd confessed that to me in the beginning. You really can't pick and choose how you obey the law. Your presence almost makes you accessories after the fact.'

'I don't believe so,' said Isaac. 'They were not privy to the secrets of Moth's murderer.'

'All right,' said Anders. 'I'll turn a blind eye to that for the moment. But what's all this got to do with Gaius Pritchard?'

'He was there,' said Quest. 'Oh no, not in the room. But in the Water Lanes that night. Just a few yards from the entrance of the court where Moth lived. Talking to a rough-looking youth. Almost certainly minutes after Moth was killed.'

'A coincidence...'

'But ask yourself, Anders. What would a respectable man about town be doing at that time of night in a rookery? You're right. It could be a coincidence. I'd believe it might be, but for the behaviour of Faden in the moments of his death. And isn't it interesting that Pritchard happened to be in the workhouse infirmary, just at the time when Davy was throttled? Yet another coincidence?'

'It was of course, Inspector, Gaius Pritchard who was most responsible for inviting Mr John Lardiner to York,' said Isaac. 'The invitation that has created so many mysteries...'

Anders threw up his hands.

'I can hardly question Pritchard on such scant evidence,' he said. 'It's not unlawful to be out at night on the streets of York. Nor to be present in a workhouse where you have full authority to be. I'll need far more than that.'

Isaac gave him a broad smile.

'Yes, and that's why I've spent the past day or so trailing Mr Gaius Pritchard around this place,' he said.

'You've been doing what?'

'Putting the dodge on him,' said Isaac. 'I don't think he's detected his watchdog. For all that I'm old and fat and out of practice. Not that my endeavours have produced much evidence to condemn the man. He's spent much of the time at his home in Goodram Gate. Apart from his little expedition last night in the company of his brother. And I do wonder just why Gaius Pritchard was so keen to be there... in at the kill at it were? Determined to see Faden brought to book?'

Anders walked a few yards away, his face turned towards the heavens.

He turned back.

'You people are unbelievable!' he said. 'It's not your task to trail suspects. If you were spotted you could throw my entire investigation. If Gaius Pritchard needs to be watched, well... then it's the responsibility of the police.'

'I understand the city police are very below strength at the moment,' said Isaac.

'Hardly the point...' thundered Anders.

'Inspector,' Quest interrupted the tirade that was obviously coming. 'Far better that Isaac undertakes this task. Even Pritchard might notice a uniformed constable on his tail. Being a lawyer, he'd know the face of every detective in York, in or out of uniform...'

'He happens to know Mr Isaac Critzman too!'

'Yes, but Isaac is so much better at this sort of thing than the average policeman,' said Quest.

Anders took in a deep breath.

'Quest,' he said. 'You are a bloody menace!'

'It's been remarked upon before,' Quest replied. 'But I'm sure you must see how essential it is that we discover just what Pritchard's game is?'

Anders paced up and down, deep in thought.

'Very well,' he said. 'Mr Critzman might continue to trail Gaius Pritchard. But from now on I want to know everything you find out, Quest. With no omissions. You understand that?'

'I'd never want it another way,' said Quest. 'Now if you gents will excuse me, I've an appointment with Reuben Dudgeon and Nat Cooper. They're going to walk me again around the vicinity of Grape Lane.'

He smiled at them both and walked away.

'You must forgive Will his indiscretions, Inspector,' said Isaac. 'He doesn't mean to be so brusque. He's had a very bad time these past few weeks.'

'I'm aware of that, sir. But you know I can't condone lawbreaking. However much I understand the temptation. Seems to me we must delve into so many puzzles. We still don't know whether or not there's a connection between Lardiner's vanishing and all these other matters at all.'

'My instinct tells me there is,' said Isaac.

'Mine too,' admitted Anders.

He gazed out from the high walls across the city, across the jumbled medieval streets to the high towers of the Minster.

'Somewhere out there's the resolution to this puzzle,' he said. 'In one of those buildings is some individual who can tell us why Lardiner vanished. And why Decker had to die, and why an attempt had to be made on the life of your friend Quest.'

'It's a beautiful city in so many ways,' Isaac reflected.

'I've seldom seen a place quite as engaging,' said Anders. 'Sprawling medieval streets. A sense of history all around. You get a real feeling of walking through the past. But...'

'But?'

'But we shouldn't let that vision of the past blind us to the fact that it's 1854. The menaces of the present century are as real here as in the filthiest and most depraved streets of London.'

Anders waved an arm towards the vista.

'I've seldom felt such a sense of danger as here in York,' he said. 'There's a dark shadow hanging over this place. Something almost intangible, because I can't see the motives behind much that's happened. That's why I'm being tolerant towards you and your associates. Because I don't believe that ordinary police work *will* expose the menaces of this place. If we are to dispel the dark shadow so that we might see the light, we need to use your unorthodox methods.'

'You're a very wise man, Inspector,' said Isaac.

Anders faced him.

'Please don't believe that what's between us is anything more than an armed truce. I still intend to slam the gates of Newgate Gaol on you all at the earliest opportunity.'

Fourteen

The man looked down at Marcus with some surprise.

'We don't encourage beggars to come to our door,' he said. 'This isn't the workhouse, boy. Be off with you!'

Marcus had carried the message from Mrs Booth to the offices of a manufactory on the other side of York. He'd tapped on the great oaken door. Bolts had been pulled back, and this small but authoritative wide-eyed figure had confronted him.

Marcus pulled off and twisted his canvas cap.

'Not beggin', sir,' he protested. 'Got this message. From a lady. Mrs Booth. Asked to bring it here. I'm to wait for a reply.'

The clerk looked him up and down again with a great air of suspicion. He held out his hand and took the letter from Marcus, examined the writing on the outside and considered the boy again.

'You say that Mrs Booth gave you this?'

'Yessir.'

'Wait here, boy. I'll give it to my master.'

The door was slammed shut in Marcus's face, and he heard the man draw the bolts. Marcus paced up and down in the sunlight. Looking along the street, he could see Clifford's Tower up on its mound and the forbidding buildings of the nearby prison. Some twenty minutes passed, and he began to think that the man had forgotten all about him. He sat for a while on the doorstep and then paced up and down for what seemed an eternity.

At last, Marcus heard the bolts pulled back. The door opened and the clerk stood at the top of the step and looked down at him. A small man, Marcus thought. No bigger than himself. Marcus didn't like the way the clerk regarded him. As though he were a rat come up from the sewers.

'You say you've been instructed to take a message back to Mrs Booth?' the man said.

'Yessir.'

'Then here it is,' the man said, holding out a letter. 'You are to take it to her straight away. And don't dawdle, boy. This letter is of the utmost importance.'

'Yessir.'

The man slammed the door shut with such ferocity that Marcus almost tumbled off the doorstep. He heard the now familiar sound of the bolts being pulled. He glanced down briefly at the letter, its folded pages held with a great lump of impressed red sealing wax.

~

Constable Charles Barratt had found it difficult to sleep after the events of the night. Every time he drifted towards slumber, he'd remembered the excitement of the chase through the streets of York. Saw Faden fall to the ground as Sergeant Starkey brought him down.

This was real police work. A villain, who'd been a stain on the fair face of York, put out of circulation for ever.

Anders had seemed satisfied with Barratt's work, though he'd done little more than organise the sweep of the uniformed men through the narrow lanes and ginnels of the city.

As dawn broke, Barratt wondered what it would be like to be a detective at Scotland Yard? Working alongside the famous Inspector Abraham Anders? Better than treading a beat in York, where there were so few opportunities for promotion...

Unable to sleep at all, he'd got up to examine his collection of walking sticks, some of them made by his own father.

There were quite a few now. Mostly good old-fashioned walking canes, though he'd recently added a poacher's shooting stick to his long rack of examples, as well as a sword-stick he'd confiscated from a Water Lanes rascal: the latter stolen, no doubt, though no legitimate owner had come forward.

Then Barratt remembered Mrs Booth's splendid stick, with the carved and unusual eagle's head. An eagle of such a stylised design, like nothing he'd seen before.

He remembered the promise to himself to try and identify the unusual bird, so took down his *Compendium of World Birds*, a book that had belonged to his father, who'd had an interest in such matters.

Barratt found the chapter on eagles and hawks and perused the pages for a considerable time. He was on the verge of giving up in disappointment, for there was no wild eagle quite like the bird's head on the old walking stick.

He was turning to the index to see if it might be listed elsewhere, thumbing his way through the large volume's many appendices. By chance, he noticed the section entitled 'Birds and Symbolism'; a particularly arid chapter of the book, though there were many illustrations.

It was there that he came upon a bird resembling the eagle, though it was different in that it showed the creature with two heads, each facing away from the other on what was obviously some type of coat of arms. Barratt read the superscription. He looked at the colourful illustration again, trawling through his memory of the walking stick's head to make sure he'd got it right.

It was undoubtedly the same eagle's head, even if it was just a singular example, missing its fellow. He read the whole of the next page, which described the origins of the eagle's use on that particular coat of arms.

Alongside the coat of arms was another illustration. A view painted of the centre of a far-off city, with a great religious building at its heart. An odd-looking place to worship God. So different from the bluff outlines of York's ancient Minster.

Barratt felt a warm glow of satisfaction which took away all of his tiredness. He'd have to see the walking stick again to make sure, but he was almost certain.

And what an odd coincidence that a walking stick with just such a bird should appear in York at that particular time.

~

'I can't see where the mystery is,' said Reuben Dudgeon as he, Quest and Nathaniel Cooper walked up and down Grape Lane. 'If John Lardiner came this way, he could have vanished into any number of places...'

'Or even just run out of the street altogether,' added Cooper. 'There's nothing special about Grape Lane, except that it's quieter than some streets in York.'

Quest leaned back against a wall.

'I agree. Nothing special at all,' he said. 'We'll learn nothing here. Inspector Anders said the real mystery is why someone needed to murder Joshua Marples with such expedition. I've a feeling that the vanishing of John Lardiner is a chimera - not so important in itself anyway, but rather a minor piece of some wider puzzle.'

'He was invited to York to discuss ways of using his influence to end the war against Russia,' said Dudgeon. 'We should ask ourselves who that might be a problem for? If the one man who had such influence vanishes, then there has to be a connection.'

'Undoubtedly,' said Quest, 'but what? And...'

He was interrupted by a shout from along the street. The Reverend Clews waved a hand and crossed to join them.

'I do apologise for my delay,' he said. 'I had business elsewhere. I'd very much hoped to walk this place with you. Have you come to any conclusions?'

'None whatever,' said Quest.

'I fear we'll never know the answer,' said Clews. 'And the wretched war will go on. I'm still shook up by the events of last night. Seeing that poor devil die in front of me. This is a wicked world.'

'It certainly can be,' said Cooper. 'You might all care to return to my tavern to seek some refreshment?'

Clews looked uncertain.

'Ordinarily, I would welcome it,' he said. 'But it's early in the day and perhaps, as a clergyman and a servant of Archbishop Musgrave, I shouldn't be seen imbibing in a public house?'

'It would be in my private quarters...' said Cooper.

'Well, in that case...' said Clews.

~

Mrs Booth sat in her window in Tanner Row and looked across the street to where the passengers were leaving the railway station.

Not many on the afternoon train from London, but she always took an interest. It was one of the reasons why she'd been so keen to engage a property nearby.

Not that she could watch every train, but she usually engineered her perambulations around the city so that she might be at home when the trains from London arrived. And when she had to be out, Dolly would keep a watch. The use of Marcus to carry messages meant that Mrs Booth didn't have to be away quite so often.

But no, there was no passenger from London on this train to disturb her equilibrium.

Mrs Booth read again the letter that Marcus had brought back in reply to her own missive. All very well. Perhaps this sojourn in York might soon come to an end...

A figure passed the window, walking hesitatingly up and down, a police constable looking as if he was considering tapping at her door. As he turned towards the house, reaching for the knocker in the shape of a fox's head, she recognised the visitor as Constable Barratt, the policeman who'd intervened in the matter of Long Ted and his daughter.

Mrs Booth felt alarmed.

What could he want?

She dreaded the neighbours' gossip at the thought that she might live in a house where the police frequently came knocking. What right had he to cause such bother?

Mrs Booth heard Dolly open the door. A moment later that slattern entered the room.

'Constable Barr...' she began.

'Yes, please show the policeman in, Dolly.'

She sat back in her chair in the shady corner of the room, tapping her stick on the carpet as Barratt entered.

'Good day, Constable.'

'Ma'am... as I was passing, I thought I might just call in,' Barratt said. 'Just to make sure that villain Long Ted hasn't been a bother to you?'

It seemed a reasonable excuse for a visit, Mrs Booth considered, but it seemed to her just that – an excuse. There was no conviction in the way Barratt uttered the words.

She noticed the way he was looking not so much at her but at her walking stick. He'd expressed an interest once before, Mrs Booth recalled. Something about his father making walking canes...

'I've seen nothing of this Long Ted,' said Mrs Booth. She was silent for a while, then... 'You seem to have a great fascination for my walking stick, Constable?'

'Sorry, ma'am... I didn't mean to stare. It's just that I've rarely seen such a well-made cane. And I find that eagle's head very interesting. Since I saw it the other day, I looked it up in a volume I have in my rooms. Not a British eagle, I think?'

'I really wouldn't know, Constable. As I told you, it was a present from my late husband.'

135

'Most interesting,' Barratt said. 'But I'll intrude on you no longer, ma'am. If Long Ted should bother you, please do send word at once. In the meantime, I'll keep a weather eye on your property as I'm about my beat.'

'So very kind, Constable. Good day to you.'

As Barratt turned, he noticed the painting above the fireplace.

'What a splendid picture, ma'am,' he said. 'I believe I've seen a very similar view quite recently. Did you paint it, yourself?'

'Ah, you are the second person to admire my little effort in one day, Constable,' said Mrs Booth. 'My messenger boy seemed interested in it only this morning. Yes, I painted it from life. A long time ago. I suppose I shouldn't display my own amateur daub quite so prominently, but it brings back such memories.'

Barratt couldn't help notice the pride in the old lady's voice. A pride belying any consideration that the painting was badly done.

'A strange looking building, ma'am?' he said.

'It's a cathedral...'

'Yes, I can see it must be a holy place. Where...?

The door was flung open and the maid Dolly burst into the room.

'I was to remind you, ma'am, about your appointment...'

'My goodness! Is that the time?'

Mrs Booth examined the clock on the nearby table.

'You'll forgive me, Constable,' she said. 'I should have left for my appointment several minutes ago...'

'Then I apologise for delaying you, ma'am...'

He gave a little bow and left the room.

When Dolly had seen him out, she came back into Mrs Booth's sitting room.

'You were listening at the door, Dolly!'

'I thought it best to intrude.'

'Very wise,' said Mrs Booth. 'I was nearly indiscreet. There's an atmosphere in these English towns that can tempt you to drop your guard.'

'He'll come again, that policeman,' said Dolly.

'I fear he will,' the old lady replied. 'If only to catch another glimpse of my painting and my stick.' She let out a deep breath. 'Dolly, keep an eye out for the boy. If you see him, tell him I have another message for him to deliver.'

~

Gaius Pritchard sat in the study of his house in Goodram Gate, examining the dark piece of prehistorically-worked flint that was one of his favourite possessions.

He'd washed away the blood that had covered it from the time of his last feeling of shame and frustration. An exercise undertaken very often.

All morning he'd dwelt on the events of the previous night, for Faden's attack on him had stirred feelings not only of fear, but also of excitement.

He might have perished just a few hours ago, been slashed to death by the great blade of Faden's dagger. Now that would have been a silly end for a respectable lawyer and man about town. Too much was being risked by way of nocturnal adventures. He had spent many hours since, nervous at the prospect of going into the streets and alleys of old York during the hours of darkness.

There were others like Faden, haunting the dark shadows.

Gaius Pritchard sipped some more brandy, holding the sharp edges of the flint harder than he needed to. Sometimes, pain could help focus the mind so clearly.

For go out, he must.

He'd done all he could to distract himself, but he couldn't put off his journey much longer.

Pritchard glanced through the window.

Would the night *never* come?

Fifteen

'Matters are coming to a head, Relkin,' said Mr Carver. 'But there are now considerable dangers too. I'm pleased that Faden's been removed from the scene, but that's only bought us a little time.'

He leaned forward in his chair.

'The archbishop is travelling to London in a week's time, to take part in a debate in the House of Lords. Those opposed to the war are making their move. They may well carry the day.'

'I hadn't realised that Archbishop Musgrave had quite that much influence, sir?' Relkin replied. 'Isn't he just one of many voices crying in the wilderness?'

'A chance we cannot take...'

'Then what are we to do?'

'Too many questions are being asked, Relkin. York's a small place where everyone knows everyone. It's a miracle we've kept up the deception for so long. It's becoming increasingly dangerous for those of us obliged to live a double life. I'm determined that the archbishop should never reach London.'

'You'll attend to the matter yourself?'

'I dread the thought, but hopefully our associate will' said Mr Carver. 'No doubt *he* would love to do it.'

'Are you under suspicion, sir?' asked Relkin.

Carver laughed.

'Not at all,' he said. 'Our opponents are particularly stupid and clueless. They haven't an inkling what it's really all about. But I fear we must act swiftly, lest the light penetrates their dim brains.'

~

'Mr Quest, sir?'

Quest was walking along Stonegate towards the Minster, when he felt a tap on the shoulder. He turned to find an anxious-looking Constable Barratt a pace behind him.

Quest smiled.

He couldn't quite get used to policemen seeking out his company in such a friendly way.

'Constable?'

'Sorry to bother you, sir. It's just that...'

'You've discovered something of importance?'

Quest could detect the signs of excitement...

'Well, I don't know that I have,' said Barratt. 'Not really. It might well be all quite innocent, but...'

'Your instinct tells you that something's wrong?'

Quest was a great believer in instinct. Such feelings had saved his liberty and life on numerous occasions.

'I've thought about this matter for a while. And dismissed it. I wasn't going to say anything at all. Just a coincidence, after all. Yet I've this nagging doubt... I thought you might be the person to come to...'

'If it's pertinent to the investigation, Constable, perhaps you should relate your worry to Inspector Anders or Sergeant Starkey...'

'They'd probably think it was nothing...'

Quest smiled again. He could understand how young men were frightened of putting themselves out on a limb. He remembered his early days with the Monkshood secret society, when he'd shied away from relating his own concerns to the Critzman brothers, or Albert Sticks or Jasper Feedle.

He patted the constable on the arm.

'I've a duty to attend to in a short while with Isaac Critzman,' he said. 'But I've time to take a turn with you around the Minster. Tell me everything about the matter, Constable. Hold nothing back. Tell me what the matter is, as though you'd only just considered it for the first time.'

They were walking out of Stonegate as Barratt began to relate some recent events.

'Well, Mr Quest, sir. There's this old lady...'

~

Mrs Booth read the reply to her letter. It was not what she wanted to hear. So annoyed was she at the information therein, that she almost forgot the boy standing patiently by the door. She turned as he gave a little cough.

'Marcus, you must forgive me...'

Mrs Booth took a coin from the table and held it out.

'There'll be no more messages today, Marcus.'

'Very well, ma'am.'

'But come first thing tomorrow, boy,' she added. 'I'll have a reply to send by then. Are you returning to your lodging house?'

Marcus screwed his cap in his hands.

'Not just yet, ma'am,' he said. 'There's the late train from London to attend to... always a busy one.'

'Yes, of course...'

She gave a nod of dismissal and crossed to the window to watch the boy cross Tanner Row to the station. He'd scarcely gone through the gates when she heard the noise of the arriving train, accompanied by a great plume of steam from the hollow of the platform.

The London passengers poured out in one great burst through the gates. She could see Marcus carrying the luggage of some young man and woman. A newly-wed couple, Mrs Booth surmised, by the way they were clutching at each other.

Mrs Booth watched the passengers depart, and was just returning to her chair when another solitary traveller came through the gates, accompanied by the station master. Mrs Booth watched as the railwayman pointed in the direction of the town, obviously explaining how to get to his accommodation.

Mrs Booth thought nothing of it at first and had started to turn away, when something in the now hurrying figure struck a note of recognition. Fatter than the last time he'd been encountered, if it was who...

But still, Mrs Booth was not sure. He'd certainly gained a lot of weight. But there was something about those features...

The passenger halted by the entrance of the railway station yard, removing his tall hat and rubbing his head. Mrs Booth saw that he had been wounded, and quite recently for the bandage was still in place. He looked flustered, agitated, annoyed...

As though he was expecting to be met and nobody had turned up. The fat man was about to hail a nearby cabriolet, when a very thin man rushed along the street, shouting some words of greeting.

The two men shook hands and walked off together in the direction of North Street, chatting as they moved away.

Mrs Booth took in a great breath, for she'd recognised the second man as well.

There was no doubt about it.

Mrs Booth's most feared enemy had arrived in York.

Sixteen

'You must have endless patience, Isaac,' said Quest, as they concealed themselves by a twisting wall a hundred yards from Gaius Pritchard's house in Goodram Gate. 'How long have you been here?'

'Only an hour or two,' said Isaac. 'Since it got dark.'

'How did you know that Pritchard wouldn't go out in the daylight? Or undertake his secret mission from somewhere else?'

'I didn't know.'

'He might have slipped out already...'

'He might have,' said Isaac. 'But that was a chance that had to be taken. I couldn't watch him every minute of the day. I've been counting on the fact that you saw him at the Water Lanes during the hours of darkness. In my experience, what a man does once, he'll do again. Besides, Gaius Pritchard's well known in this place. If he's involved in nefarious deeds, he'll undertake them in the dark. Less chance of being seen.'

'There's something in that,' Quest agreed. 'Where's Josef?'

'Ah, my brother had to run an errand to the railway station. To meet another new visitor to this place. He'll be entertaining him to supper about now.'

'What new visitor?'

'Well, it's an old...'

He stopped talking and raised a finger to his lips.

'Our man's on the move,' he said.

Quest looked along the street in time to see Gaius Pritchard shut the door of his home, descend the steps and walk speedily away in the opposite direction.

'In a hurry,' said Quest.

In moments, Pritchard had turned into Colliergate and vanished from their sight. The two men set off in pursuit, the air around them dinning with noise as all the church bells struck eleven.

'Very much in a hurry,' said Isaac.

Pritchard was almost out of sight by the junction with Pavement, even as they strode along Colliergate.

'Well, I should say he's not just out for an evening stroll,' said Isaac drily. 'There's a purpose to his perambulation. We must go faster, my friend, lest we lose him in a ginnel.'

Quest and Isaac Critzman increased their speed, winding their way around the many pedestrians who, even at that hour, were thronging the street. As Pritchard reached the street called Pavement, he crossed that wide thoroughfare, then almost instantly crossed back again.

They watched as their man halted and lit a cigar. They saw its smoke rise and mingle with the steam from the gas lamps for several minutes. There was no doubt about it. Gaius Pritchard was searching, looking all about him.

'Pritchard doesn't think he's being followed, but he's taking no chances,' said Quest.

'Only men with something to hide take precautions like that,' said Isaac. 'Your theory might be correct, Will. Ah, he's on the move.'

Gaius Pritchard had looked at his pocket watch. The way he threw his head about, as he conned the street. suggested that the person he'd come to meet was late arriving. Pritchard had thrown the cigar to the ground, and was walking onwards. Not so fast now and more warily. Every now and then he would halt, his back to the buildings, looking all around.

'Still considering that he may be being watched,' suggested Isaac.

'Mm, but not just that,' said Quest. 'I do believe friend Pritchard's looking out for someone in particular. He's come out on the streets to meet an acquaintance. And whoever it is seems to be late...'

Quest and Critzman hung back, though the street was still busy and there was little chance of being seen. But nearly twenty minutes passed, twenty minutes of Pritchard pacing up and down, while his two pursuers strolled in company with fellow pedestrians almost to the end of the street, so that they didn't draw attention to themselves.

And then, just as they sauntered back again, they saw Pritchard wave a hand to someone approaching him from the other end of Pavement. They watched as the youth looked all around and then walked straight up to Pritchard.

There was some animated conversation, the younger man waving an arm in the direction of Coppergate. After a few moments, the two began to walk towards that narrower street.

'Is it the youth he met before?' Isaac asked Quest.

'I believe so. About the same build, though he was under a gas-lamp the last time I saw him, so I couldn't swear that his hair's quite as fair.

Whoever he is, friend Pritchard doesn't seem to want to be seen with him...'

The youth was definitely leading the way down Coppergate, though always keeping a couple of yards ahead of the lawyer. But there was a determination in their matching steps. No experienced pursuer putting the dodge on a tail could be mistaken in the assumption that the two were together.

At Castle Gate, the road running along the top of the Water Lanes, Gaius Pritchard and the youth turned left, walking in the direction of the old castle. But after a few yards, they crossed the road and headed towards the third of the narrow and disreputable lanes.

'That's where I saw them meet before,' said Quest. 'At the top of the lane and under the gas lamp. Just a few paces from where Moth was murdered.'

'A wild-looking place,' muttered Isaac. 'Dark and sinister. Not the sort of alley you'd expect to be frequented by a respectable lawyer. We'd best close up, Will, lest we lose them...'

They were just seconds behind Pritchard and the youth, who were now walking side by side. As they headed down towards the river, Quest indicated to Isaac the door of the building where Moth was killed. But it was clear that Pritchard and the boy had further to go.

Then they stopped dead.

Quest pulled Isaac to one side, in to the shelter of an old wooden barrow, propped up against the wall of a house. A drunk snored beneath it, his only lodging on what was clearly going to be a cold night.

When they looked down the alley again, Pritchard and the youth had vanished.

'Have they left the alley?' asked Isaac.

'They might have turned the corner on to the staith,' said Quest. 'But I doubt they had time. Or there's a pair of doors they might have gone in...'

'Best check the staith,' suggested Isaac.

They walked out on to the cobbled King's Staith. There were wharfingers unloading boats moored on the Ouse river, whistling under their burdens as they carried crates and barrels through a great pair of open gates.

But no sign of Pritchard and the young lad in that direction. Quest and Isaac turned and looked the other way towards the Ouse Bridge.

143

There were a few strollers on its parapets, and a handful of drinkers had gathered outside a tavern, carolling some old shanty very loudly.

'They couldn't have covered that space anyway,' said Quest. 'Not in the time it took us to come round the corner. Best to have a look at that pair of doors.'

They turned back up the lane to the two side-by-side entrances. The upper door was very firmly fastened. The building rose three storeys and had clearly once been some common lodging house. Now it seemed derelict, though a nearby broken window suggested that the homeless and desperate still used it for its original purpose.

'Not that one,' said Isaac. 'That's a heavy door. We'd have heard it open and slam after them. And it's not likely they'd have clambered through the window.'

The lower of the doors stood slightly ajar, and a dim light came from somewhere within. They heard voices, low but excited. Someone with a soft country burr; the other voice was the polished tones of Gaius Pritchard.

They turned into a narrow corridor which ended in a flight of stairs, though there were three doors on the ground level. Another lodging house of sorts, but clearly one where the tenants got rooms to themselves.

Quest and Isaac Critzman could hear the voices coming from the third door along, quieter now as though Gaius Pritchard and the youth were muttering something.

'So, what do we do?' whispered Isaac. 'Wait outside and follow them in turn when they leave? Or go in?'

Quest considered.

'Somehow we've got to bring this mystery to a head. There's no lock on the door, though they may have bolted it on the inside. Let's just push it open if we can and see what friend Gaius is all about.'

Isaac nodded agreement.

The door was not bolted. Quest swung it wide open and stopped dead in his tracks.

Gaius Pritchard and the youth had their arms wrapped around each other in a tight embrace, kissing so passionately that they didn't realise for a moment they'd been interrupted.

Then they sprang apart.

'Quest...'

144

Pritchard spat out the word.

Then he disengaged from the youth and almost collapsed on to a wooden form that ran along one wall. Apart from a bed, the long seat was the only furniture in the room.

Gaius Pritchard regarded the two intruders with a terrible expression of fear, his face had turned very pale and his eyes seemed to blaze in the light of the three candles which lit the little room.

~

'You're never going out?' said Dolly. 'Not at this hour...'

'What choice do I have?' said Mrs Booth. 'I have to know what that man is doing here. Why should he be in York of all places? It can't be a coincidence. I have to know if he's gone to join the others...'

'But it's the dead of night. We've been so careful. You'll be noticed the moment you go out into the Row.'

'There really is no alternative.'

'Leave it to the morning,' Dolly almost pleaded. 'Send the lad with a message. If this man's such a threat, then let someone else deal with him.'

'But what can be done? If he's killed, we are as good as showing them there's something to investigate in York... we daren't take the risk. Far better that we find new lodgings somewhere else. The place has become too difficult...'

'But you'll be seen...'

Mrs Booth raised her head and gave her a thin smile.

'There's no one else I can trust. Not at this hour. I'll leave by the back door. In the old way, Dolly...'

Dolly gasped with a sudden realisation of what was meant.

'It's sheer bloody folly!' she yelled.

~

'What can I say?' said Gaius Pritchard.

Quest and Isaac sat down on the form on either side of him. Pritchard had slipped the youth a coin and asked him to leave his room for a good hour.

'We all have our needs,' Pritchard went on. 'This is mine. I doubt a man like you would ever understand, Quest?'

'These attachments are not unfamiliar to those of us who come from London,' Quest replied. 'There are as many boys as girls selling themselves on the streets. Something our precious society keeps very quiet about. But in London, men of your station in life are more likely to visit one of the molly houses to ease their lusts.'

'Lust? You think that's all this is, Quest?'

There was outrage in Pritchard's voice.

'What else?'

Pritchard noticed the gentleness in Quest's tone.

'I'm sorry, Quest. You're right in a way. This liaison began in just such a manner. Tommy was desperate for money and haunted the streets for just such custom. I sought out a boy for exactly the reason you state. It began like that. But now it's more, Quest. So much more...'

'You've fallen in love with him?' stated Isaac.

Gaius Pritchard nodded.

'Does anyone else know?'

'I've kept my desires from most,' said Pritchard, 'though it was simpler when I travelled abroad. I fear my brother Sebastian suspects. He wouldn't approve. He's a cold fish where emotions are concerned. He shows no interest in any form of desire. The only person who ever knew was John Lardiner, my oldest acquaintance...'

'And was he?...' Quest began.

Pritchard stifled a little laugh.

'Like me? No, Quest, not like me. Not this anyway...'

They were all silent for a while.

'I'm aware of the penalties for sodomy,' said Pritchard. 'I'm a lawyer, after all. Now I suppose I shall have to face up to such obligations. My reputation destroyed. Long years in the gaol. All for something I've tried to resist, but really can't help.'

'Are there not molly houses in York?' asked Isaac.

'There are, and worthier gentlemen than I frequent them. But at such a terrific risk to their place in society and well-being. I was never brave enough to take such a risk. I've always had to seek out the rough trade of the town. I never believed my higher emotions would become engaged... and then I met Tommy.'

'How long have you been seeing him? asked Quest.

146

'A few weeks. Since he came up from the country. He was obliged to leave his village for showing similar sentiments. He came to seek work in York. But the boy's fragile, Quest. Not up to the efforts that the hard labour of the working world demands. So he was obliged to turn his finer feelings into a commercial transaction. Fortunately, he met me...'

'I see...'

'Do you, Quest? I wonder when...'

Gaius Pritchard turned on Quest with a sudden anger.

'Why are you following me, Quest? What business is my private life to you, that you should come here?'

'I saw you meet this boy the other day. I thought your actions suspicious. I'm in York to investigate Lardiner's vanishing and I thought there might be something you hadn't revealed.'

Pritchard put his face in his hands and was silent for a long while.

'There is, I suppose,' he said at last, 'though I saw nothing sinister in it. The situation with John Lardiner is as I revealed it to you. I wrote inviting John here. But I omitted one detail...'

'Which was?'

'Well, the desire to come to York came initially from John and not from me. We had several communications before he made the journey here. A while before, I was summoned to meet him in London. I hadn't encountered John since before he went to Russia the last time. He told me he desperately needed to come to York. Not just to get away from the stifling atmosphere of his Wiltshire parish, but... well, he said there were other reasons.'

'Did he say what these reasons were?'

'He did not,' said Pritchard. 'Only that they were vitally important to him. John seemed to me to be... agitated. As a man might be if he had a great many concerns upon his mind.'

'Do you mean he was suffering from some mental exhaustion?'

'Not exactly. More like a frustration. As though the business he was referring to could hardly wait...'

'And he gave you no indication what that business was?'

'Only that there was a great urgency that he began its undertaking.'

'That's all?'

Gaius Pritchard was silent for a long while, as though he was trying to summon up exact memories.

'He was not the John Lardiner I knew in my early travels abroad with him. There was an anger in him, Quest. He seemed to be an individual running out of time. And he made an extraordinary request at our meeting...'

'Go on...'

'He told me... well, he wanted to come to York and remain *incognito*. That nobody should know that he was here. John wanted me to find him quiet lodgings. He said it would assist him in the work he had to undertake.'

'You offered that help?' asked Isaac Critzman.

'How could I? John's a man of considerable reputation. Very well known. His volumes on Russia and wider travel are much read. There is a frontispiece illustration of him in every volume. He's had his portrait painted by some of our leading artists. There are even photographic likenesses of the man about... You might as well try to hide Prince Albert in York...'

'Then you told him it was impossible?'

'I did,' said Pritchard. 'He got angry, Quest. More than that. There was a fury about him I'd never seen before. A violent anger. He pressed me against the wall and told me that my secret life might have to be revealed, if I didn't assist him in this way.'

'And you think of him as a friend?' said Isaac.

'I'd never seen him behave like it before,' said Pritchard. 'Such was his desperation. We'd trusted each other with so many aspects of our private lives. Believe me, I knew all his secrets too. Or I thought I did. I told John not to be a fool. Said that I could destroy his reputation as easily as he could wipe out mine. In any case, I told him, it was too late in the day for him to issue such threats.'

'Why?' asked Quest.

Gaius Pritchard smiled.

'Because I'd already been indiscreet,' he said. 'I'd told Archbishop Musgrave that this famous man was desirous of coming to York. The archbishop told a great many others. To be fair to me, John had made no request in his correspondences that I shouldn't mention it. I thought it reasonable to tell the greatest man in York. Archbishop Musgrave is taking a strong line of opposition to the war in the Crimea, and was most anxious to speak at first hand to someone close to the Tsar.'

'How did Lardiner react to that news?' asked Quest.

'He went very quiet for a long while,' said Pritchard. 'Then his mood seemed to change all in an instant. He became amiable again, more like the old John. He patted me on the shoulder and apologised profusely for his behaviour. Said that his anger was all due to tiredness, but that he shouldn't have taken his annoyance out on me. He hoped I'd overlook his behaviour and said he'd be delighted to come to York as the archbishop's honoured guest.'

'Was that the conclusion of your meeting?'

'We dined together at my club,' said Pritchard. 'He seemed in good cheer now that the matter was settled. Though towards the end of the evening he seemed distracted, but pleasant enough. Took a great interest in who was there. Later, in the smoking room, some of the others were discussing the war, and Sebastopol in particular. Knowing that John had spent time there before the conflict, I thought he might intervene in their talk. One or two of them positively invited John to share his views, but he seemed reluctant to do so. Said he hadn't been there for many years...'

'Yet...' Quest said.

'It was a lie, Quest. John Lardiner was very familiar with Sebastopol. He was there when the present war broke out, and might have been charged as a spy if the Tsar had not personally intervened. John's lie seemed pointless to me. Everyone in the know was aware that John had been in Sebastopol. But his comment was the end of our evening together. He said he was tired and wanted to withdraw for an early night.'

'It is a great puzzle,' said Isaac.

Quest was silent for a long while, noticing Gaius Pritchard's obvious distress. But the shock of discovery had made the man loquacious. He knew he had to press Pritchard even further.

'So why didn't you meet Lardiner when he arrived in York?'

'I would have done,' said Pritchard, 'but I was requested to be present at a meeting of the workhouse overseers. There had been an accident on the premises and I was asked to give a legal opinion. Fortunately, my brother was available. He too, knew John Lardiner quite well...'

'The other night, when Faden was killed...'

'A ghastly business,' said Pritchard. 'I've never seen a man slain violently before...'

149

'Faden attacked you...'

'I was quite horrified. I've never been the object of a man's violence before, though given my proclivities, it's always been a possibility I've dreaded.'

'Why do you think he charged at you?'

Gaius Pritchard looked baffled.

'I'm not sure what you mean?'

'Well, of all the men in that alley, he came in your direction...'

'He did. My God, I can picture his face now. The anger in his expression. His eyes so wild. It was almost as though I wasn't there as a person. That I was just an obstruction in his path of escape.'

'Faden called you a bastard,' said Quest,

'He yelled out the word, Quest. That's for certain. But I'm not sure he meant me in particular. I took it to be the curse of a furious and desperate man.'

'Did you ever know Faden?'

'Many in York have long been aware of Faden by his notoriety. But he never appeared in court when I was still practising law. As far as I'm aware, I'd never set eyes on the villain before the other night.'

There was something in the tone of Pritchard's voice which convinced Quest he was telling the truth. For a moment he felt a surge of frustration. His best theory as to the vanishing of John Lardiner was dashed.

Quest stood.

'We'll leave you alone, Pritchard,' he said. 'Your friend should be returning, and I feel sure you have much to talk about.'

Gaius Pritchard looked up at him.

'What is to happen to me, Quest? Am I disgraced?'

Quest smiled.

'As far as we are concerned, this incident never happened,' he said. 'How you live your life's none of our business. But I would urge you to discretion. There are some very cruel people in this world.'

Pritchard grasped his hand.

'Thank you, Quest.'

Quest and Isaac Critzman walked out into the alley and back up towards Coppergate.

'What a mess people get into because of their wants,' said Isaac, as they paced up the cobbles.

'You seemed uneasy with the situation, old friend,' said Quest.

Isaac sighed.

'I'm not unfamiliar with men such as Gaius Pritchard. I've encountered a great many over the years. My religion condemns the physical expression of such desires. I can't help my upbringing, Will. You seemed admirably compassionate?'

'I'd rather people loved than hated,' said Quest. 'Gaius Pritchard's secret will remain safe with us. Nor do I believe he knows more about the mystery of John Lardiner's disappearance than he's told. My favoured explanation for the mystery has vanished as suddenly as the man himself.'

A cold breeze swept along Coppergate as they made their way back towards the heart of the city. Its chill halted their conversation, giving Quest time to consider everything Gaius Pritchard had told him. He replayed the scene in his mind of Pritchard's last encounter with John Lardiner. Then his mind wondered to the events in Grape Lane, then to the slaying of the footpad Faden.

The clocks of the many churches chimed the midnight hour, their noise evicting the concatenation of mixed thoughts from Quest's mind, leaving one simple but obvious solution to the mystery of many of these events in York.

A staggering and almost unbelievable key that unlocked everything puzzling Quest about the vanishing of Mr John Lardiner.

Seventeen

Clouds crept across the moon, leaving only the gas-lamps to illuminate Tanner Row. A chilly breeze swept along the street, causing Constable Charles Barratt to shiver as he leaned against the wall by the railway station. He had finished his evening beat two hours before and was now working on his own behalf, and at the suggestion of that strange individual, Mr William Quest.

The last railway train had arrived some hours before and the railway station was silent; its employees had long ago gone home, apart from Aaron Slack, the watchman – a genial individual who sometimes shared a pot of tea with Barratt in the lonely hours of the night. As Tanner Row seemed to be quiet, he'd indulged in just such a treat an hour before.

'I see her about, 'course, that Mrs Booth' said Slack. 'Not that she's much of a word for me. Her maid used to come over to get late parcels. Never much liked the look of her. No better than she should be, and a face that'd stop the London fast train.'

Aaron Slack gave Barratt a toothless chuckle.

'All changed though, Charlie. They use young Marcus to run errands now. Runnin' here and there all over the town. Fetchin' and carryin' for 'em.'

'I've seen the lad about,' said Barratt. 'Does he still do his duties here at the station?'

'Aye, he does. When the trains are in and out. But I suspicion that Mrs Booth pays young Marcus more than he ever gets here. Certainly eatin' better and had a new jacket on this morning.'

Barratt considered.

'When would be the best time to have a word with Marcus?'

'Tomorrow,' said Slack. 'While he's a-waitin' for the early train. But you'll have to be prompt, for there'll be a lot of passengers. There's a convention in the city the day after. There's people arrivin' for that...'

'Convention?'

'Men opposed to the war. The archbishop's gettin' them here for a big meetin' before his nibs goes down to Lunnon to speechify in Parliament.'

Barratt considered what he'd been told, as he wrapped his long coat tighter to keep away the midnight breeze. He looked across at Mrs

Booth's house on the opposite side of Tanner Row. A light still burned in the downstairs front room and there was the hint of an illumination in the bedroom above. The old lady certainly kept long hours – something he'd noticed on previous nights when he'd walked this particular beat.

Gone twelve now, and not much point in lingering any longer. Barratt began to wonder why he'd bothered with the surveillance. Old ladies seldom walked the dark streets of York so late at night and he could hardly visit her at such a time.

Barratt was starting to walk back towards North Street when the wind carried the noise of footsteps and the tap of a walking stick towards him. Someone very late about. He hugged the wall again, concealed in its shadows, as the pedestrian walked up towards him, though on the opposite side of the Row.

A well-dressed man of middle years, Barratt surmised by the energy of his walk, though he could see nothing of the face in the dim gaslight. A late reveller come back from dining out, he considered, or a gentleman who'd been enjoying the more nefarious pleasures of the town.

But just as Barratt stepped out of the dark shadow, the man halted hard by the step of Mrs Booth's house. There was something about the way he looked hastily in both directions, that triggered a suspicion in Barratt's mind. Then the man went up the step and rapped gently on the door.

After a moment, the door opened and he saw the maid standing there, still dressed for the day, though her fist stifled a yawn. She opened the door a tad wider, and then said something Barratt couldn't hear, though her voice was raised and she didn't seem to be very happy with this nocturnal visitor.

The man muttered something in response and it became clear that he had every intention of entering the property. He almost pushed both the door and the maid to one side as he stepped into the hallway.

But as he did so he turned, looking back into the street. Glancing across Tanner Row at Barratt, who stood near to the opposite gas-lamp.

Mrs Booth's late visitor stood regarding him for what seemed an age to Barratt, before he pushed the door shut very gently.

Barratt looked on at the closed door for quite a while, wondering just why he felt so uneasy?

Then a thought dawned on him that seemed incredible.

He must talk to the boy Marcus.

Then seek out Inspector Anders.

No, not Anders. Not yet, anyhow, lest he might be making a ghastly mistake. Better to confide again in William Quest, who'd been so understanding when they'd had their previous discussion.

Barratt smiled.

If he could prove what he half-suspected, then his ambitions within the police might know no bounds.

~

Quest was late from his bed after his wanderings of the previous night. He'd woken to find Nat Cooper tapping on the door, summoning him to breakfast. When he went downstairs in the Stonegate tavern, he found Reuben Dudgeon there with a message.

'Met your friends Isaac and Josef outside the Minster, William,' said Dudgeon. 'They've summoned a meeting for all interested parties at the Reverend Clews' house for midday.'

Quest yawned.

There was a time he could stay awake and aware for many hours on end. He recognised that he must be getting older. He sipped Nat Cooper's best tea and wished that Rosa Stanton was there. He ached for her company, and it was hardly a fortnight. Part of him wanted to jump on to the train back to London and seek her out.

But he remembered their agreement. Those few months away from him that she'd demanded. The thought of months without her seemed like staring into the jaws of an eternity.

Quest looked through the window, out on to Stonegate, a street already crammed with pedestrians. An interesting city, but he knew he dared not be away from London for much longer. Rosa's acting put her so much in the limelight, and there were great risks involved in being so much in the public eye.

Even if he couldn't see her, he could keep a watchful eye open.

He yawned again, and then ate more of Cooper's excellent breakfast, so that he wouldn't feel obliged to talk. He'd lain awake for many hours of the night, gnawing at the idea he'd had walking along Coppergate.

Was it conceivable, this solution that had come flooding into his head, with the ringing of the church bells? After turning again and again in his bed, he'd felt inclined to dismiss the notion as too fanciful. The whole premise was quite ridiculous, and yet?

It could account for so much, even though he found it hard to understand the motivation behind it. Despite all, he still couldn't produce the wretched Mr John Lardiner. And without Lardiner, there really was no explanation at all.

The long-case clock in the corner of the room chimed the half after eleven, its gentle peal taken up immediately by the great bells of the Minster. He checked the time against his own pocket watch.

'Time to go,' he said to Dudgeon and Cooper.

~

Marcus had been up and about, greeting the early trains, before returning to the lodging house just across from the House of Correction in Toft Green, to make himself a late breakfast. Mrs Booth's maid had signalled to him as he'd left the railway station, and passed him a written message as he stood obediently on the step.

'Usual place,' Dolly had grunted. 'Don't hang around.'

But the boy had been hungry, and thought that there would be time to eat something before he delivered the missive. So Marcus walked briskly along Tanner Row in the direction of his diggings.

Dolly had been closing the door, but halted when she saw the boy walking in the opposite direction to the obvious route. At first she though he might just cross to the railway station, but the boy stayed on the nearer pavement.

'He's going home, little bastard!' she muttered to herself.

'What is it?'

She turned to find Mrs Booth standing behind her.

'Probably nothing,' Mrs Booth said, after Dolly had reported the boy's refusal to obey orders. 'The common people often do get slack in their duties after making an initial attempt to impress. But best to make sure, Dolly. Get after him and see where he goes...'

Dolly put on her cape and stepped outside, remaining at some distance as the boy sped along Tanner Row.

~

'I've business in the town, Relkin,' said Mr Carver. 'I may not be back for a considerable time. But if there are any messages, you know how to deliver them.'

Relkin passed his employer his walking cane, hat and gloves, and nodded.

'These are busy times, sir,' he said.

'Indeed they are, Relkin. Alarming times as well. I do believe our business in York is coming to a conclusion. There have been so many complications, but I do feel that we've weathered the storm.'

'I do hope so, sir.'

'Make your plans to move on, anyway. We might get very little notice. You have no questions?'

'It's all clear enough, sir,' said Relkin.

~

Marcus strode speedily along the street and had just crossed the junction with Barker Lane, when he felt the heavy hand on his shoulder.

'Not so fast, boy,' said Barratt, as he pulled the lad out of Tanner Row and into the narrower lane.

'I've done nothing,' he protested. 'I'm honest...'

'Sure you are, Marcus. I just want a word.'

'But I got to deliver this message...' said Marcus, holding out the sealed letter.

'Where to?'

'I can't tell you that,' said Marcus. 'It's private...'

'Nothing's private when a policeman asks you a question,' said Barratt. 'So look sharp and give me an answer.'

'But I...'

'Marcus, lad. You live opposite the House of Correction, don't you? Do you want to find yourself in there for a spell? Or the prison, perhaps? Or Botany Bay?'

'I don't...'

'Give me that,' Barratt said, seizing the message.

He broke the seal and unfolded the paper, then sighed with frustration. This was no regular letter. Some of it was written in odd letters, in a language he couldn't understand. But he guessed what language it was. Then there was a long central paragraph comprising a sequence of numbers, divided into fours. A code. Well of course it would be...

'You didn't ought to have done that,' said Marcus. 'Mrs Booth'll think I opened the letter. She'll never trust me again.' He looked up hopefully at the constable. 'You'll come round and see her? Explain what you've done?'

'I very probably will,' said Barratt. 'Now, lad. You were taking this note where?'

'Can't tell you that...'

'It'll be hard work, Marcus. All those hours on the treadmill. And underfed boys like you might well die on the voyage to Botany Bay. So are you going to show me? And on the way you can tell me everything you know about Mrs Booth and her maid.'

~

Dolly trailed the policeman and the boy as they walked across the city. Not a difficult task at this time of day, for the streets were crammed with pedestrians.

The constable had the boy firmly by his collar and was clearly interrogating his captive. Marcus was talking, really such a lot. This was far more than general conversation. The boy was spilling everything he knew. And Dolly had seen the constable put her employer's message in his own pocket.

For a moment Dolly was torn as to whether to keep up her pursuit of the pair. If the traps knew everything, then best to report back so that she and her employer might have time to get away. There might be very little time...

It was, after all, very clear where Marcus was taking this inquisitive policeman. They were walking the obvious streets to the building not so far away from York Castle and Clifford's Tower.

Dolly wished she'd a brace of pistols with her. An ambush as they passed the dark entrance to a ginnel. One shot for the policeman and another for the dreadful child.

She'd mistrusted the brat from the very start. But Mrs Booth had known better. Or said so. They had had such a secure place to hide in this foul city. Taking on the boy had been a very great mistake.

Her employer should really have heeded her warnings.

~

'This is the place?' asked Barratt.

He and Marcus stood outside a red-bricked building, not dissimilar to a dozen others in the same row. A business premise, the subsidiary office of a company well known throughout the land, though the plaque by the door proclaimed only the trading name:

Thore and Kirkby Consolidated
London, Birmingham, Leeds, York,
New York, Paris and Hanover

At first glance it might have been the registered office of a firm of lawyers, such was its modesty.

But these traders were very well known, even to Barratt, who saw the company mentioned very often in the business pages of the Leeds *Intelligencer* and the London *Times*, both of which circulated in the rest room of the police office.

'You tap on that door?'

Marcus nodded.

'Who answers?'

'Don't know his name. A very little man.'

'Do you go in?'

'Into the hallway,' said Marcus. 'He's a clerk, I think, the little man. He reads the message. Sometimes writes on it, notes like. There's often somethin' to take back to Mrs Booth.'

Panic crossed Marcus's face.

'What am I to do now?' he cried. 'The old lady'll never trust me again. I daren't go back there.'

'Wiser if you didn't,' said Barratt. 'Come along o'me.'

Still holding the boy by the collar, he led him along Castle Gate until they reached Ousegate, where he came across Constable Marsh on his beat.

'What's this, Charlie?' asked Marsh 'Caught the lad dipping?'

'Not exactly,' Barratt replied. 'This is Marcus Braithwaite. You might describe him as a witness to a crime. I want you to take him to the police office and keep him safe there until I get back in touch.'

'Why, where are you going?'

158

'I've some unfinished business in Tanner Row. And something else, Sid. After you've seen him safe at the office, I want you to run an urgent message to the Reverend Clews' house by the Minster. You know it?'

'I know it. A message for the reverend?'

'No, not for him, but for a Mr Quest who'll be there about now. This is very important, Sid. It's got to get there as soon as you can. We'll go into this shop here and borrow their counter while I write it out. And I've got this other message to travel with it.'

'What if this Quest bloke ain't there?'

'Then you're to give it to Inspector Anders.'

'Him from Scotland Yard?'

Barratt nodded.

'But Mr Quest for preference, got that?'

'I got it.'

Barratt led the others into a stationery shop nearby, whose owner he knew particularly well. Borrowing paper and ink, he wrote out a long explanation of what he'd found out and what he needed Quest to do next.

Then he watched as Constable Marsh and Marcus went off in the direction of the police office.

When they were safely out of sight, he walked quickly back across the Ouse Bridge towards Tanner Row. Time to go a-visiting Mrs Booth.

Time to make his mark on these proceedings.

Time to really make a good impression on the renowned detective from Scotland Yard.

~

'We're a trifle late,' said Quest, as he, Reuben Dudgeon and Nat Cooper were admitted to the house of the Reverend Clews. 'It sounds as though the meeting's begun.'

They could hear some sort of debate going on in Clews' drawing room, as the servant led them across the hallway and opened the door.

'Ah, here they are,' said Isaac Critzman as they entered the room.

But his words were lost on Quest, who'd seen the large man with the bandaged head, sitting in the winged armchair in the corner of the room.

An old opponent whom Quest had last seen in London just a couple of weeks before.

In distressing circumstances...

'You'll forgive me if I don't stand to greet you, Quest,' said Benjamin Wissilcraft, touching the bandage. 'As you can see, I'm not quite recovered from my injury.'

Quest nodded his head and looked angrily in Isaac's direction.

'I wasn't aware I'd requested the assistance of Queen Victoria's Spymaster,' he said. 'Forgive me, Wissilcraft, but I can't understand why you've been summoned?'

'Summoned!' Wissilcraft roared. 'Do you believe I need your permission to go anywhere I like, Quest? Your arrogance will get you hanged. I'm here because I choose to be. I was intending to come to York, long before I received Critzman's request.'

'Gentlemen, please,' interceded Josef Critzman. 'Civil words, I beg you...'

The old man turned to Quest.

'William, Mr Wissilcraft has come to York for the same reason we are all here. To discover the whereabouts of Mr John Lardiner. And he has information which might aid us in our own investigation. He was about to tell us what he knows. Please do him the courtesy of listening...'

Quest might have snapped back had Isaac uttered such an admonishment, but he could never talk angrily to Isaac's frail brother.

'Go on, Wissilcraft. What's your interest in Lardiner? Have you come to find him too?'

Wissilcraft rubbed a hand across his chin, deep in thought. Quest got the impression that the spymaster was still considering whether to share his confidences.

He gave Quest a grim smile.

'Yes, Quest,' he said at last. 'I've come to York to find the wretched Lardiner. My associates have been seeking him out since he decamped from his Wiltshire parish. Had he remained there, we'd have him already.'

'Have him?'

'Have him in our custody, Quest. Under arrest. Arraigned at the Old Bailey. Though a secret trial might have been arranged... But that would have depended upon Lord Palmerston's instructions.'

'On what charge?' demanded Quest.

'The greatest charge of all,' said Wissilcraft. 'A charge of High Treason.'

Eighteen

It had been a long time since Constable Barratt had explored the narrow passage leading along the rear of the row of houses in Tanner Row.

It was scarcely a public alley, but rather an old path which led from All Saints Church in North Street along a winding course to Barker Lane, a path so narrow that it forced a man to walk sideways just to get by in places. Two similarly small ginnels led from it to the busier street of Micklegate, but only the desperate would ever have sought out their dark corners.

The passage twisted and turned in all directions, an occasional gate leading to the back of the Tanner Row properties, its only illumination coming from above the wall on that side. Otherwise, the path was so black a hundred villains might have been concealed in its shadows.

It took Barratt a while to work out just where he was in relation to the individual houses in Tanner Row. Only the slightly different tiles on the home of Mrs Booth gave him a clue, as they sloped steeply down to a long disused back yard.

There was no gate. Barratt was obliged to scramble over the wall, bracing his feet against the opposite side of the passage. He'd scarcely surmounted the wall, when a cat of obvious great age, crusted in filth, sped away with a ferocious meowing. The surprise of its presence almost caused Barratt's heart to stop.

The yard was stacked with old furniture from the house, much of it rotting away, and other assorted rubbish. As there was no gate into the passage beyond, it had been dumped there to decay. There was no sign that anyone had used the yard for some time.

The door of an ancient privy was ajar. Barratt looked in – it had obviously not been used since more modern sanitary arrangements had been installed in Mrs Booth's property.

There were two windows at this ground level of the house, with a door set between them. The window glass was so dirty that Barratt could see nothing within. The sluttish maid had obviously never made any attempt to clean any windows out of sight of Tanner Row. The front and back of the building might have been in two very separate worlds.

There seemed to be no lock on the back door, though Barratt had brought pick-locks with him in case they were needed. No doubt generations of owners thought the property secure enough, given that there was no ready access to the outside world.

The police constable in Barratt made him shrug in dismay. Had the house's owners so little imagination that they couldn't envisage anyone climbing the wall as he had?

Perhaps they thought the passage to the rear was so unpleasant that not even the denizens of the York underworld would penetrate those disgusting recesses? More likely that in the house's glory days, there would always have been servants busily at work in these unpleasant nether regions.

The door opened into a slight corridor leading into the heart of the house. There were doors on either side; one into what had obviously once been a servant's lodging, the other into the kitchen which was still the domain of the maid. A kettle was boiling over an open fire, and there was the stale smell of recently cooked food.

At the end of the corridor was a heavy door, no doubt placed there to separate the domain of the householder from the world of the servants a long time ago. It was shut, and Barratt wondered whether it could be opened without making a din?

But that was where he needed to be, for it was the sitting room at the front of the house that he badly wanted to examine, the place where he'd interviewed Mrs Booth and seen that interesting picture on the wall.

He turned the doorknob very carefully. To his surprise, the door made no noise at all as he eased it open. The hinges had clearly been oiled very recently. The wood of the door-frame had been planed, so that the door didn't stick as it was opened.

The old lady obviously hated unnecessary noise. Barratt remembered how quiet the property had been on his own visits.

Even the clocks had ticked quietly.

Barratt paused and caught his breath.

He could hear someone talking in another part of the house. He stood still for several moments, holding the door lest it slammed shut and betrayed his presence.

The distant talk stopped.

He began to wonder whether the house was actually empty and whether the voices he'd heard were coming from outside in the street. As he listened, that seemed very likely. He eased the door shut and walked across to the main entrance to the house.

Putting an ear against the front door, Barratt could hear lots of voices. He glanced at his pocket watch. The midday train must have been on time. Passengers were alighting, walking out into Tanner Row and making their way towards the heart of the city.

He moved away from the door and hearkened to the house itself.

So peaceful.

So still.

A real feeling of emptiness.

Good fortune if he'd timed his exploration in a period when both Mrs Booth and the maid were away from the house. Barratt remained still for a few minutes.

Not a sound.

Not a whisper.

The door of Mrs Booth's sitting room stood open. He walked in. Empty and, despite the chilly morning, the fire was not lit. He paused by the picture on the wall, and smiled as he examined it afresh. There was no doubt about it. The lady had painted it from almost exactly the same viewpoint as the artist in the book he'd seen.

The Cathedral of Vasily the Blessed, its author had written, though western guidebooks preferred St Basil's Cathedral. Whatever, it was in Moscow. The old lady must have travelled far in her time to turn out what she'd described as an "amateur daub" from the life.

Game old girl, thought Barratt.

But what was her game?

Despite the messages conveyed by Marcus to the offices by the castle, it could all be perfectly innocent and have no connection with the other recent happenings in York.

Sudden doubt filled his mind.

Here he was, a constable of the city force, to all effects and purposes housebreaking. Intruding into the home of a widow woman, with no warrant from a Justice, and scant evidence of any real wrongdoing.

Being found in such circumstances, would not only lead to the shameful end of a promising career in the police, but perhaps even a spell in the city gaol.

Perhaps better to leave now. The way he'd come. Before anyone might discover this act of malfeasance...

And yet?

Barratt recaptured his initial suspicions, tried to weigh them against the doubts. Tried to...

He was there in the empty property. The deed of illicit entry had been done. He might as well conclude the business. His instinct told him that there was something wrong...

He recalled the words of the note he'd sent round to William Quest. Remembered how sure he was when he'd penned it, hardly only an hour or two before.

Barratt went back into the hall, with the intention of examining the room on the opposite side. A carved stand stood by the front door. There was one of those new-fangled umbrellas standing upright within. And next to it that extraordinary carved walking cane with the eagle's head.

He pulled it out and examined it more closely.

He couldn't work out how to shoot out the hidden blade, twist the stick as he might. A deadly weapon for an old lady. Though he could understand just why her late husband would have equipped her with it. These were perilous and lawless times.

But he smiled as he examined the eagle's head in more detail. His book had been right about that...

Barratt eased the stick back into the stand, and then he took the two paces across the hall to the doorway on the far side. The door was ajar and he put his head around it. The room was almost empty, except for a pair of hard chairs and a long table. Evidently not used much. Mrs Booth probably used it for very formal interviews.

And still the house was quiet. Not a creak of a floorboard or a whisper of conversation. The street outside seemed silent now, in the interval between arriving trains at the railway station opposite.

This tranquillity reinforced his initial courage. He recalled the zest with which he'd set out on this illicit adventure. He had no doubt that the intrepid William Quest wouldn't give up now... nor, very probably, Inspector Abraham Anders.

Barratt looked towards the narrow stairway and made the decision to explore the upstairs of this quiet house in Tanner Row.

On the first step he halted and listened very carefully. There were no sounds coming from anywhere in the house. But then it was the middle of the day. A time when it was most likely that Mrs Booth and her maid might both be out.

Barratt considered, for a moment, what might happen if they arrived home while he was upstairs? There could be no real excuses for his intrusion. It would mean the end of his career in the city police force. He briefly thought that he might claim to have entered because he had spotted an intruder...

A barefaced lie, and extremely unlikely. The front door was firmly shut, and he could hardly explain just why he'd come along the narrow passage to the rear, clambered over the wall and broken in through the back door.

A terrible risk, being caught here... and yet?

Barratt's instinct suggested that he was right to be suspicious of this old lady and her maid. If he could only find some proof to show to Inspector Anders.

He might then be commended and not condemned for his initiative.

Without even realising it, Barratt had reached the top of the flight of stairs on to the landing which ran across the width of the house.

There was really no going back now.

An even narrower set of stairs, not far off a ladder led to the rooms in the roof. No doubt an attic for servants. Apart from that, there were four doors leading from the landing, to rooms at the front and the back of the house.

All four doors stood wide open.

Barratt thought that this shouldn't take long.

The one nearest him, to the rear, had a single bed, a washstand and a chest of drawers. Simple and cheap furniture. Something told Barratt that it was the maid's room. Generous of the old dear not to consign her maid to the attic...

The room opposite was completely empty, bare boards, not even a cupboard. There were bars on the window, the kind some previous householder might have installed to protect his children in their nursery.

Barratt stopped and listened again.

There was some distant noise from the railway station. A train must have arrived. He thought for a moment. There wasn't a passenger train due. Must be a goods train...

But the house was still quiet.

He walked slowly along the landing to the front of this house. There was a long window at the end giving a view down into Tanner Row and across to the station.

It lets in plenty of light, Barratt thought.

What a strange thing to note in the circumstances, he smiled. As though he was some casual visitor rather than an interloper. Like some gent who'd been invited over for luncheon...

Barratt was level now with the two doors leading to the front of the house. He hardly glanced at the one on the left, but he noted that it stood empty. He swung fully round to face the door opposite.

A lady's bedroom.

Not a single bed, he noted. Mrs Booth obviously liked her comforts. A chest of drawers, a washstand, a small writing desk, a wardrobe, a free-standing mirror. And...

There was a noise from within. He'd have to ease back the door a few more inches to see that end of the room, the window was out of sight, though the light shining through it was reflected in the mirror.

The noise came again. The tutting noise that people make when they are impatient.

Time to back away.

Time to leave.

Someone was at home.

As Barratt took a step backwards, it gave him a full view of the mirror. Both ends of the room were exposed to his view in the mirror's reflection. It took him a long moment to comprehend what he was seeing...

Something so unbelievable that he gasped out loud.

The blow caught him unawares. Somebody had hit the small of his back with a considerable punch. It seemed to shove all of the air out of his lungs. His right hand flew instinctively round to his chest. He noted that his fingers were screwed up into a tight fist.

His fingers brushed the thin end of the blade that was protruding out of his chest. In a moment, his hand and wrist were wet with his own blood.

He couldn't seem to grasp what was happening. His mind was whirling and a darkness seemed to be banishing the light from the landing window and the mirror's reflection.

Barratt wanted to ask a question... what was in the mirror was such a puzzle to him. How could any of this be possible? So incredible that he thought he was losing his reason with his blood.

He looked again, but the darkness had banished the mirror from his sight. His eyes seemed to be revolving in his head. He could see nothing... nothing...

Barratt knew he had tumbled on to his knees, then on to his side.

He could hear an angry voice... shrill... outraged...

Saying?

He couldn't make out the words...

The darkness swept away every last thought.

~

'Before you begin, Mr Wissilcraft, I'd like to point out that John Lardiner's a friend of mine,' said Gaius Pritchard. 'For all his faults, I'm still loyal to him.'

There was a mumbling from several others in the crowded room.

Archbishop Musgrave was nodding his head in agreement.

'I find your allegation hard to accept, Wissilcraft,' he said.

Wissilcraft twisted round in the big armchair and looked askance at the archbishop.

'I'm sure this is painful for both of you gentlemen,' he said. 'But as Her Majesty's Spymaster, I have to deal in facts, not loyal opinions. My department's been watching the activities of John Lardiner for several years.'

'Are you seriously suggesting that Lardiner's a traitor? Working for our enemy, Russia?' asked Sebastian Clews.

Wissilcraft waved a hand in the air.

'Oh, that it were that simple!' he said.

'Come on, Wissilcraft, tell us what it's all about?' said Quest. 'Is Lardiner working for the Tsar?'

'In a word, no,' the Spymaster replied.

'Then he's hardly a traitor!' Pritchard protested.

Wissilcraft sat back in his chair and rubbed his wounded head.

'With respect, you gentlemen seem to have a simple opinion of just what constitutes treachery,' he said. 'There are a multitude of ways that a man may sell out his country. Working for the enemy is one...'

'And the others?' asked Quest.

Wissilcraft smiled, 'Working for your own self-interest.'

'That's outrageous,' yelled Gaius Pritchard. 'I've known John Lardiner for many years. I'm not saying he's the most perfect of individuals, but where the welfare of others is concerned, he's almost a saint! You are hunting him down because he's opposed to this foul war. That's quite obvious.'

The archbishop leaned forward in his chair.

'I do feel Pritchard has a point, Wissilcraft. If your only grounds to seek the apprehension of John Lardiner is that he's opposed to the conflict in the Crimea, well, then you'll have to charge a great many millions with treachery. I, myself, am opposed to the war. Even Prince Albert...'

'Well, there's no doubt that the Prince Consort had his reservations at the beginning, but he's since come round to the realities of the international situation.'

'If I may interrupt, gentlemen, perhaps we should let Wissilcraft explain his position,' said Josef Critzman. 'He says he has facts about John Lardiner's supposed treachery. I would like to hear just what these facts are?'

~

'This is an infernal nuisance,' said Mrs Booth, looking down at the body of Charles Barratt. 'Not easy to dispose of the body of a constable . I must consider...'

'You think he told anyone he was coming here?' asked Dolly, as she pulled the long dagger out of the policeman's back. 'He did have to die...'

Mrs Booth nodded.

'Oh yes, he did have to die. He saw everything. Quite clear he'd been suspicious of our little household for some time. But I admit I expected him to visit us more officially. Had he done so, I might have fended him off.'

'And now?'

Mrs Booth sighed.

'Our sojourn in York was coming to an end anyway,' she said. 'We will have to hasten our departure. You killed this intruder with great efficiency, but they'll put a rope round both our necks, if they find us with his corpse.'

'We could try and bury him in the back yard,' Dolly suggested.

'Hard cobbles. It would take hours to get to the earth beneath. Far better to lock his body in one of the rooms and depart. If he told his superiors what he was doing, they might be here at any time. If he acted alone, then it might be weeks before they find him. In any case, we must leave Tanner Row within the hour.'

'They might be watching the railway trains. And the inns from where the coaches depart,' said Dolly. 'How much do they know?'

'I've really no idea,' said Mrs Booth. 'But there's safety in assuming a great deal. We'll go to the offices in the city and seek out our man there. He can arrange for a private carriage to take us away from York. As soon as I've done my most important deed. The one we came here for.'

'Is it worth it?' asked Dolly. 'He's only one man.'

'But a very influential one. A man who must be silenced. Or our paymasters might refuse to give us our deserved reward. Removing him was our ultimate goal.'

'Better that we fail than our necks be stretched.'

Mrs Booth gave the maid an unusual smile.

'Oh, we shan't fail, Dolly. Don't you know who I am?'

~

Constable Marsh rapped on the door of the home of the Reverend Clews.

Jessop, the servant, had been hovering in the hallway in case his master rang for refreshments. He opened the door straight away to hush the noise of the visitor.

'This is for Mr Quest, if he's here,' he said, holding out the letter Barratt had written just a few hours before, and forcing his way into the house.

'He's in conference with m'lord the archbishop and certain other gents,' said Jessop, 'but I'll make sure he gets it as soon as they've finished their business.'

'I'd rather he was given it now,' Marsh insisted. 'Its sender said that it's extremely urgent. Is Inspector Anders of Scotland Yard here?'

'He is.'

'Then I'd also appreciate a word with him as soon as the gents have finished their discussion. I'll wait here in the meantime, in case Mr Quest has need of me.'

Jessop looked annoyed. He'd previously served in a house where even senior members of the police were directed to the tradesmen's entrance. He wasn't used to having his peaceful routine disturbed by a constable barking orders.

He waved Marsh to a chair beside the door.

'You may sit there,' he said. 'I'll take in this... package.'

Nineteen

'You obviously feel the war should go on, Wissilcraft?' said Pritchard.

'What *I* feel is irrelevant,' Wissilcraft replied. 'My entire role in life is to obey the orders given by my masters. That's what I do. I look with suspicion at anyone opposing the war.'

'Even me?' said Archbishop Musgrave.

Wissilcraft gave the churchman a wry smile.

'Particularly you, my lord. You intend to speak out against the war in London in a few days. You've a lot of influence, so you are a particular danger to this country. I'm well aware you've friends in Sweden who are prepared to negotiate with the Tsar.'

'So does that make me a traitor?' asked Musgrave.

'Opinions are free, my lord,' said Wissilcraft. 'But there's a line drawn in the sand. I advise you and your friends not to step across it.' He gave a weary sigh. 'But Mr John Lardiner's a different proposition...'

'Why so?' said Clews. 'He opposes the war as much as any of us.'

'Does he?'

Quest noticed the irony in Wissilcraft's voice as the spymaster spat out the two words.

'You've evidence to the contrary?' said Isaac Critzman.

'My department's long had an interest in our Mr Lardiner, but we've had our failings in keeping tabs on him. As some of you will know, my predecessor as spymaster, Raikes, was a treacherous individual playing both sides at once. He purposely buried much of the truth about Lardiner. They were associates, allies of the very worst kind.'

'From what I've heard of Lardiner, that seems incredible,' said Quest. 'I had my own dealings with Raikes. But since I arrived in York, I've been led to believe that Lardiner rose above personal ambition in the interests of good and justice.'

Wissilcraft threw up his hands in a gesture of mock despair.

'Ah, that's the trouble with you and your sort, Quest. Everything's so black and white to you seekers after a better world. But the truth is that Lardiner's one of the most despicable villains ever to walk the earth.'

'I must protest!' roared Pritchard, turning to the archbishop. 'My lord, must we listen to these lies? To slander a good man, when he's not here to defend himself, is contemptible. I've my own criticisms of

John Lardiner, but I've never doubted his integrity on the matter of peace and universal brotherhood. Wissilcraft's clearly a warmonger, desperate to keep the present conflict going. Please put an end to these disgraceful proceedings now.'

Archbishop Musgrave rested his head in his hands and seemed lost in thought. The room went quiet as nobody seemed willing to disturb him.

An age seemed to pass before he spoke.

'I'm inclined to agree with Pritchard, Wissilcraft. I take it that you can substantiate your accusations?'

Quest thought that the spymaster looked very tired, as though weary of the whole business. But, he recalled, Wissilcraft had not only recently been wounded, but had also had an appalling tragedy in his own life.

'If you mean can I show you written proof against Lardiner, well, no, for all of that comes under the heading of state secrets. If necessary, I'd be prepared to share our records with you, my lord archbishop. The rest of you will just have to listen and accept what I say to you now.'

'Do you believe Lardiner's alive?' asked Quest.

'Very much so,' said Wissilcraft.

'And in York?'

'More than likely.'

'Do you know where he is?'

'I can't say I do. Lardiner came to York for several reasons. Firstly, not least, because he needed to flee from Wiltshire, where word must have reached him that there was a warrant out for his arrest. York's not only a long way from there, but it happens to be a place where his employers have the organisation to look after him.'

'His employers?' said Clews.

'I'll come to them in a moment,' said Wissilcraft.

'You said that was his first reason for coming to York?' said Archbishop Musgrave. 'There's another?'

Wissilcraft grinned, and turned to face the archbishop.

'John Lardiner came to York to murder you, my lord.'

~

'He won't be here yet,' said Dolly, as she and Mrs Booth approached the tall office building, in its long row of similar business premises. 'There's a terrible risk in this...'

'Well, we could hardly remain where we were...'

Mrs Booth rapped on the door with the metal ferrule of her eagle-headed walking cane.

For a long time there was no answer, then they could hear steps approaching the door. A bolt was drawn and a key turned.

The door partly opened, and they saw a little man gazing out at them, giving them a look of complete astonishment.

Relkin took in a great gasp of breath, swinging the door wide open to admit them. Then he slammed the door shut, turning the key and pushing over the great bolt.

'This isn't wise...' he said.

'We'd no choice,' said Mrs Booth. 'Is he here yet?'

Relkin shook his head.

'Well then, when do you expect him?' Mrs Booth persisted.

'He's still in the meeting, I assume, though I expect him shortly. With respect, you are taking a great risk coming here today.'

'Tell him...' Mrs Booth instructed the maid.

Dolly related to Relkin the recent events in Tanner Row.

'That's appalling,' said Relkin. 'It's all up then?'

'How can it be up?' said Mrs Booth. 'Our task is not completed. Though if Carver had been more efficient, we could have been done by now. He could have undertook the work himself and saved us all a great deal of time and effort.'

'He's not used to killing,' said Relkin. 'That's why he always used that wretch Faden.'

'He'll have to learn to be,' said Mrs Booth. 'If this girl here can silence an enemy, then why can't Carver?'

'The circumstances are quite different to the casual slaying of a constable,' Relkin blustered. 'The other man is almost never alone...'

'Carver turns molehills into mountains,' said Mrs Booth. 'It was always a shortcoming of his. But for his incompetence, we could have been done here a week ago, and safely across to France. Have you heard anything about the money?'

'The draft's in a bank in Paris,' said Relkin. 'It will be released as soon as our masters receive word the deed's done. But I don't see how it can be? If the police know, then all is lost...'

'Pull yourself together!' said Mrs Booth. 'They might not know. I got the measure of that constable when he interviewed me. An ambitious young pup. More than likely, he was working alone. But there's a greater danger than the police...'

'Greater danger?'

'Wissilcraft is in York.'

'My God!'

'He arrived at the railway station last night,' said Mrs Booth. 'He's joined the little party surrounding the archbishop. By now they'll know everything. So we have to contend with him and the detective, Anders. And thanks to Carver messing up the destruction of this character Quest, the odds are very much against us.'

'Let's escape York then, while there's still time,' said Relkin.

'You fool! Do you think I've gone all through this to walk away without any reward? Now, right at this last moment, just when they feel their forces are mustered and overwhelming. They'll all believe they're safe enough. This is the moment when we must strike.'

Relkin fell back on to a chair.

'We will, of course, wait for Mr Carver?'

Mrs Booth hit the bare boards with her walking stick.

'No we will not!' she said. 'Their meeting will adjourn soon. They'll be full of themselves, confident of their power. They'll scatter in all directions. This might be the one chance we'll get.'

'You'll do it?' asked Relkin.

'Who else is there now?'

'But what about us?' asked Dolly.

Mrs Booth took the maid's hand in both of hers.

'I rely on you and Relkin to make preparations for our escape,' she said. 'A closed carriage to get us swiftly out of this wretched city. We'll avoid the railway trains. They're traps between stations, and they'll be watching those. We'll make our way across country to Hull. We need the schooner there, Relkin, waiting for us. Send a coded message by the electric telegraph. Tell the captain to prepare.'

'Where will you be?' asked Dolly.

'I'll undertake this last mission,' said Mrs Booth. 'No one else can do it now. What weapons do you have upstairs, Relkin?'

'A brace of pistols, that's all.'

'They will do.'

'You should wait for Carver,' said Dolly. 'Let him do it. It's safer for him. He can go among them unimpeded. Let's just get away from here...'

Mrs Booth took the maid's right hand in her own and squeezed it very tightly.

'Hold your nerve, girl! You've achieved so much today. Brought us some precious time. You are needed to ensure our safe farewell from York and England. Wait for me here. If I can achieve this, it won't take long. If I can't, well... we shall still need to show our enemies a clean pair of heels.'

Twenty

'You must be insane, Wissilcraft!' said Gaius Pritchard. 'Why would John Lardiner wish to murder the archbishop? There'd be no logic to it. They're both working for the cause of peace.'

'Are they?'

There was a note of exhaustion in Wissilcraft's voice.

'You've evidence that Lardiner's developed a contrary view?' asked the archbishop.

'Not a contrary view,' said Wissilcraft. 'But I do have evidence that Lardiner's never given a damn - I beg your pardon, my lord - never cared less about peace, but only about John Lardiner.'

'It can't be true,' said Clews.

Wissilcraft sat back in the chair.

'I'm afraid it is, gentlemen,' he said. 'John Lardiner has no interest in peace, nor yet in patriotism. His only concern's to make himself rich, and to win power for his own nefarious ends. Far from loving the prospect of peace and ending the war in the Crimea, Lardiner cares only about keeping the war going for as long as possible.'

'But why should he?' asked Pritchard.

'I'll try and explain this in the simplest terms,' said Wissilcraft.

He reached out to the nearby table and took up a glass of water. As he sipped, Jessop came into the room and passed the written note to Quest.

Wissilcraft held the empty glass between his fingers, as though the object was somehow helping him define the painful words he had to utter. As he did so, Quest speedily read the note written just a while before by Constable Barratt. He read it once more, and passed it to Inspector Anders, who read it and gave it to Sergeant Starkey.

'John Lardiner, as you know him, my lord, is not so much an individual as a myth,' said Wissilcraft. 'The great saintly diplomat who's above international squabbles. The friend of kings and emperors. The champion of the common man. A being who hates war so much, seeing it as a regressive trait of the human race. So much so, that he wants all the countries of the world to live in harmony.'

'You talk as though such desires are a sin?' said Josef Critzman.

'Such sentiments would certainly be a sin coming from John Lardiner,' said Wissilcraft. 'I'm amazed anyone ever took seriously this new Sermon on the Mount, even as it poured from Lardiner's lips!'

'Your comments are close to blasphemy!' said Clews. 'Be warned...'

The archbishop held up a hand to silence him.

'I do hope, Wissilcraft, that you're able to justify your words,' he said.

'I believe so, my lord. My department's been watching Lardiner for several years. We don't like what we've discovered, particularly as our findings concern a man so universally popular.'

'But your employer, Lord Palmerston, brought Lardiner out of Russia,' said Quest. 'Though the Tsar was probably reluctant to see him go. If you thought him a traitor, why didn't you arrest him then?'

'Because he *is* John Lardiner,' said Wissilcraft. 'He has friends in some very high places. While we had our suspicions, we had no real evidence against him.'

'And now you do?' asked Quest.

'For some time, we've been investigating manufactories of armaments. We've had some concern that there are firms in this nation who don't take the war seriously. Companies quite prepared to sell their guns to every single country involved in the conflict.'

'Now that would be treason,' said Isaac Critzman.

'It would indeed,' said Wissilcraft.

'Then why not bring these villains to book?' asked the archbishop.

'Evidence is hard to obtain,' said Wissilcraft. 'At least the kind that might stand up at the Old Bailey. But as you'll appreciate, these companies have – for their own profit – a real interest in keeping the war going for as long as possible.'

'But what's this to do with John Lardiner?' asked Pritchard.

Wissilcraft gave another weary sigh.

'Let's just say that one particular British arms company was a trifle careless in letting some of its records fall into our hands. One of my agents happened to spy a ledger in the time he worked undercover at their office in Hanover. The ledger showed substantial payments being made to John Lardiner.'

Gaius Pritchard sank back on to the window seat. Quest thought that Lardiner's friend seemed near to collapse. He poured Pritchard a glass of water and put it into his hand.

'You have this ledger?' asked the archbishop.

'We do,' said Wissilcraft. 'You'll understand that we needed the actual volume, if we were ever able to bring a prosecution against the company concerned. We are about to do just that. And against Lardiner as well. We thought we'd a little time in hand to round up all the individuals concerned.'

'But they discovered the ledger was missing?' said Quest.

'Apparently so,' said Wissilcraft. 'Just a few days later, John Lardiner also went missing from his Wiltshire parish. Vanished without trace. It was only when I received the message from Mr Isaac Critzman, requesting my assistance, that we knew he'd probably come to York.'

'For a meeting with me,' said the archbishop. 'About bringing the war to an end...'

Wissilcraft shook his head.

'There'd be no profit in that for Lardiner. He came to York, I believe, with the intention of murdering you. You may have noted the recent deaths of several men who've sought to bring the war to an end. But no one opposes it quite like you. The end of the war would bring to a conclusion a very lucrative trade for arms dealers. Lardiner came here to kill you.'

'This arms company?' said Quest.

'I sent a message to my associates... its offices are to be raided today. Later, I intend to borrow several of Sergeant Starkey's constables and descend upon their premises in York. You might care to come along, Quest. I might have need of your services. The company is called...'

'Thore and Kirkby Consolidated,' said Quest.

'How the devil do you know that?'

Anders passed Barratt's note to Wissilcraft.

'There are dark deeds afoot here,' Anders said.

He turned to Sergeant Starkey.

'Sergeant, you'd better get some men down to Tanner Row to apprehend this Mrs Booth. I've no idea what part she's playing in these machinations, but your Constable Barratt's words at least put her under suspicion. I'll go with Wissilcraft and Quest.'

Anders turned to the archbishop.

'My lord, I think you should remain here. We'll post a constable on the door. If Wissilcraft's right about Lardiner, we must take no chances.'

'I'll not skulk here like a cornered rat,' said Archbishop Musgrave. 'These matters have caused me a great upset. I intend to go into the Minster and pray for peace, and a resolution to these dreadful matters. You may bring me news there. I'll be safe enough in the House of God.'

~

'I fear for Constable Barratt,' said Anders, as they assembled outside Clews' house, having watched the archbishop set out for the Minster. 'Sergeant Starkey, please summon some constables, and we'll put Wissilcraft's mission to the test.'

Quest gave a nod to Reuben Dudgeon and Nathaniel Cooper, who wandered away, seemingly deep in conversation.

'If it's true about Lardiner...' said Clews. 'I find it hard to believe.' He gave a deep sigh. 'If you gentlemen will forgive me, I've official business at the workhouse.'

Clews strode off past the Minster.

'This has hit my step-brother hard,' said Pritchard. 'He thought very highly of John Lardiner. Except...'

'Except?' said Anders.

'Nothing, Inspector. I fear that Wissilcraft has spoken true. It upsets me.'

'Could I have a word, Gaius?' Quest said very gently, leading the lawyer to one side.

'Quest?'

'When we had our talk in the Water Lanes, you said that Lardiner threatened you, but you countered by promising to reveal personal details about Lardiner, in turn, should the situation arise. I've a suspicion what they might be...'

Noticing Anders drawing closer, Quest whispered the words to Pritchard.

'How did you know?'

Pritchard gave Quest a look of astonishment.

'Just a suspicion, based on evidence gathered by Constable Barratt,' said Quest. 'He wrote down his thoughts in a note that was passed to me, though he seemingly hadn't grasped the whole truth.'

He drew Pritchard a few yards further away.

'It was John Lardiner's greatest secret,' said the lawyer. 'From when he was a youth at the university. He said he couldn't help himself. John always insisted he was not like me... in my habits. But that society would never understand his needs. And there were elements in the Russian court who indulged in similar behaviour. It was one reason the Tsar kept John close to him. The emperor feared that John Lardiner might spread the word of such doings. Oh, Quest, am I ruined?'

Quest put a hand on the lawyer's shoulder.

'I think not,' he said. 'If Lardiner's apprehended, and should he turn on you, I'll tell the world that you've been working for me and that Lardiner found out. That his accusations are vicious attempts to discredit his enemies.'

'Bless you, Quest.'

'Perhaps you'd wait in the house and keep the Critzman brothers company,' said Quest. 'There's nothing you can do now. Best to lie low, while I go with Anders and Wissilcraft.'

Gaius Pritchard went inside.

Quest turned and found Anders standing nearby.

'Why is it I feel you always know more that you're telling?' he asked.

Quest smiled.

'You've read Barratt's note,' he said. 'You know as much as I do.'

'I saw that nod you gave Dudgeon and Cooper,' said Anders. 'Where've they gone to? And don't suggest they strolled back to Cooper's tavern. I've seen that look in men's eyes when they've a purpose about them. And what were you saying to Pritchard?'

'I was simply asking Gaius to keep a watch on the Critzman brothers. They tend to get into mischief if left alone.'

'And your two other rascally associates?'

'Well, they're investigating a theory of my own,' said Quest. 'They are on the trail of the Reverend Sebastian Clews.'

'*Clews?*'

'Yes, Clews,' said Quest.

'But why on earth would they...'

'We've a moment before the constables arrive, so I'll tell you, Anders. Ever since I arrived in York, we've been wrong-footed in this investigation. As though the opposition knew all about our plans. Note the speed with which Albert Decker was murdered. He'd only been in the city a few hours. Then, only a trifle later, there was the attempt on my own life.'

'But why would Clews want to...'

'To cover the back of John Lardiner...'

'It doesn't make sense,' Anders said. 'Clews was partly responsible for bringing Lardiner to York. For heaven's sake, Quest, he was bringing Lardiner to the archbishop when the man vanished! Why would that happen if they were associates?'

Quest gave the detective a grim look.

'We've only Clews' word that Lardiner vanished in Grape Lane. What if Lardiner never reached Grape Lane? How would it be if Clews manufactured the whole incident? Oh, yes, Lardiner came to York all right, but for his own ends, as Wissilcraft suggested. But he had to vanish, so that he had the freedom to pursue his own treacherous undertakings. And knowing Wissilcraft was after him, he could hardly just appear as a guest of Archbishop Musgrave.'

Anders turned away, deep in thought.

It was a full minute before he turned back to face Quest.

'But there's a flaw in your fantastic theory, Quest. Clews didn't go alone to fetch Lardiner from the railway station. The archbishop sent Joshua Marples, his clerk, with Clews as a delegation of welcome...'

'He certainly sent him,' said Quest.

Quest saw the realisation of what probably happened on Anders' face.

'So that's why Marples had to die,' said Anders.

'And speedily too, so that Clews could report his fiction about the vanishing of John Lardiner without challenge. I'm only surmising, but I suspect that Clews insisted Marples remain at the Minster. He probably played on the old man's poor health, suggesting that he rested. I don't believe that Lardiner arrived in York that day at all. I think he arrived earlier.'

'But Clews would have taken one hell of a chance,' said Anders. 'He's well known in this place. Sergeant Starkey said they'd interviewed the drayman who was unloading casks at the corner of Grape Lane. The man remembered seeing the archbishop's brougham and Clews. He said he'd seen Clews running frantically down Grape Lane...'

'So he did,' said Quest. 'I'm sure that Clews went through all the motions of taking the brougham to the railway station, then through the city to Grape Lane. Then he acted out the pantomime of chasing after Lardiner down the lane. Just to give a verisimilitude to the tale he was to tell so much later. To make sure people saw him about his errand. But it all depended on poor Marples being slain.'

'You think Clews murdered him?'

'No, I don't,' said Quest. 'I doubt that man ever gets his own hands dirty. He'd never have had the time. Given his explanation of Lardiner's vanishing, he could hardly justify being seen in the Minster, instead of reporting back to his house where the archbishop was waiting.'

'Faden or Moth did it then?'

'Rats from the Water Lanes?' said Quest. 'I doubt it. They could hardly wander into the Minster without being noticed. No, I believe that poor Marples was murdered by John Lardiner.'

Anders paced a few yards along the pavement.

'I can see one flaw in your case, Quest,' he said. 'You maintain that the murder of Joshua Marples was arranged in advance? Yet we know he was throttled by a piece of bell rope casually left lying on the Minster floor. His killer would surely have taken his own garrotte?'

'I'm sure Lardiner did,' said Quest. 'But then by a stroke of good fortune, he saw the bell rope lying there and used it instead. A very good stroke of fortune as far as Marples' killer was concerned. It removed all suggestion that the murder was planned in advance.'

'I must say, you make a compelling case, though it's a tad short of hard evidence against Lardiner or Clews.'

'Ah, but you remember the other night? When Sergeant Starkey shot Faden dead?'

Anders nodded, 'Hard to forget. We had the villain cornered and he attacked Pritchard.'

'I recall it very well,' said Quest. 'Faden was surrounded. He had no way of escape. Then suddenly he veers in the direction of Pritchard, who happened to be standing in front of Clews.'

'But, Quest, you've tried to sell me this line before! Only then you suggested that Pritchard was Faden's target? Faden charged the man, yelling out the word "bastard". Now you suggest he was really after Clews?'

'I was mistaken about Pritchard. It was Clews that Faden was trying to get at.'

'How can you be sure of that?' said Anders.

'Because Faden did nothing for a while when he was surrounded, even though both Pritchard and Clews were closest to him. If he recognised someone he wanted vengeance against, why didn't he charge there and then?'

'Because cornered men rarely act rationally,' countered Anders. 'When we had this discussion before, you were very keen to put Pritchard in the frame. You implied that Faden only recognised Pritchard when he heard his voice. Reasonable if Pritchard had always been in disguise when they'd met, and we know that someone hired Faden as a killer. No, you've no case against Clews, Quest. If I had to go with one of your theories, then I'd back the earlier one against Pritchard. You said you'd seen him acting suspiciously around the Water Lanes on the night Moth was killed? I might discuss that with friend Pritchard later.'

Quest waved a hand dismissively.

'Take my word for it, Anders. Gaius Pritchard's visit to the Water Lanes was perfectly innocent. I've found out just why he was there. It was nothing to do with this business.'

'Why was he there?'

'I can't tell you.'

'Not helpful, Quest. Has he acted criminally?'

'Not in my eyes.'

'So, on your word, I'm supposed to dismiss your own original belief that Pritchard was the guilty man? I need more than your word, man!'

'Very well,' said Quest. 'I'll try and oblige you. Reflect again on the moments before Starkey shot Faden. I've no doubt that Faden determined to attack Pritchard, but when he did launch his assault, he seemed to me to be fighting to get past Pritchard. He was attacking Pritchard only because he was obstructing his real target.'

'Perhaps...'

'To get at Clews.'

'Who could be sure?'

'You remember the word Faden yelled?'

'Bastard?'

'No, the other word, beginning with J?'

'Just a scream as he charged, surely?'

'I think the word he was starting to yell before he was shot was "Judas",' said Quest. 'Aimed at Sebastian Clews.'

'We'll never know,' Anders replied.

'I always remember the look on men's faces when they confront death, Anders. Faden was grieved by Pritchard's words, and no doubt thought him an ideal last prey. You'll remember I was starting forward with my cosh to protect Pritchard, when Starkey fired his pistol.'

'I recall you stepping forward...'

'It was then I saw the look on Faden's face, saw it change from anger to astonishment. Saw it change when Clews yelled out, warning his step-brother of his imminent danger. Saw it change because Faden heard a voice he recognised. No, Clews was the man in disguise who must have hired Faden for heaven knows how many slayings, including the murder of poor Albert Decker.'

Anders took off his hat and rubbed a hand through his white hair.

'It makes for interesting speculation, Quest, but no more than that. I can hardly build a prosecution on someone's tone of voice or the look on another man's face. As you're playing the role of detective, perhaps you could explain the killing of Davy in the workhouse infirmary ward? Clews had left a long time before that death, but Gaius Pritchard was definitely in the workhouse at the time. Nobody would have questioned his presence anywhere in the building.'

'He came downstairs and joined us on hearing the news,' said Quest. 'The infirmary ward can't be reached from above. Pritchard would have had to walk twice past Constable Parfitt to undertake such a killing. No, I believe Lardiner murdered Davy, probably posing as a visitor to the ward.'

Anders racked his brain to recall what Parfitt had said about visitors to the infirmary, but couldn't bring his report to mind. He'd need to consult his notebook later.

'And Moth?' asked Anders.

'Moth was garrotted,' said Quest. 'In much the same way as poor Joshua Marples. By the same killer. I believe his death was also the work of John Lardiner.'

A group of constables were approaching across the Minster Green.

'It's still all speculation,' Anders said. 'We'll review this matter when we've undertaken Wissilcraft's errand. But I need facts, Quest. And I still want to hear Pritchard's excuses. Now, let's get the present business underway.'

Twenty-one

Relkin jumped visibly at the frantic hammering on the door. He walked across the plush carpet of the hallway, his face pale and both his hands shaking.

'Don't you bloody open it!'

Dolly snarled out the words, putting a hand against the little clerk's chest.

'I have to open it,' Relkin said. 'That noise will bring everyone in the street to our door. There's nothing I can do but open it.'

'Leave it closed,' said Dolly. 'We'll get out of here through the back door. We still have time...'

'If it's the police or Wissilcraft, they'll have surrounded the building,' said Relkin. 'There's no escape...'

Dolly gave the clerk a contemptuous glance. The little man seemed close to tears.

The banging on the door came again.

A voice demanded that it be opened.

Relkin looked relieved.

'It's Mr Carver,' he gasped.

Rushing across, he turned the key and pulled back the double bolts.

The door was flung open.

A figure in black charged into the room, slamming the door behind him.

'You fool!' yelled Dolly. 'To come here now. Dressed like that. Where is your great coat? Where is your cloak?'

The Reverend Sebastian Clews fell back against the wall, struggling for breath.

'It's all up,' he said. 'There's no point in further pretence. The fiction of Mr Carver's all in the past. They know too much. Wissilcraft and the police are on their way here. I've come only to warn John Lardiner, for I was meant to meet him here this day. Relkin, you must destroy any documents that'll put our necks in the noose. Burn them all.'

'But Mr Carver...'

'Carver's dead to the world,' said Clews. 'But there are papers here that might suggest his presence. I fear I'm already under suspicion. But if they can't find any links between Carver and...'

He paused and looked along the hallway to the stairs.

'Is Lardiner not here?' he said.

'Do you think John a fool?' said Dolly. 'My husband's long gone. One last task and he'll be out of York. Do our masters know about this disaster?'

'I assumed you'd have sent a message by the electric telegraph,' said Clews. 'I'd no time to do it...'

'I was told to,' said Relkin. 'There hasn't been time...'

'This is a catastrophe,' said Clews. 'Anyway, I'm not stopping here. I'm sure they've no proof against me... where is...?'

Dolly gave him a humourless smile.

'Mrs Booth's gone to the Minster,' she said. 'The archbishop always prays alone in the Choir at this time. One last chance. More of a man than any of you...'

'It's folly!' said Clews.

'You weren't prepared to do it,' said Dolly. 'If you'd only been prepared to get your hands dirty, none of this would have happened. We've all had to take risks because of your cowardice...'

'I was instructed only to organise,' said Clews. 'Nothing more than that!'

'Coward!'

Clews ignored her and turned to Relkin.

'Get upstairs and burn those documents,' he said. 'Then get away from here. I don't want to see any more of you. Carver's dead to the world, but I intend to absorb myself back into my other life.'

Clews turned and grasped the door handle.

'I must get back,' he said. 'I'm supposed to be administering prayers at the workhouse. I'll not see either of you again. And when you see John Lardiner, tell him to keep away from me. He tempted me into this, against all my better judgement. He may have brought me to ruin. If he has, I'll turn Queen's Evidence and destroy you all.'

He reached up and drew back the first of the bolts.

But even as his fingers grasped it, there was a thudding against the door.

'Open in the name of the Queen!'

Clews turned, his mouth open as he struggled to breathe.

The thudding came again.

'Open in the name of the Queen!'

'God Almighty!' shouted Clews. 'Oh God, spare me!'

'You can ask him, coward!' said Dolly.

She grasped Mrs Booth's walking cane, clicking the device which lowered the blade at its end.

Dolly thrust it forwards with great velocity into the heart of Sebastian Clews. Then she pulled it free, holding it out towards the door.

Clews slid on to the thick carpet, astonishment in his eyes and the word God on his lips.

'There's a bastard who won't peach!' she screamed at Relkin.

The little man hardly heard what she said. He sat trembling on the bottom step of the stairs.

Trembling and trying hard not to vomit.

~

'Do you have the place surrounded?'

Wissilcraft seemed particularly impatient, Quest thought. An unusual trait for a spymaster, who would so often stalk his prey over long periods of time.

'We do,' said Sergeant Starkey.

'Are your men armed?' asked Anders.

Starkey shook his head.

'There aren't the guns in the police office to arm them all,' he said. 'But they have their sticks, and one man in each party has a pistol.'

'I want whoever's in there alive,' said Wissilcraft. 'There are other bigger beasts I want brought to the Old Bailey. I need someone in there who'll peach.'

'I'll see if I can oblige you, but I'm not risking the safety of my men,' said Starkey. 'And we can't just barge in there. I must rap the door and give them time to yield.'

'They may destroy evidence while you play with these niceties of the law. Smash down that door, man. We're in hot pursuit and there'll be no awkward questions asked.'

'This is York, sir. It's not how matters are handled here,' said Starkey.

Wissilcraft was about to remonstrate, when Constable Marsh ran up to them. He looked pale and there was blood on his uniform.

'Are you wounded, Constable?' asked Anders.

'No, Inspector,' Marsh gasped for breath.

'Then whose blood is that?'

'The blood... it's... Barratt's blood, sir. The bastards have butchered him. In Tanner Row. We found his body when we broke into the house. Stabbed through the chest. He was upstairs... on the landing. Poor Charlie! They've butchered him, sir.'

'Was Mrs Booth there?' asked Quest.

'The house was deserted,' said Marsh. 'They'd left in a hurry. Nobody there. Just poor Charlie's...'

Anders looked grim.

'We'd better hope Mrs Booth's in there,' he pointed at the wooden door before them. He turned to Marsh. 'Constable, take the men you have with you. To the railway station, and to the coaching inns. Just in case Mrs Booth tries to flee the town.'

Marsh touched his forehead and went off.

'Hot pursuit, Anders!' said Wissilcraft. 'They've murdered one of your own, Sergeant Starkey. Get in there, man!'

'Whatever the offence, I must rap the door,' said Starkey.

'Damn you...' said Wissilcraft.

Starkey bashed the door with his billy-stick.

'Open in the name of the Queen!' he shouted.

After a moment he delivered the command again.

'The other way then, Sergeant,' said Anders, very quietly.

Starkey summoned two of the constables. They carried a long piece of wood picked up a long time before from a riverside staith. Wood that had broken down many doors in the city of York.

They crashed it five times against the thick door of Thore and Kirkby Consolidated, before the lock and bolts were broken away from their mountings.

~

Mrs Booth, walking rapidly across the city, was quite missing that helpful stick. There was a faint remembrance of passing it to Dolly. It was a mistake to come away without it. It would have been useful now, on this fast journey on hard pavements. Its concealed and deadly delights might well have helped if the other means of murder failed.

There was a smile on the face beneath the veil. There was time to achieve much. The dreams thought out for so long still burned brightly. Still time to kill and get away.

~

Gaius Pritchard looked out through the window of his step-brother's house, across a street dark-shadowed by the mighty walls of the Minster. The road outside was as quiet as the house, now that everyone else had departed.

There was that awful menacing stillness that comes in the moments before a thunderstorm. Pritchard felt sick inside, as he realised the growing number of men who knew his secret. While he had faith in Quest, and the fighter Reuben Dudgeon, he hadn't liked the way that Inspector Anders had glanced across at him.

As though the detective was reading the secrets of his heart and soul. Not just ruin if his personal mystery was revealed, but long years in the prison.

Why is the world so cruel to men who only want to love?

A solitary bell rang somewhere in the Minster, as though tolling a personal death-knell for him.

It had been such a long time since he'd knelt down and prayed, but he felt a need for it now. He took up his hat, cloak and stick, quietly closing the door behind him, and made his way towards the great cathedral.

~

'For the love of God!'

Relkin was clutching the bannister, as though he might fall away into hell without it. He'd vomited on the plush carpet as the first blows from the battering ram struck the door. Seeing nothing but a hood being placed over his head and the rope drawn tightly across the soft flesh of his throat.

'God help us all!' he screamed.

'Shut your bloody face!'

Dolly clutched his right hand and bent the fingers back, but he noticed no pain, so deep was his fear.

'Get up those stairs,' said Dolly. 'Burn those documents....'

But Relkin was looking past her, to where the mountings of the bolts were shearing away from the wall. He watched as the key fell from the lock. Saw the hasp break away, the wood of the door turning into long splinters.

'My God!'

Dolly turned as the men charged into the hall. She held out Mrs Booth's stick, forcing the red-blooded blade into the arm of the nearest constable.

She might have struck a deadlier blow, had not Quest brought his cosh crashing down on her wrist, breaking the bones. She screamed hatred at him as Starkey and two of the constables seized her arms and forced her down on the floor.

'Get her outside,' said Anders.

He looked at the pitiful figure at the foot of the stairs.

Relkin was vomiting again. He drew a hand across his mouth and looked up at the detective.

'Queen's Evidence,' said Relkin. 'I want to turn Queen's Evidence...'

'Anders,' said Quest.

The detective turned, noticing for the first time the dark figure lying dead in the corner of the hallway.

The corpse of the Reverend Sebastian Clews.

'It seems you were right, Quest,' said Anders.

'Who killed that man?' Starkey yelled at Relkin.

'It wasn't me! It wasn't me! It was her!'

He pointed at the doorway, as the constables led the murderess away.

Wissilcraft bent over the little man.

'Where is John Lardiner?' he asked.

'Mr Lardiner is dead,' said Relkin, giving them a bizarre grin.

He seemed almost mesmerised as he clung harder to the bannister.

Quest reached inside his fob pocket and produced the slip of paper which had started him out on this dangerous adventure. The paper that bore those four very words. He held it before Relkin's eyes.

'Did you write this?'

The little man nodded furiously, pointing at Clews' body.

'Yes! Yes! he wanted someone whose handwriting wouldn't be recognised. He thought it might buy time. You see he has shares in this company and is retained under the name of Carver to further its policies in the north. He was in debt, the reverend there. Easy prey for the owners of this company. He posted that note through his own letterbox.'

'I ask you again,' said Wissilcraft, 'where is John Lardiner?'

Relkin gave him a wide-eyed glance.

'On the way to hell, I hope,' he said.

Quest knelt down and rested a hand on Relkin's shoulder. Tears were pouring down Relkin's face.

'I'll help you,' said Quest. 'But you must tell me the truth.'

'I will, sir, I will. I'll peach on them all. But don't let them hang me or put me away. I'm a clerk. Just a clerk. I write and sign documents. That's all I do, sir, honest to God!'

'Where is Mrs Booth?' asked Quest.

Relkin's eyes seem to widen even further. His mouth was agape. He nodded as he considered the question. Then the words came out like a child reciting a catechism.

'Oh, Mrs Booth was here, but she's gone now. Gone for good, I hope. Gone to the Minster to kill the archbishop. Don't you know all about Mrs Booth? Quite the lady, Mrs Booth.'

Relkin gave a great burst of laughter.

It ended in a great sob as more tears poured down his cheeks.

'Is Mrs Booth armed?' asked Quest.

'I produced a brace of pistols,' said Relkin. 'Nasty things. Dreadful things. I might work for a company that creates them, but I can't stand the thought of them. I'll tell you something, sir...'

He whispered into Quest's ear.

Twenty-two

Archbishop Musgrave did not sit on the *cathedra* to pray, not wishing to use the throne except on formal occasions. He preferred to draw a little stool up to the reading desk in the middle of the Choir from which the litany was read.

He glanced up at a small pillar of brass nearby, which formed the head of an eagle with expanded wings. On this, when a service was being held, a Bible was placed, so that the lessons might be read.

He'd never really liked it, thought it both ugly and ostentatious, though he loved the history behind it. But it lacked the simplicity he'd come to prefer in his old age. Musgrave had never felt truly at ease in this great cathedral. He envied those parsons in the diocese who preached in simple country churches.

Nor did he particularly care for the Minster's huge Bibles, preferring to clutch the simple prayer book given to him when he first began his Ministry.

In the quiet of the cathedral he knelt and prayed, relieved that there were no visitors about to distract him from his devotions. He prayed here nearly every day when he was in York, and always seemed surprised that his prayers were never interrupted.

He was unaware that the cathedral's own police, who kept order within the cathedral's precincts, distinct from the city constables, politely steered visitors away from the Choir when the archbishop was present.

That day, Musgrave prayed for strength, so that he might deliver his great speech against the evils of war. He prayed that destruction might never come to the great Minster, as it nearly had a quarter of a century before when fire had threatened the building.

Musgrave prayed for the soldiers dying or in peril on the battlefields of the Crimea. He prayed that politicians might open their hearts and listen to the compassionate message of Almighty God.

He prayed for the soul of John Lardiner.

Could that man Wissilcraft really be right in his condemnation of a living saint? Musgrave hoped to God it was all a misunderstanding. If there was such deceit in the hearts of men, was there any point in praying?

He glanced at the brass eagle, which seemed to have so little to do with Christianity.

A shadow seemed to fall across its head and outspread wings.

Then something swept down past his eyes.

There was a tightness in his throat. The dim light of the cathedral Choir seemed to darken as Archbishop Thomas Musgrave struggled to get a breath.

~

'You can't go through there,' said the cathedral constable as Gaius Pritchard walked away from the few visitors towards the sanctity of the Choir.

He turned, and the constable recognised him.

'Oh, it's you, sir. His Grace isn't done with his prayers yet, though he shouldn't be a moment. Are you to meet him?'

'Not really,' said Pritchard. 'I'll wait by the entrance to the Choir. I'll not disturb him. I've come to pray there myself. It's the place I love the best.'

The constable bowed his head.

'A peaceful place indeed, sir. I like to sit there. I was ten years in the city police before transferring here. Not much to do and I've gotten to liking this old pile.'

Gaius Pritchard smiled and walked on to the Choir's entrance. He wondered what the archbishop and the constable would think if they knew the truth?

Behind him there were noisy voices near the great west door of the Minster. He turned briefly and noticed the constable hurrying off in that direction. Not such a peaceful place after all.

He came to the entrance of the Choir and paused.

The archbishop was kneeling by the litany desk, but the sounds the old man uttered were not prayers but choking gasps.

A figure, all in black, was bent over the churchman.

It took Pritchard a long moment to realise what was happening.

Then he shouted, a great shout that reverberated back and forth along the length of the cathedral.

'No!'

~

The cathedral constable rushed to the west door, convinced that some of the riff-raff of the town must be invading the building, such was the commotion being made by the body of men who entered. He saw the other duty constable was already there, deep in conversation with an elderly man with white hair.

He relaxed when he noticed that, amid the collection of men, were city policemen in uniform and the familiar figure of Sergeant Starkey. Despite breathing a sigh of relief, he felt a mild annoyance that the city police were intruding on his own particular preserve.

~

'No!'

Gaius Pritchard yelled again, the horrified cry beating up to the high ceiling of the building and back down again. A cry so loud that it seemed to shake the Minster's medieval stones.

Mrs Booth relaxed the ligature and pushed the archbishop's head forward. Mrs Booth dropped the length of cord and produced a pistol from somewhere.

Pritchard saw that it was pointed at him.

'No!' he said, more quietly now.

'Gaius Pritchard!' exclaimed Mrs Booth. 'Haven't they sent you down yet? Don't they know your little ways as well as I do? You might as well let me go about my business, Gaius. For if I'm took, I'll make sure all the world knows about you.'

'I don't care!' Pritchard retorted. 'You're a villain! Let that old man alone!'

'Oh, Gaius. It'd be a shame to kill you after all these years. But I will. I've a brace of pistols, both charged and loaded. I'll kill you and then him. There's no ending to this matter but the way *I* want it to be ended.'

'You harm the archbishop and I'll kill you,' said Pritchard.

'In a holy place like this?' said Mrs Booth. 'What a sinner you are! Now back away Gaius. This old man's as good as dead.'

'I don't think so!'

Mrs Booth swung round.

A white haired man was regarding the scene from the other end of the Choir.

'I don't believe we've been formally introduced?' said Mrs Booth

'I'm Inspector Anders. From Scotland Yard. And you are under arrest.'

Mrs Booth gave a great burst of laughter.

'I think not, Anders. Not while I hold this pistol at the archbishop's head. I came here to kill him. How soon that will be depends on whether you let me leave this place.'

'The game's up.'

Mrs Booth turned the other way.

A man with dark hair had walked past Pritchard, coming nearer down the Choir.

'You're Quest!' said Mrs Booth. 'I've had you pointed out to me in the street. You'd be dead now but for the incompetence of Clews and his lackeys.'

Quest walked nearer, his hand held out for the pistol.

'The game's up, Lardiner!' he said.

'What?'

Anders held his arms out in a gesture of astonishment.

'Let me introduce you, Anders. To the famous living saint, Mr John Lardiner,' said Quest. 'Not so saintly now, Lardiner.'

John Lardiner tore off the veil and the grey wig.

'It was fun while it lasted.'

'A habit of yours, I believe, Lardiner?' said Quest. 'I'm told this interesting side to your personality caused much amusement at the Russian Court?'

'We all have our wants, Quest. But don't imagine I'm like some people I could mention.' He looked towards Pritchard, drawing a hand down the black mourning gown. 'My interests are only towards women. This is just something I enjoy. My wife would confirm that, though you'll not get the chance to ask her.'

'We have her, Lardiner,' said Quest. 'She murdered Clews, so she'll swing. You will too, so give me that pistol.'

Lardiner took in a great breath.

'Then I'll trade you this old man's life for hers,' he said.

'There'll be no deals,' said Anders

'Then I've nothing to lose...' he said.

He put the pistol against the archbishop's head.

Quest walked a step closer, even as Lardiner pulled out the other pistol and aimed it at him.

'You've nothing to gain, either, Lardiner. I'll prove it to you. Shoot me down first...'

'What?'

'Shoot me down...'

Quest could see first puzzlement and then doubt on Lardiner's face.

'What do you mean?'

'Pull the trigger, Lardiner!'

Lardiner raised the pistol and...

The hammer clicked down on the percussion cap.

But Quest still stood in front of him, hand held out.

'What is this?' Lardiner demanded.

'You'll find exactly the same will happen if you discharge the other pistol. His Grace might get a burn from the percussion cap, but that's all the harm you'll do him,' said Quest.

'Relkin...'

'Yes, Relkin,' said Quest. 'I asked him if you'd gone on your errand bearing firearms? He told me he'd given you a brace of pistols. You assumed he'd loaded them for you. Well, they certainly had percussion caps in them. But neither pistol was loaded with a ball. You see, Relkin was just a clerk. He wrote and signed documents. Nobody ever instructed him in the task of loading a pistol.'

'Damn the little clerk,' said Lardiner.

He put the two pistols down on the litany table. He laid the stretch of cord next to them.

'Rope from Russia, I believe?' said Quest.

'The last of a goodly supply,' said Lardiner. 'It's given cord burns to a good few throats, though the last time I murdered here was with some bell rope. Far too thick. Nowhere near as efficient. The archbishop's clerk took longer to die than I'd have wished. Then there was Moth. He was drunk. So much easier. Davy was harder to kill. Difficult to penetrate the workhouse infirmary. I went in as a younger woman there. Hovered by the bedside of a man dying of the consumption. They all thought I was his wife...'

He laughed hysterically.

'Come on, Lardiner, time to go,' said Anders.

'Oh, I don't think so,' Lardiner replied. 'The game's not quite up.' He laughed again. 'A lady always comes well equipped.'

He reached into his black cape. In a second he was holding a small dagger with a thin but deadly blade at the archbishop's throat. With his other arm he pulled the churchman to his feet.

'I believe we should negotiate...' he said.

'Don't listen to him,' Archbishop Musgrave said. 'It's the cause that matters, not me.'

'Oh, brave words Your Grace, brave words. But these gents know I can cut your throat before they can get anywhere near. Now it's time for our little walk...' said Lardiner.

'You're not going anywhere,' said Anders.

'I never said I was,' said Lardiner. 'That's not the game we're playing, you see. I intend to remain in this building until you bring my wife to me. Then three of us will leave, in the fast carriage you'll provide. I shan't let the archbishop go until we're well clear of York.'

Quest took a step nearer.

'But you came here with the sole intention of murdering him,' he said. 'You'll never let the archbishop live.'

'It isn't going to happen, Lardiner,' said Anders. 'There's no future in this. Put down that dagger.'

'I think not,' said Lardiner. 'Let us go for a little walk, Your Grace.'

He pulled the archbishop to his feet and pulled him backwards.

'And do remember, gentlemen, that I can plunge this blade into the archbishop's throat in a moment. He'll bleed to death before you can do anything.'

He walked backwards, the others following him at a distance.

'Lardiner's gone mad,' said Anders.

'I fear so,' said Quest.

'If he leaves here, he'll not only kill the archbishop, but might be a danger to others.' Anders glanced at Quest. 'I suspect you have a pistol with you?'

Quest nodded.

'Then if you can, bring that man down,' said Anders. 'The law will protect you from any consequences.'

'Just like the last time,' said Quest. 'Only I can't argue self-defence.'

'It's permitted. With the sanction of a detective officer in the execution of his duty. To save the lives of others,' said Anders.

Lardiner was walking with his back to the wall near the south entrance to the Minster. There was a doorway. He turned to face them as he reached it.

'I'm going through here,' he shouted. 'I intend to lock the door after me. The archbishop and I are ascending to heaven!'

He gave a deranged burst of laughter.

'I do believe he's insane,' said Sergeant Starkey. 'He'll dodge the gallows if they judge him to be unsound in his mind.'

'No, he won't!' said Anders. 'What's through that door?'

'A winding staircase,' said Starkey. 'Two hundred and seventy three winding steps to the top of the central tower. That's the heaven he's talking about.'

'If he gets up there, we'll not get close,' said Quest. 'He won't need to stab the archbishop. He'll just be able to throw him down into the Minster yard.'

'A far more impressive gesture for a man out of his mind,' said Anders.

'Come on, my lord archbishop...' said Lardiner.

Gripping the archbishop around the chest, he took away his hand from the churchman's throat, reaching behind him to turn the latch. He kicked the door open with a foot and turned to face them once more.

But the turning away was Lardiner's undoing.

Gaius Pritchard seemed to come from nowhere. Quest had thought the lawyer was behind them, but guessed he must have left the building and come back in through the south entrance.

His move took Lardiner completely by surprise.

Before the strange figure in black could put the dagger back at the archbishop's throat, Pritchard had seized Lardiner's hand and was fighting him for the knife. The archbishop fell clear on to the hard stones of the Minster floor.

Quest dashed forward in time to catch Gaius Pritchard as he fell.

'Damn you, Gaius!' yelled Lardiner.

He turned and fled through the door.

Quest heard the fugitive's footsteps echoing in the narrow stairwell.

'Are you hurt, Gaius?' said Quest.

The lawyer looked up at him, then to where the dagger was sticking out from his shoulder.

'Get this man to a surgeon,' Quest said to Starkey. 'Don't try and remove the knife, lest he bleeds to death.'

He looked at Anders.

'You're younger than I am, Quest,' said the detective. 'Alive if you can, dead if you can't. But don't take any chances. Who knows what other weapons he's got hidden away. Bring him down with your pistol, Quest. If that's what it takes...'

The stairwell was winding and narrow. But Lardiner clearly didn't intend to mount an ambush there. Quest could hear the footsteps of his quarry running upwards at a fast pace. He wondered, vaguely, how the man could move with such speed in a widow's weeds.

He took out his little percussion-cap pistol and followed Lardiner up the steps.

The top of the crenelated tower reminded Quest of castles he'd visited. The weather had cleared and there was a fine view over the entire city of York. Pedestrians far below, looking like ants, were gawping up at the Minster, unaware of the drama being played out above their heads.

John Lardiner stood in the farthest corner of the tower, somehow looking absurd in the widow's weeds without the accompanying grey wig and veil.

Quest walked around the edge of the wall, until he was just a yard away.

Lardiner gave him a broad smile.

'No hope for me, is there?' he said.

'None at all.'

'Will they really string up my wife? Poor Dorinda. That's what she's called, you know? The wife of my bosom. How she hated the "Dolly" and having to play the maid. She really killed Clews?'

'She did.'

'The loathsome bastard deserved it,' said Lardiner. 'He led a double life that was far in excess of mine. Always put money before his precious God. But never had the courage to shed blood. Always the way with him. I met him first many years ago, at a foxhunt organised by his dear papa. You should have seen Sebastian retch. How pale he turned. Always very good at organising death, but never liked to be in at the kill.'

'You made up for that, Lardiner. A deadly saint you turned out to be.'

'I walked through the courts of Europe and they all adored me, Quest. And why not? I always knew I was far above all the kings and emperors I ever met. I was worth all of them, but they lived in wealth and idleness while I had to struggle with poverty, despite my reputation.'

'Are you going to come down this tower?' asked Quest.

Lardiner took in a deep breath.

'I do believe I'd like to live a tad longer, Quest,' he said. 'And shall I tell you what? I do believe I shall beat the gallows.'

'I wouldn't wager on that.'

Lardiner brushed his hands down the black dress.

'They'll say I'm mad, Quest. And they don't top lunatics, do they? As for my wife, well, she'll no doubt argue she killed Clews while defending herself. The jury may well believe her. I do love my Dorinda, I really do. I shan't see her again. I doubt they'll let me have visitors in the asylum. But I'll find it peaceful enough. There are worse fates for a man like me.'

'Are you coming down?'

Lardiner nodded.

'You know, I might have escaped justice but for Gaius Pritchard. He always was a most dreadful, interfering chap. But I'll tell you what? He'll pay a heavy price for his meddling. I'll shout his dirty little secret from the dock. And while I'm away in some peaceful little asylum, I'll get great satisfaction knowing he's rotting in gaol.'

'I thought he was your friend?'

Lardiner smirked.

'Just someone to be used...'

Quest stepped forward and grasped Lardiner by the black crape of the mourning dress.

'You needn't seize me, Quest,' Lardiner said. 'I'll come quiet...'

'You'll really sell out Pritchard?'

'Well of course I will,' said Lardiner. 'Why not? He's disposable. Just like crushing an ant. Nobody really matters to me, Quest. Dorinda, yes. But mostly it's hard to think beyond myself.'

Lardiner laughed.

But the humour died on his lips.

Quest raised him high in the air and forced him backwards through a crenelated gap in the tower wall. Quest took one hand from Lardiner's chest and pushed hard under the man's chin, forcing Lardiner to look down at the Minster Yard so far below.

Quest could see the terror on Lardiner's face.

'You'd really peach on Gaius?' demanded Quest.

'Just my jest,' said Lardiner, pale-faced as he looked down at the pedestrians so far below. 'I'll not betray poor Gaius. You have my vow. I would never...'

'Sorry, Lardiner, I don't believe you.'

Reaching down, Quest put a hand under Lardiner's leg and forced him even further through the gap.

'For the love of God...' Lardiner screamed.

The pedestrians in the Minster Yard, gazing up towards the sunlight, thought they saw a great black bird high on the central tower. It seemed to hover for a moment on the old stonework, before coming down to the ground, splayed out like some sinister old scarecrow caught up in an autumn gale.

Twenty-three

'So why do you think they killed Constable Barratt?' asked Anders.

He and Quest were taking an evening stroll around the city walls.

'Barratt broke in to the house in Tanner Row,' said Quest. 'Overstepping the mark in the eyes of your precious law, Anders. But it's the kind of thing I'd have done myself. I fear he came across Lardiner in the widow's weeds, but without the wig and veil.'

'But who killed him? Lardiner or his wife?'

'We'll never know,' said Quest. 'He was stabbed in the back, so I'd wager it was the woman – the real woman. We know from the note he wrote, that Barratt saw Lardiner at night on the doorstep of the house. Wondered just why a man would be carrying Mrs Booth's eagle-headed walking cane? But the truth didn't dawn on the constable until it was too late.'

They strolled a little further, admiring the sun as it set behind the great towers of the Minster.

'The worst of it,' said Quest, 'is that the men behind this crime, the war profiteers and creatures of business, will walk away. As usual. It's always the minions who get caught, never the individuals they work for. Such is our corrupt society.'

Anders said, 'Not perhaps on this occasion, though. In the offices of Thore and Kirkby Consolidated, we found a great book, with a lot of incriminating evidence. The little clerk, Relkin – who, by the way, is singing like a canary to save his neck – was a meticulous keeper of records.'

They walked on a little further.

'Well, I'm returning to London tomorrow,' Quest said. 'I've other business to attend to.'

'I'm well aware of the kind of business you have in mind,' said Anders. He turned towards him. 'You should throw it up, man. You are too valuable to society to put your head in a noose.'

Quest smiled but said nothing.

'So our truce is over...' said Anders.

'I wasn't aware we had a truce...'

'We've worked well together, here in York.'

'We have!'

'It'd pain me to see you hanged, Quest.'

'It'd pain me more.'

Anders laughed.

'Tell me, Quest? About how Lardiner died, up there on the tower?'

'What's there to tell?' said Quest.

'Did you give him a chance to surrender?'

'He could have come down and faced trial,' said Quest. 'He chose not to do so. Now it doesn't matter, does it? The mystery of John Lardiner's vanishing is solved.'

'I'd like an answer, Quest... just between ourselves...'

William Quest contemplated the sunset for a moment or two.

He smiled.

'I can only give you this, Anders,' he said.

Quest dug into his fob pocket and produced a slip of paper.

He handed it to the detective, who read it once more and laughed.

It read:

Mr Lardiner is dead.

THE END
But William Quest will return...

Books by John Bainbridge

THE SHADOW OF WILLIAM QUEST - A mysterious stranger carrying a swordstick walks the gaslit alleys and night houses of Victorian London. What is he seeking? London in 1853 - a mist-shrouded city where the grand houses of the wealthy lie a stone's throw from the vilest slums and rookeries of the poor. Who is this man, so determined to fight for justice against all the wrongs of Victorian society? What are the origins of the mysterious William Quest? In a pursuit from the teeming streets of London to the lonely coast of Norfolk, Inspector Anders of Scotland Yard is determined to uncover the truth. To an explosive climax where only one man can walk away...

DEADLY QUEST - A reign of terror sweeps through the Victorian underworld as a menacing figure seeks to impose his will on the criminals of London. On the abandoned wharves of the docklands and in the dangerous gaslit alleys of Whitechapel, hardened villains are being murdered, dealers in stolen goods and brothel keepers threatened. The cobbles of the old city running with blood, as pistol shots bark out death to any who resist. Who can fight back to protect the poor and the oppressed? The detectives of Scotland Yard are baffled as the death toll mounts. There is, of course, William Quest – Victorian avenger. A man brought up to know both sides of the law. But Quest faces dangers of his own. Sinister watchers are dogging his footsteps through the fog, as Quest becomes the prey in a deadly manhunt, threatened by a vicious enemy, fighting for his life in a thrilling climax in the most dangerous rookery in Victorian London. Dead Quest or deadly quest?

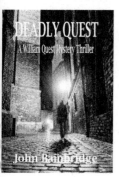

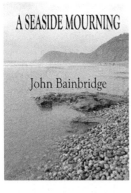

A SEASIDE MOURNING - An atmospheric Victorian murder mystery.

Devonshire 1873. In the sleepy seaside resort of Seaborough, a leading resident may have been poisoned, Still coming to terms with his own mourning, Inspector Abbs is sent to uncover the truth. Behind the Nottingham lace curtains, certain residents have their secrets. Under growing pressure, Abbs and Sergeant Reeve must search the past for answers as they try to unmask a killer.

A CHRISTMAS MALICE - Christmas 1873. Inspector Abbs is visiting his sister in a lonely village on the edge of the Norfolk Fens. He is hoping for a quiet week while he thinks over a decision about his future. However all is not well in Aylmer. Someone has been playing malicious tricks on the inhabitants. With time on his hands and concerned for his sister, Abbs feels compelled to investigate..

This complete mystery is a novella of around 33,000 words. The events take place shortly after the first full-length Inspector Abbs novel, *A Seaside Mourning.*

THE SEAFRONT CORPSE - Set in 1931, newly promoted Inspector Eddie Chance is back in his home town. Reunited with his old pal Sergeant Bishop in the sleepy Sussex town of Tennysham-on-Sea. The only cloud on their horizon is a young police-woman with ambitions to be a detective. The seaside resort is getting ready for the first day trippers of the season. When the body of a stranger is found on the promenade, Inspector Chance is faced with a baffling murder... A traditional 1930s murder mystery set in a vanished England of typewriters, telephone boxes and tweeds.

THE HOLLY HOUSE MYSTERY - A 1930s murder mystery novella. A girl lay dead in the freezing grounds, near the ruins of an ancient priory. How was she killed... with only one set of footprints in the snow? Inspector Chance investigates death at the Big House in a snow-bound Downland village. As New Year approaches, can he unmask the murderer before the house-party ends? The Holly House Mystery is a complete novella of 34,000 words and an affectionate homage to the Golden Age of country house murder.

BALMORAL KILL - How do you hunt down a faceless assassin before his ultimate kill?

You get Sean Miller... Sniper. Mercenary. Adventurer. He'll stop at nothing. Do whatever it takes. As the shadow of the Nazis falls across Europe, a sinister conspiracy begins a secret war closer to home. Miller's chase leads from the dangerous alleys of London's East End to the lonely glens of the Scottish Highlands. But where do his loyalties really lie? Who will take the final shot in the Balmoral Kill?

THE CHRONICLES OF ROBIN HOOD SERIES - A hooded man has come to the forest. Sherwood Forest. Come to fight for the poor and desperate. Come to fight for freedom against the overlords imposing tyranny on those who can't fight back. Embittered after a failed rebellion, armed with a longbow and a sword, Robin of Loxley faces his greatest challenge – defeating the despotic Sheriff of Nottingham, the deadly Sir Guy of Gisborne and the cruel Master of Newark Castle, Sir Brian du Bois. Proclaimed wolfshead in Sherwood, Loxley becomes Robin Hood. In the struggle against injustice Robin Hood fights alongside the other wolfsheads of Sherwood. Their deeds will become legendary. The series continues with *Wolfshead* and *Villain.*

If you've enjoyed this book, please consider leaving a quick review on the Amazon site. All independent authors appreciate your help in spreading the word about our books. Thank you.

Connect with John at his website:

www.johnbainbridgebooks.weebly.com

and John's writing blog:

www.johnbainbridgewriter.wordpress.com

or on Twitter at:

@stravaigerjohn

Follow John on Goodreads:

https://www.goodreads.com/author/show/73470.John_Bainbridge

Printed in Great Britain
by Amazon

44207070R00121